ASWAN!

ASWAN!

A novel by

MICHAEL HEIM

Translated from the German by
J. Maxwell Brownjohn

Alfred A. Knopf   New York   1972

Copyright © 1972 in the English translation, William Collins Sons & Co., Ltd., London.
All rights reserved under International and Pan-American Copyright Conventions. Published in the United States by Alfred A. Knopf, Inc., New York. Distributed by Random House, Inc., New York. Originally published in Germany as *Assuan Wenn der Damm bricht* by Verlag Kurt Desch GmbH, Munich. Copyright © 1971 by Verlag Kurt Desch GmbH. Published in Great Britain by William Collins Sons & Co., Ltd., London.

Library of Congress Cataloging in Publication Data

Heim, Michael.
  Aswan!

  Translation of Assuan. Wenn der Damm bricht.
  I. Title.
PZ4.H465As3 [PT2668.E36] 833'.9'14 76-178959
ISBN 0-394-47908-4

Manufactured in the United States of America

FIRST AMERICAN EDITION

For Michael and Susanne, Peter and Annette—

that they need never be witnesses to this catastrophe

Contents

Part One

TOO LITTLE

The High Dam at Aswan (*Sadd el Ali*)

—is an earth dam situated at the intersection of the Nile Valley and latitude 24°N.;

—consists of 52 million cubic yards of rock, sand, and mud filling;

—has a volume seventeen times that of the Great Pyramid of Khufu;

—is 3,937 yards long and 1,071 yards wide at base;

—measures 131 feet across the crest;

—rises 364 feet above the bed of the Nile and 643 feet above sea level;

—has a maximum water level 597 feet above sea level;

—is 550 miles from Cairo;

—forms a reservoir, Lake Nasser, which impounds 5,800 billion cubic feet of water and is 310 miles long;

—has an outlet channel blasted through granite at its east abutment;

—supplies water to a hydroelectric power station whose twelve turbines are fed by six penstocks.

(Details of seepage volume, velocity, and pressure form part of a pseudo-documentary treatment and are thus fictitious.)

THE FIRST STAR OF DAVID FLAG was found impaled in the crest of the dam a hundred yards east of the tomb of Gamal Abdel Nasser. The metal shaft had been driven into the ground between blocks of stone so firmly that it took three soldiers to pull it out. The second flag was found after daybreak, during recovery operations. It lay among loose stones at the foot of the south face, its torn cloth lapped by the waters of the lake.

The crew of machine-gun post No. 3 stated in evidence that their searchlight had been rotating at normal speed. The beam took three minutes to complete a single revolution and the mechanism was synchronized with the searchlights of machine-gun posts Nos. 2 and 4, so that no beams intersected on the face of the dam. Section Commander Fechwat stated that his men had not been dazzled by other lights at any time during the night.

Private Alim, who was the first to open fire with his submachine gun, said, "I thought I saw a figure in the beam. There was no reply to my challenge, so I fired at once." Fechwat estimated that it took one and a half minutes to switch off the traversing mechanism and crank the searchlight back. It was impossible to leave the nest of sandbags and take up the chase, because the crew of post No. 2 also opened fire on the crest of the dam a few seconds after the incident. At least fifteen ricochets were found embedded in the sandbag barrier surrounding post No. 3.

The signaler who notified Command Post Aswan East by

field telephone, thus initiating a general alert, told the board of inquiry that he had heard a metallic sound in the interval between the searchlight's leaving the crest of the dam and the alleged appearance of a figure in its beam.

The search for the Israeli commandos who were presumed to have planted the flag on the High Dam was called off well before midday. After consulting General Mortchov, the senior Soviet adviser who was directing operations from his headquarters at the military base of El Shallal, Colonel Naguil, the Egyptian commander of the central sector, provisionally reopened the Daraw-Aswan road to allow the passage of five trucks laden with perishable foodstuffs. The early train to Cairo left Aswan three hours late. At Aswan airport, a Boeing-727 of Uganda Airlines received permission to take off.

The last army helicopter returned to Talc, the air base in the mountains east of Aswan, by 11:20 a.m. General Mortchov sent off a coded signal to the Soviet Embassy in Cairo and drove by jeep to Command Post Aswan East. In a range of hills three miles east of the generating station, a patrol found some tire tracks leading off the road into a side valley.

At noon, the ground personnel of the SAM-3 missile bases at Ras el Aqaba, Samut, and Sirir um Batikh were relieved and flown in Soviet helicopters to Aswan. A runner brought Colonel Naguil the latest batch of radar reports. The commander of a platoon assigned to guard the reservoir on the island of Elephantine in the Nile notified his company commander that a lance corporal named Musallom had been missing since midnight.

The Star of David flags were examined in the officers' mess at Aswan East. The poles consisted of spear-shaped mild steel shafts seven feet long. The Stars of David were appliquéd on rectangles of linen and measured ten inches from tip to tip. The flags themselves were hemmed with strips of leather and affixed to the steel shafts by five countersunk screws. Only the pole of the flag which the soldiers had pulled out of the crest of the dam showed much distortion at the tip. Its surface was scarred three inches below the flag, presumably by a bullet from Private Alim's Tommy gun. The second flagpole, which had been lying at the foot of the embankment, was bent in the middle.

"One thing can be ruled out," Naguil said. "It's quite inconceivable that an Israeli commando force planted that flag on the crest of the dam last night. Even if every single one of our men had been asleep, no Israeli would have got past the flare pots and trip wires."

General Mortchov tossed the steel shaft onto the table. "Spare me the technicalities, Naguil. The fact remains that a Zionist flag was waving on the High Dam—in the heart of Egypt."

"But there's no sign of any hammer blows on the end of the shaft. Are you telling me the Israelis drove it between the parapet stones with their bare hands? It took three of my men to pull it out."

"Congratulations. They obviously don't believe in exerting themselves too much."

"It's quite possible the flags were dropped from an Israeli aircraft," Naguil said. "Notice how the poles taper toward the top? The center of gravity is somewhere down here. Let them fall free and they'd stick in the ground sharp end first. The leather hems are another pointer in the same direction. They'd be strong enough to prevent the slipstream from ripping the material."

"Oh, yes, and who's going to fly to Aswan and back through a triple radar network?"

"Any pilot who's prepared to duck the umbrella by

underflying the ranges on each bank. The plane probably approached from the south and dropped the flags in series. One of them stuck in the crest—that's no great feat, with sixty-eight thousand square yards to aim at. There is a second possibility. . . ."

"Of course. There may be subversives in your ranks—people who are deliberately trying to spread panic."

"Panic? If that is an aspersion on the Egyptian army, I reject it."

"I'm sorry, Colonel, I'm sorry. So you're looking for more flags. If you find half a dozen in the river, my embassy will accept your theory. Call in frogmen. Start with the submerged outline of the dam and work upstream. In three months, your divers will be in the Sudan."

"I can't send divers to inspect the base of the dam, General Mortchov. The underwater currents are growing stronger every day—they'd be sucked into clefts or fissures in the base. It's now 2:10 p.m. In an hour's time, we'll try our luck with boats and mine detectors."

At that moment, sirens wailed over Aswan.

Three Nubians fishing upriver of the Aswan Dam, on a level with Nag'el Shima, found a buoy bobbing in an inlet and retrieved it from the water. Their attention had been drawn to it when a wave sent it clattering against some blocks of sandstone.

The cast-aluminum float had a snap hook riveted to the underside. A steel tube ran lengthwise through the float itself, which was the size of a pumpkin, and inserted in this was a Star of David flag.

The fishermen stopped an army convoy seven miles short of Nag'el Shima and handed the buoy with the flag to an

6

officer in the leading vehicle. A signal from Nag'el Shima reached Command Post Aswan East at 1:50 p.m. During the next twenty minutes, similar finds were reported from Abu Hor, Nag'gad Kol, Garf Husein, El Malk, and Diwan, where two buoys had been found. At 2:10 p.m., the duty officer issued a submarine alert.

At Talc, tractors towed five flights of MIG-21 fighters from the transverse galleries of a disused mine. Fountains of sand erupted from the runway as their engines roared into life. The Soviet pilots took off at thirty-second intervals and headed northwest.

Air traffic control at Aswan civil airport canceled permission for an Ilyushin from Cairo to land when it was already approaching at three thousand feet.

"Are you crazy?" demanded the pilot. "I've got Defense Minister Nachram on board."

The flight controller said, "The Israelis are here. We're already blocking the runways with trucks. Go back to Luxor."

General Mortchov and Colonel Naguil left the command bunker just as the third flight of MIGs thundered over the crest of the dam. They ran past the penstocks to the south cofferdam, keeping in the lee of the cement store. A patrol boat was circling a thousand yards off the outlet channel. The machine gunners in post No. 1 shouted to the two officers. Naguil turned as he ran and saw their arms pointing skyward.

"They must drop depth charges—a pattern from here to Kalabsha," panted Mortchov. He stumbled and lost his cap.

On the dam, a jeep skidded wildly near post No. 8 and somersaulted down the embankment. The patrol boat had turned and was racing toward the dam, trailing foam.

Mortchov and Naguil pounded across the cofferdam and leapt onto a landing stage composed of heavy planks and oil drums. In the center of the lake, a squadron of motor torpedo boats had fanned out and was proceeding upstream with the crews tugging the covers off their guns. Mortchov was bleeding from both palms. He said, "They shouldn't go so far from the dam."

A military helicopter roared over the valley and disappeared behind reddish hills on the west bank. Someone on the dam loosed off a burst of automatic fire. The two officers on the landing stage could see little jets of dust rise where the ricochets had struck.

"I must get in touch with Senior Adviser Falin at the El Timsah SAM base," Mortchov said, "urgently."

The approaching patrol boat throttled back and glided in a wide arc toward the landing stage.

"Take my binoculars, General Mortchov! There's another buoy with an Israeli flag drifting out there."

"It's a trick. There aren't any submarines. The Israelis are coming from up top, straight out of the sun . . ."

A red signal rocket rose above the generating station, burned out, and fell back leaving a haze of white smoke behind it. The fourth flight of MIGs shot over the crest of the dam so abruptly that the two officers flinched.

"Believe me," said Mortchov, "there aren't any submarines. We'll drop depth charges all the same. From here to Khartoum if necessary."

Naguil caught the rope which a sailor threw from the patrol boat and wound it round a bollard. The boat's propellers churned the water as it reversed to a standstill. Naguil was first across the rail. The sailor saluted.

"Get me Command Post Aswan East!" Naguil shouted.

He hurled himself at the radio set. A Red Crescent ambulance was racing along the crest of the dam.

"Communications center Aswan East."

"Naguil here. I want the sonar station. Yes, this is Naguil —Naguil, I said. Well, what can you tell me?"

"We heard nothing at first, sir."

"And now?"

"Lots of propeller noise."

"Of course, but what sort?"

"High-speed engines, sir."

"Did you pinpoint any submarines earlier?"

"Submarines? No."

Mortchov stepped up to the radio.

"Let me speak to Senior Adviser Falin."

The boat headed out into the lake. Naguil was just about to remove the headphones when a voice said, "Sonar station Nag'el Sibu has just reported a powerful underwater detonation, probably near the east bank. And now the station at Nag'Qurta. . . ."

"All right, man. Over and out."

Naguil handed the microphone to the Soviet general.

"This is it, Mortchov."

Falin came through on Channel 9 three minutes later.

"Are you ready to open fire?" asked Mortchov.

"Yes, apart from the fifth SAM battery. One of the generators isn't functioning."

"Are you in touch with the radar stations on the Red Sea?"

"Yes."

"Well?"

"Nothing. Absolutely nothing."

"Listen, Falin, we haven't allowed for this contingency

before. Could you fire your gadgets into the lake from those three positions up top?"

"Theoretically, General, yes."

"What do you mean, theoretically?"

"We might just about manage the trajectory, but it would damage the mountings."

"Very well, stay on listening watch. Out."

"Out."

"You'll have to recall those boats," Mortchov told Naguil. "We must bombard the approaches at all costs."

"Not a single depth charge gets dropped near the dam."

"Why the hell not?"

"Because if anyone puts Egypt under water, it isn't going to be me."

"You refuse?"

"I shall not give orders to drop depth charges. The torpedo boats on the lake are under Egyptian command."

"You're mad, Naguil. I'll have you court-martialed."

"Sonar station here," quacked a voice in the headphones, "sonar station here. The underwater detonation was caused by the crash of a MIG. Nag'el Sibu has just reported . . ."

"Why won't you drop depth charges?" Mortchov persisted. "The swine may be lying down there on the bottom, releasing their buoys. Why not crack them open?"

"Because we've only computed a shock-wave frequency which didn't exceed the dam's tolerance level when it was completely intact. The base of the dam has been so badly eroded in the last few months that the shock waves from a single depth charge might combine to cause—"

"So you'd rather the High Dam was destroyed by Israeli torpedoes?"

"It's a matter of personal taste. As an Egyptian, yes, I would."

"I offer you a compromise, Colonel. If the Israelis really

have introduced some one-man submarines into this accursed river, their only hope is to operate in the area between the submarine nets and the body of the dam itself. We'll raise the nets and examine them. If we find some buoys inside the cordon, it'll mean they've already penetrated it. If the nets are undamaged, you win."

"Agreed," said Naguil.

At 3:12 p.m., Falin reported on Channel 9:

"The generator at SAM Battery No. 5 is functioning again. Some cretin forgot to preheat the diesel engine."

Seven MIG fighters thundered over the patrol boat at low altitude. The general went to the bridge and described a semicircle in the air with his right arm. The boat turned and raced back toward the dam. As they passed over the marker line, which was held near the surface by a row of white cork floats, Naguil had the engines stopped. The bow sank abruptly as the boat lost speed. The four soldiers who were manning the machine gun on the roof of the bridge lay on their bellies and stared down at the deck. Astern, a headless sheep bobbed in the boat's wake, four legs stiffly erect above a distended carcass.

"If you want a close-up of the Star of David, you'd better step over to the rail, General." Naguil hung his binoculars on a life-belt hook. The diminishing bow wave washed over the small aluminum buoy and caused the white-and-blue flag to undulate. "We're now about fifteen hundred feet beyond the submarine nets," Naguil said. A green signal rocket rose above the penstocks of the generating station. The sonar control center reported that the pilot of the MIG which crashed near Nag'el Sibu had been hauled out of the water by a ferryman. Both his legs were smashed, and the commander at Nag'el Sibu had sent for a medical corps helicopter.

11

"In that case, we can raise the nets," said Naguil. "The buoys were dropped by air, sank to the bottom, and were released at midday by some sort of timing device. Scare tactics, that's all."

"Very well, but what if it's a double bluff? What if the Israelis are lying there on the bottom, waiting for us to open up?"

"I thought we'd agreed on a compromise, General."

The hydraulic winches on each bank tautened the upper cable until it hissed to the surface and sprang clear. The water seethed and a line of foam scored the lake from side to side. Then the winches took a grip on the main cable and raised the net.

Naguil and Mortchov flew along the wall of glistening black mesh in a helicopter. In the third row of links, with his arms sucked through them by the current, hung a dead man. Tattered clothing bellied out in the helicopter's downdraft, which tore the corpse free of the net. As it flopped into the water, Mortchov glanced sidewise at the Egyptian colonel.

"Remarkable," he said. "The system appears to be intact."

While collecting deck chairs at about seven o'clock that evening, a page boy at the Hurghada Hotel on the Red Sea found an ownerless beach robe and handbag and deposited them at the reception desk. After dinner, the hotel management was informed by Paul Pabst, a MER tour leader from Frankfurt, that Fräulein Hofft was missing. It was thought better to await the return of the coach from Bur Safaga. The members of the MER party sat in the bar, with its canopy of fishermen's nets suspended from bamboo poles, until 9 p.m. An accountant from Wiesbaden insisted that Fräulein Hofft had not gone to Bur Safaga at all. She had apparently intimated, two days earlier, that she planned to visit the Coptic monasteries of St. Anthony and St. Paul on the South Galala plateau. Ahmed Galil, the hotel manager, sent the page boy down to the beach with a flashlight. Half an hour later, Galil had the floodlights removed from the hotel terrace and transferred to a point near the beach huts. Two electricians arrived from Hurghada with extension cables.

The coach from Bur Safaga drove along the coast road and drew up outside the hotel at 10 p.m. The passengers comprised two married couples from Cairo; Professor Nuredin Saber, a lecturer in marine biology at Mansura University; and his assistants, Drs. Elbrem and Moher. They had been assigned to study the latest chemostructural changes in the coral reefs along the coast between Hurghada and Foul Bay.

After consulting the prefect of police at Hurghada by phone, Galil opened the handbag that had been left at reception. From a side pocket he removed a purse and a passport issued by the local authorities at Waiblingen, near Stuttgart. The passport's essential particulars were as follows:

Anneliese Hofft, born March 23, 1931, German citizen, unmarried, height 5 ft. 5 in., color of eyes green, special peculiarities none.

Firemen from Hurghada began the search for Anneliese Hofft an hour before midnight. Torches held high, they paddled up and down the bathing beach in rubber dinghies. Dr. Moher checked his diving gear on the hotel terrace. Five German tourists sat perched on the keel of an upturned fishing boat by the water's edge, smoking. The tour leader ran back to the bar and fetched himself a bottle of mineral water. Ropes and grappling hooks arrived from Hurghada in a fire brigade jeep. The prefect of police requested the commander of the garrison at Quseir to send two naval divers.

ASWAN!

General Shraga Waitzinger of the Israeli air force stated during an interview: "Within the next six months at latest, we shall again be in a position to drive the Egyptians into the sea—if I may be permitted to borrow from their own vocabulary. We shall not do so, of course. If necessary, however, we can always bring the sea to them."

The search for Anneliese Hofft was still in progress as dawn broke. Militiamen sealed off the beach and two army launches towed grappling hooks along the bottom. Paul Pabst sent a cable to inform his head office in Frankfurt that Fräulein Hofft had disappeared.

The hotel management posted a notice inviting all guests to a free tour of the emerald mines at Wadi um Dalfa. At midday, one of the grappling irons lodged in a reef and the cable linking the two launches snapped. The prefect of police gave orders for the recovery operation to be discontinued.

Dr. Mario Angelo, of 6065A Calle del Cristo, Venice, entered the Questura at 1:55 p.m. After pacing up and down the landing for five minutes, he knocked at a door marked "Paolo Menegon, Inspector of Police." He sat in a wicker chair facing the inspector's desk while being questioned, with his elbows clamped against his hips because he felt too uncomfortable to prop them on the armrests that jutted at right angles from the chair back. His fingers were splayed across the briefcase on his knees.

"Are you still working at Ispra?" asked Menegon.

"No, I was in the first batch of redundancies from Euratom. That was four years ago."

"I'm sorry. You come from Tuscany, I see. How old are you?"

"Born April 14, 1918. Height five feet six inches, aquiline nose, firm jaw, gray-green eyes. And dog-tired, just for the record."

"I don't quite follow what you were trying to do in Saint Mark's Square the night before last. Neither did the tourists. They thought it was some kind of gag."

"I meant them to take it seriously," said Dr. Angelo.

"The municipal sanitation department reported you to us on account of those plastic sheets you spread in front of the church. What were you planning to do, stifle the pigeons?"

"I waited until it was dark and the pigeons had gone. Then I got a couple of men to carry the bundles of plastic from the mole to the square. For a fee, of course. After that we took bags of corn and wrote—or sprinkled, whichever— the word 'HUNGER' on the paving stones in big letters six feet high. Then we covered the letters with plastic sheeting."

"I still don't get it," said Menegon.

"My assumption was that early next morning, when the sheets were removed by the municipal refuse collectors and the first tourists arrived in Saint Mark's Square, the pigeons would pounce on the corn. Hundreds of pigeons spelling out the word 'hunger' on that godforsaken square, don't you see? Hundreds of jostling pigeons forming the word 'hunger.' If one tourist in ten had snapped the scene at the right moment—well, it would have made a unique picture."

"You meant it to be a protest against hunger—an appeal for more aid to underdeveloped countries, and so on? You obviously don't spend the whole day recording protests against world hunger in pigeon food. They tell me you buy large quantities of vegetables and take them home. Is that your contribution to the fight against hunger?"

"Yes, I use them for experimental purposes."

"I get the feeling you're in the wrong place."

"I felt that as soon as I entered this office."

15

"Did you take any research notes with you when you left Ispra?"

"I had every right to. Some of them related to personal experiments."

"Conducted in the Euratom laboratories."

"And inside my head."

"This business with the plastic sheets . . ."

Dr. Angelo let go of his briefcase for the first time and pulled his chair nearer the desk. "My patience deserts me sometimes, Inspector. The plastic sheet idea was a gimmick. I've made a scientific discovery which I somehow have to sell. I need publicity. I have a process for the preservation of agricultural products. No cans, no gamma rays, no freeze-drying, or anything like that. I preserve agricultural products by inhibiting the evaporation process. If fluid can be retained in vegetable tissue, a fruit remains in good condition. It doesn't dry up or go bad."

"In other words, you could ship tomatoes to India."

"Precisely," said Dr. Angelo.

"What's the trick?"

"At Ispra, I looked for a preparation which would reinforce the surface tension of a fluid and, as I told you, prevent atoms and molecules from breaking away. At long last, I stumbled on perymethylene ether. If I spray an orange with perymethylene ether, the fluid inside can't evaporate. In theory, I could coat blocks of arctic ice with the stuff and ship them to the Congo as drinking water."

"And in practice you could discuss the whole idea with a psychiatrist," said the inspector. "Who do you plan to sell it to?"

"Sell isn't the right word. I must publicize it. I owe it to the fight against hunger. I've been trying for months to contact the Secretary-General of the United Nations. Also,

I'm hoping to address the next Congress on World Hunger at Khartoum."

Menegon glanced at his watch and pushed his chair back. He said, as Dr. Angelo reached for his briefcase, "Let's hope they give you a better hearing in Khartoum."

Lance Corporal Musallom was last seen on the island of Elephantine as he left his post shortly after midnight and went down to the river. Propping his rifle against the north wall of the reservoir, Musallom called to a sentry that he had heard the hum of an aircraft and was going to fetch his night glass from the patrol boat.

Musallom's platoon commander waited until midday before reporting his absence. The search for the missing N.C.O. was discontinued at 2:10 p.m., when Command Post Aswan East issued its submarine alert. It was not resumed. Since a dinghy had also disappeared, the immediate inference was that Musallom had deserted.

He was found a week later, on the bank near the old Nilometer, by a soldier who had smelt putrefaction and gone to investigate. Musallom was lying prone on the sand with his arms flung wide and his head twisted sidewise. The water was lapping round his legs at knee level and one of his boots was missing. The steel shaft with its Star of David flag had obviously caught him as he ran, penetrating his body via the right shoulder blade and emerging under the heart. The impact had been so great that the dead man's body was pinned to the ground. Colonel Naguil phoned instructions that nothing was to be moved and sent an army photographer to the island.

. . .

Naguil showed General Mortchov the prints that evening in the mess. "It must have been this way," he said. "The pilot flew down the Nile Valley at very low altitude. He throttled back his engines just before reaching the dam and started to drop the flags and buoys. By the time he overflew the dam, he'd already had a good chance of planting at least one flag in the heart of Egypt—to quote your own words. All the others sank into the mud. At midday, the delayed-action buoys rose to the surface, and the ruse designed to conjure up the presence of Israeli commandos was complete."

"May I have a couple of these prints?" asked Mortchov. "For my memoirs, just in case." He stared at the sprawled figure with the flagpole sprouting from its back. "If you ever think of erecting an unknown soldier's tomb at Aswan after the war, you might do worse than fill it with the remains of Lance Corporal Musallom."

Fewa Mansyut, a girl student who had been staying at the resthouse of the Egyptian Hunting and Angling Club, drowned before the eyes of fellow-bathers at the Red Sea resort of Marsa'Alam.

Beach attendants rowed out to the girl as she screamed and thrashed the water. Questioned later, they said that Fewa Mansyut had obviously been attacked by cramps. No sharks had appeared at the scene of the accident. Lookouts in the boat beyond the reef had flown a blue flag throughout the morning. Fewa Mansyut sank eighty yards from the shore. The spot was marked by a buoy. That evening, the local commander at Marsa'Alam informed the Ministry of the Interior in Cairo that two amateur frogmen who had gone in search of the girl's body had not returned to their hotel.

.   .   .

At a press conference in the Tel Aviv Hilton, Premier Moshe Dayan was asked whether General Waitzinger's remark about "bringing the sea to the Egyptians" was an allusion to the possibility of bombing the Aswan Dam.

"Lake Nasser represents an important factor in our defense plans," said Dayan. "President Sadat of Egypt knows this and so do the members of his General Staff. President Nasser also knew this but refused to come to terms with the idea. If ever a day dawned when our national survival was in jeopardy—but only then—we should attack the dam."

"With bulldozers?" asked a correspondent.

"Stored in the upper reaches of the Nile Valley is a bomb whose explosive power almost rivals that of America's nuclear potential. When Lake Nasser is full, the dam has to withstand the pressure of 5,800 billion cubic feet of water. That means 164 billion metric tons, not including mud. The dam is 3,937 yards long and 364 feet high. The base measures 1,071 yards across, the crest 131 feet. That makes a total volume of 52 million cubic yards. So much for the detonator of this bomb. Since our army doesn't maintain a unit capable of producing man-made earthquakes, we should simply scratch the surface of the High Dam. Water pressure would do the rest."

"Would you drop aerial torpedoes?"

"Who knows? We might even use the bulldozers you mentioned just now."

"Would you agree that your statement might be construed as one of the grossest examples of political blackmail in the history of mankind?"

"Of course not. I'd prefer to call it a form of insurance."

"And if the dam breaks?"

"You must ask the Swiss flood experts about that. They estimate that Cairo would be engulfed by a wall of water thirty-nine feet high."

"So it would mean the annihilation of an entire country?"

"Since eighty-five per cent of the Egyptian population live in the Nile Valley—yes, I suppose it would."

"What is your personal reaction to such a possibility?"

"If the High Dam were situated in the Jordan Valley, I should be suffering from insomnia."

While stacking deck chairs, the page boy of the Hurghada Hotel found a terry towel, a tin of Nivea, and the upper half of a flowered bikini. A second member of the MER party was found to be missing, this time Annedore Ehlsen, a thirty-two-year-old civil servant. In a hut on the edge of Oil Field IV, police arrested an engineer from Port Said whom beach attendants had allegedly seen loitering near the bathing huts.

That evening, the guests of the Hurghada Hotel were summoned to the dining room by the prefect of police and asked to abandon their sand castles on the beach. "After the incidents here and at Marsa'Alam," he explained, "it seems logical to suspect a pattern of some sort. Sharks were not responsible, so far as we can tell at present."

Fräulein Ehlsen's room was sealed after a preliminary search. A police jeep took the page boy into town for questioning. Anneliese Hofft's brother arrived in Hurghada on the night bus. The Admiralty in Cairo sent an underwater camera to aid the search for the missing tourists. Pabst, the MER tour leader, announced that his party would be cutting short their stay. In the bar, the accountant from Wiesbaden claimed to have seen a triangular dorsal fin two hundred yards from shore that afternoon.

Professor Saber's assistants, Dr. Elbrem and Dr. Moher, were diving for coral specimens from a raft moored off the beach below the Hurghada Hotel, opposite the bathing huts. The members of the MER party were waiting in the hotel foyer for a coach to take them to Luxor airport. Anneliese

Hofft's brother was sitting with some firemen in a rubber dinghy, staring at the screen of the underwater camera.

Professor Saber was on the balcony of his second-floor room, drafting an interim report to the Egyptian Admiralty. This reiterated statements by local fishermen to the effect that barracuda and lampreys were avoiding inshore areas, and drew attention to an accumulation of atrophic forms in the sea-urchin colonies inhabiting the reefs.

At 12:10 p.m., the page boy returned from Hurghada on a borrowed bicycle. Beneath an awning on the terrace, waiters were laying a table for the two married couples from Cairo. At 12:12 p.m., the hotel manager, Ahmed Galil, called the MER tour leader to the telephone.

Two boatmen rowed out to the raft with some oxygen cylinders. The coach pulled into the hotel car park. On the third floor, the prefect of police pried the seal from the door of the missing civil servant's room with a knife point and told a Nubian servant to wind up the slatted shutters.

At 12:28 p.m., the men on the raft started to shout. Professor Saber ran out into the corridor and hammered vainly on the door of the lift. Taking the stairs two at a time, he reached the foyer just as Galil was picking up the telephone. Saber caught him by the sleeve, jerking it out of his hand. The receiver dangled over the wastepaper basket by its cord. Galil bent to retrieve it, saying, "Kindly allow me to telephone."

Saber shouted, "Come to the beach. Something's happened!"

The page boy raced after the two men as they crossed the terrace and made for the beach huts. He groped beneath the boardwalk and pulled out a pair of oars.

"We must turn the boat over and slide it into the water," Saber told the manager. In the car park, the tourists had descended from their coach and were staring down at the beach. The figures on the raft waved madly. A beach attendant ran up just as Saber and Galil threw their weight against the boat, and pointed to the fire brigade's rubber dinghy, which was heading for the shore.

They reached the raft twelve minutes after the alarm had been raised. Elbrem was kneeling on the boards in his wet suit with the safety line coiled round his thighs, bracing himself with his hands. The two boatmen were standing on the edge of the raft holding the mooring rope.

"What's the matter with Moher?" Saber called from the dinghy. Elbrem shook his head.

Galil said, "He can't hear you with that rubber cap on."

The line ran off into the water at a shallow angle. Saber and Galil leapt aboard while a fireman moored the dinghy to the raft. The professor tore his assistant's diving cap from his head.

"Where's Moher?"

"He suddenly started to tug. Like this, you see? Like a big fish. Then the line went slack and tightened again."

"How long ago?"

"Since they started to shout . . ."

Saber put his hand on the line and felt it jerk. He said to Galil, "What do you think? Is it a shark?"

"I don't know, it could be."

"Did he give any signal?" Saber asked his assistant.

"That's what I thought it was, at first—a signal. Then I was jerked off my feet. The circulation in my legs has gone."

"We must see if we can haul him out," Saber said. "We'll have to mask the edge with something or the line will shear."

They passed the rope over an oxygen bottle which the page boy held against the side of the raft, tied the end to a mooring ring, and hauled.

. . .

Dr. Moher's body was recovered an hour later by the crew of a police boat which towed the raft and safety line toward the beach. After it had gone a hundred yards, resistance ceased abruptly and the line went slack. Moher floated to the surface face downward. The mouthpiece of his breathing apparatus was still clamped between his teeth, but the tube had snapped and his depth gauge was missing. A plastic bag full of coral specimens still hung from the dead man's belt.

A post-mortem examination disclosed that the professor's assistant had been strangled by the safety line, which had passed under his right arm and round his neck. No shark bites were found on the man's body. Rents in his wet suit were attributable to the coral reef.

That evening, Professor Saber telephoned the Admiralty and informed the Secretary of State. "It was quite inexplicable," he said. "The constant tension on the line must have been equivalent to at least ten times Dr. Moher's body weight. I still find it just as inexplicable that his body should have risen to the surface so abruptly."

At eight o'clock, Radio Cairo reported that an Israeli reconnaissance plane had been shot down over Aswan. The pilot bailed out and was detained by some Bedouin on the plateau west of the dam.

On orders from the Admiralty, the scene of the accident near the Hurghada Hotel was searched with the underwater camera. Two officers from the naval base at Ras Gharib directed the operation. A helicopter brought special floodlights from Cairo. These were lowered into the water on steel cables suspended from pontoons. Four scientists from the Oceanographic Institute at Alexandria arrived in Hurghada to assist Professor Saber in the evaluation of coral specimens.

Preliminary analyses of reef corals indicated that structural changes had occurred in the Madreporaria strains as a result of fluctuations in the salt content of sea water. A decline in polyp activity was observed in various reefs. During the day, the laboratory of the Hurghada research team received coral specimens from the reefs of Wadi Gimal Island and the coastal sectors Bur Safaga-Quseir, Marsa'Igla, Marsa Tundaba, and Qul'an Ras Banas.

The bodies of Anneliese Hofft and Annedore Ehlsen were found at a depth of sixty feet, lying side by side in a cleft beneath overhanging banks of coral. All the sailors manning the pontoons noticed at first was a pale patch on the screen. They maneuvered the craft carrying the camera and floodlights over the cleft and notified the officers in the hotel.

One of the dead women was lying on her back, head downward. Her arms were flattened against the rock and her long hair, as the official report noted, was floating vertically in the water. The other victim was crouching at the mouth of the cleft with her knees drawn up. The pathologist's report stressed that the bodies had been lacerated by grappling irons. It had nevertheless been possible to determine beyond doubt that abrasions and bruises had been inflicted on the women's backs and shoulders immediately prior to death. Although the events leading up to both accidents could not be established beyond doubt, it was reasonable to assume that Anneliese Hofft and Annedore Ehlsen had been dragged along the reefs by underwater currents. The death certificates issued by Dr. Ibrahim of the army medical corps recorded death by drowning in each case.

In his report to the Admiralty, Professor Saber confirmed a previous suspicion that corals in the reefs along the western coast of the Red Sea were exhibiting morbid changes. Symptoms of degeneration had already affected whole colonies and were particularly apparent in the calcareous skeleton linking individual polyps. The living substance coating the calcareous skeleton had been completely destroyed at certain points along the coast. Saber concluded his study with the following remarks:

"Taking into account three factors—first, that reef corals (Madreporaria) react predominantly to fluctuations in the salt content of sea water; secondly, that affected areas are being shunned by fish which would normally be dependent on the submarine fauna and flora indigenous to banks of coral; and, thirdly, that the said areas display a drop in water temperature, albeit not below the level that obtains in Madreporaria colonies, namely, 68.9° Fahrenheit—we must infer the existence of upwelling fresh-water currents.

"In this context, two circumstances appear to possess special significance.

"In the first place, symptoms of degeneration occur mainly at points where old riverbeds descend from the mountains of Upper Egypt to meet the coast. There appears to be a repetition of the process which probably led to the breaching of reefs subsequent to the Tertiary period. The fresh water which flowed down to the sea from the mountainous catchment areas, destroyed the banks of coral there, and incidentally paved the way for various Red Sea harbors now seems to be welling from the seabed and, because of its inferior specific gravity, to be superimposing itself on the layers of salt water. Precise measurements of salt content are impracticable because of the intermingling of both types of water.

"Secondly, the past fortnight has witnessed six fatal accidents to bathers in the area under observation. In all cases, including the deaths of a girl student and the two frogmen whose bodies have just been found at the seaside resort of Marsa'Alam, cardiac failure and circulatory disorders have been ruled out as a possible cause of death. No injuries attributable to sharks were found.

"The incidence of severe abrasions, lacerations, and bruising was common to all six cases. In that of my assistant, Dr. Moher, I was able to verify for myself the exceptional force with which the victim was pinned to the seabed. The three bodies found at Hurghada, immediately off the hotel bathing beach, were all located within a very small radius although they had vanished at different points. The two German tourists were lying in or near the same cleft in the rocks.

"From all this, it may be inferred that at certain points along the Red Sea coast, most of them coinciding with the estuaries of former rivers, there exist strong and hitherto unrecorded underwater currents coupled with corresponding suction effects. Atrophic changes in the coral reefs cannot but reinforce our supposition that these are fresh-water currents.

"In this connection, I deem it my duty to draw attention to current rumors which suggest that the bed of Lake Nasser and, allegedly, even the substructure of the High Dam itself are failing to withstand the hydrostatic pressure exerted on them—in other words, that water from the Nile is escaping via lateral fissures into the Red Sea and the Libyan Desert. These rumors coincide with statements to the effect that the latest storage targets have not been met and that the level of Lake Nasser is actually falling again. I urgently request that isotopic measurements be made to ascertain the route and volume of the water which may be escaping from Lake Nasser, coupling my request with the prognosis that any water thus escaping, which would have to drop only ninety-eight feet to reach the Red Sea but is subject to the immense pressures prevailing inside the dam, will tend to follow the course of the dried-up riverbeds referred to above."

On Monday, the Egyptian government declared Aswan a restricted area. A charter plane carrying British tourists was diverted to Luxor fifteen minutes before it was due to land there. An official from the Ministry of Tourism explained to the tour leader that severe sandstorms had been forecast for the area. It would thus be impossible for his party to visit the temples of Abu Simbel until further notice. The Ministry would, however, arrange some tours in the vicinity of Luxor; e.g., to the Valley of the Kings, the Temple of Horus at Idfu, and the crocodile tombs at Gebelen.

In a report requested by Minister of the Interior Yussuf Gidaff, the High Dam Authority acknowledged for the first time that discrepancies in water-level readings might not be attributable to wind drag.

The main gauge at Aswan registered 534.54 feet above sea level. Concurrently, the gauge at El Diwan registered 534.96 feet above sea level.

Reports from Sudanese observation posts responsible for checking gauges south of the border were transmitted direct from Khartoum to Cairo that evening because of a breakdown in the Wadi Halfa-Aswan teleprinter link.

The High Dam Authority stated: "The fact that the lake level has dropped more appreciably in the Aswan area than in the southern storage areas may be attributable to exceptionally heavy evaporation losses resulting from day temperatures ranging as high as 120° Fahrenheit. Mean day temperatures in the El Diwan sector during the past week have ranged between 107° and 111° Fahrenheit. There is certainly no evidence of any increase in subterranean seepage through the lake bed and the base of the dam. For purposes of comparison, it is worth recalling the situation in May, 1968, when evaporation losses over the entire surface of the lake were in excess of gains."

For the first time since the November armistice, specialist units of the Egyptian army, operating at company strength, crossed the Suez Canal at dawn. Preceded by a two-hour bombardment, they made the crossing in amphibious vehicles south of El Qantara, blew up an Israeli ammunition dump, and withdrew. An Israeli Phantom fighter was hit by a SAM-2 guided missile over Ismailia and crashed into the park between the town hall and the canal.

A military spokesman announced in Jerusalem that thirty-seven Israelis had been killed during an attack on a road construction unit. Two nineteen-year-old soldiers had been found with their throats cut. The bodies were in sleeping bags on the back seat of a jeep.

The Israeli midday paper *Yekhdith Haaretz* commented: "We are all mortal. We do not claim divine powers, save in one small respect: we could, if we so wished, unleash a second Flood. The only question is, should we wait until President Sadat has completed his Ark?"

Speaking at a reception in honor of the outgoing British Ambassador, Israel's Minister of Defense, Mme. Meir, said: "We should naturally have the utmost scruples about bombing the Aswan Dam. I hope, however, that if ever the occasion arises I shall be fortified by the example of your great fellow-countryman Winston Churchill, who responded to similar provocation in 1943 by destroying the Eder Dam."

By order of the Ministry of the Interior, the High Dam Authority at Aswan was instructed, as of now, to submit daily readings to the Presidential secretariat and Minister Gidaff. They took the following form:

LAKE LEVEL

PORE-WATER PRESSURE IN BODY OF DAM

Piezometric devices built into the body of the dam have the function of registering, via filter tubes and filtering material, the distribution of hydrostatic pressure exerted by the lake on individual sectors of the dam. The hydrostatic condition of the dam is measured by electronic devices, and, in the west abutment of the dam, partly by pipe gauges.

EARTH PRESSURE IN BODY OF DAM

Pressure gauges installed in the body of the dam record the pressure in the filling material by oleohydraulic or electrical means.

SEEPAGE VELOCITY

SEEPAGE OUTFLOW

On the downstream side of the dam, between the main dam and the north cofferdam, relief pipes (drain wells) have been sunk so that water percolating the body of the dam can flow away under its own excess pressure. If there were no such outlets, even small amounts of water could build up critical pressures within the body of the dam.

PARTICLES IN SEEPAGE

Suspended and alluvial matter carried from the body of the dam by the water perco-

lating it are deposited in a settling tank
situated between the main dam and the north
cofferdam.

According to rumors current in Beirut, cholera had been introduced into Upper Egypt by pilgrims from Mecca who, having boarded United Arab planes at the Saudi Arabian port of Jidda and flown back across the Red Sea to Aswan, were spending a routine nine days in quarantine at the former Cataract Hotel. The Lebanese newspaper *Oriental Star* claimed that one passenger had leapt from his coach during the trip from airport to hotel and caught the night train to Cairo. Denying this report, a spokesman for the World Health Organization in the Avenue Appia, Geneva, stated that Aswan had demonstrably not been proclaimed a restricted area because of the danger of infection.

F R I D A Y

LAKE NASSER: LEVEL FALLING

Lake level: 518.13 ft. above sea level.
Change: minus 0.88 ft. (Top water level: 597
ft.; crest of dam: 643 ft.)

PORE-WATER PRESSURE IN BODY OF DAM: DECREASING

Main piezometers	A	B	C	D	E
kg/cm^2	8.12	8.04	8.13	5.91	6.39
Change	−0.03	−0.05	−0.01	−0.05	−0.02

EARTH PRESSURE IN BODY OF DAM: DECREASING

Pressure gauges	A	B	C	D	E
kg/cm^2	18.06	17.38	17.99	7.50	12.21
Change	−0.07	−0.05	−0.02	−0.04	−0.03

```
SEEPAGE VELOCITY: INCREASING

In alluvium            (tolerance: 9 thousandths
(subterranean)                     of a mm/sec)

West bank          Valley center    East bank
5.5 thou-          5.4 thou-        5.7 thou-
sandths of a       sandths of a     sandths of a
mm/sec             mm/sec           mm/sec

Change
+0.005             +0.009           +0.001

In apron               (tolerance: 5 thousands
of dam                             of a mm/sec)

West section       Dam center       East section
3.4 thou-          3.4 thou-        3.3 thou-
sandths of a       sandths of a     sandths of a
mm/sec             mm/sec           mm/sec

Change
+0.006             +0.007           +0.003

SEEPAGE OUTFLOW: INCREASING

Drain well A    2.9       Drain well B    4.1
                1/sec                     1/sec
Change          +0.2                      +0.5

PARTICLES IN SEEPAGE (tolerance: 0.8mm). Fine
sediment, granular diameter 0.002-0.006mm.
```

Speaking at Columbia, the American marine geologist Robert Myan claimed that the Mediterranean had dried up between five and a half and twelve million years ago, because losses from evaporation exceeded the amount of water that flowed in through the Straits of Gibraltar. The basin did not become refilled until the bed of the straits sank after tectonic subsidences had occurred in the Agadir zone. The results of deep borings carried out in the Mediterranean made it possible to reconstruct this process in detail. Myan went on to state that the phenomenon which had dried up an entire sea should be viewed in current perspective. Since the geological formations on the bed of the Straits of Gibraltar were rising at an annual rate of seven or eight millimeters, permitting less water to flow in from the Atlantic, while water from the Nile was simultaneously being trapped by the High Dam at Aswan, the balance between influx and evaporation might again be upset. To put it crudely, he said, massive interference with the upper reaches of the Nile, coupled with geological changes, might once again, in the foreseeable future, transform the Mediterranean into a desert.

A local Miami newspaper commented on Myan's theory as follows: "The outlook—and not only for the Mediterranean countries directly affected—is weird as well as alarming. Just imagine—the Aegean Islands a rugged mountainscape with valleys full of rotting fish. The Maltese capital, Valetta, perched on a highland plateau. A rail crash south of Sardinia between the Sicily-Morocco mail train and the Madrid-Cairo Express . . ."

At a memorial service for the crew of the guided-missile ship *Beersheba,* sunk by Egyptian frogmen off the mole at Elath, the President of Israel declared that the countries of the Near East had spent twenty thousand million dollars on armaments in the past twenty years. All outstanding refugee problems could, he said, have been solved by the expenditure of only 5 percent of this sum. Israel had demonstrated her readiness to provide development aid in Africa, Asia, and Latin America, and was still prepared to cooperate economically with neighboring Arab countries. As long as lack of understanding prevailed on the other side, however,

Israel would strike back in response to every Arab provocation.

At dawn, the villages of El Maks el Qibli and El Maks el Bahari were inundated by water escaping northwestward from Lake Nasser through fissures running beneath its rocky banks.

The previous night, army posts at the oases of Abu Husein and Kiseiba in the south of the Kharga Depression had reported to the military commander at El Kharga that Bedouin were taking refuge on the plateau because water had been jetting from the artesian wells for several hours. The duty officer at El Kharga tried until midnight to reach the Defense Ministry and then wrote a report for delivery to Cairo by courier plane next morning.

Camel drivers who set out from El Maks el Qibli an hour before sunrise, bound for the village of Dush with a consignment of firewood, were first alerted by the behavior of their beasts. The camels, which had shown resistance while being loaded, snapped at their drivers and tried to break away from the caravan.

The leader of the party, a seventy-year-old Bedouin from the Dungul oasis, was injured when his camel shied and threw him into some rocks. It was decided to send the unconscious man back to El Maks el Qibli with two companions. While the drivers were tying him to a draft camel, they heard a great hiss as air was forced through the sand by rising water. Thinking at first that it was a storm, they drove their prancing beasts back onto the track and hurriedly continued their journey.

Ten minutes after the party had split up, water surged to the surface. The sand seethed, the camels began to bellow and galloped off up a slope. The animal carrying the unconscious man broke loose and dashed for the village. Flocks of pigeons rose from the houses, circled the fields for some minutes, and flew off eastward. Water flowed over the stones marking the track, gushed from the ground in muddy yellow fountains, spilled over dikes and into irrigation ditches, tore rushes from the sand, slapped against the bellies of camels as they waded through the flood, splashed into the faces of the men who were clinging, screaming, to their saddles, surged against mud walls, poured through windows and doorways, and tossed palm-frond roofs into the air. The first flood wave to hit El Maks el Qibli washed children and chickens into the maize fields; the second hurled men and women against walls as they waded through the waist-high water. A ram on the dike west of the village was strangled by its chain. The flood demolished huts, stripped palm trees of their foliage, and by late afternoon, when dinghies were dropped by helicopters from the garrison at Idfu, was flowing off into the Kharga Depression.

Eighty-seven children, twenty-four women, and eighteen men were drowned in the villages of El Maks el Qibli and El Maks el Bahari. That night, truckloads of engineers sent south by the commander of the El Kharga garrison used flamethrowers to cremate the carcasses of six hundred sheep and goats.

Idress Mohyeddin, the Egyptian Minister of Information, left the elevator on the third floor of the Ministry building and walked up two flights to his office on the fifth.

When he reached the outer office, his personal assistant told him that funeral processions were converging on the Presidential palace from various parts of the city. The mourners carried white coffins and were being forced into side streets by detachments of military police.

Mohyeddin recalled that he had heard rhythmical chanting in the distance as his car pulled up at some traffic lights in Gumhuriya Square on the way to the Ministry.

"It's just like the funerals of the fedayeen in 1969," said his P.A. "Except that there aren't any flags this time."

"Do they know at the Ministry of the Interior?" Mohyeddin asked.

"Minister Gidaff phoned us fifteen minutes ago."

"Who are they, members of the Moslem Brotherhood?"

"The Minister says his staff haven't turned up yet. He doesn't know, but it must be some kind of concerted action —a demonstration, he thinks. We don't even know if there are any bodies in the coffins."

"Has Gidaff notified the President?"

"Yes, half an hour ago. By phone. The President has been at Heliopolis since last night. Minister Nachram is flying back to Cairo at this moment. The palace is surrounded by men of the 3rd Brigade."

"What do they want, these people?"

"We've no idea. Apparently, the police held up a funeral procession in front of the National Assembly, about six thousand strong. It's supposed to be on its way here now. The last report came from pickets in Shari'al Zahara."

Mohyeddin leaned against the window sill and waited. His secretary brought some coffee.

"I may need you later," the Minister said.

Children were playing on the flat roofs opposite the Ministry. Women sat cross-legged beside fireplaces or lounged in the shade of walls. Freshly laundered clothes hung limp from the lines that were strung between the chimneys. Mohyeddin watched some children crawling around on a shallow-domed roof, chasing away pigeons with sticks. If it rains now, they'll probably dance in the streets, he thought.

35

The heat was making him drowsy. A telephone shrilled in the next room. He debated whether to call Gidaff. Irritatingly, the telephone continued to ring for some seconds before his P.A. picked up the receiver. He tossed a lump of sugar into his cup, missed, and found the ashtray instead. He could hear the murmur of his assistant's voice. The pigeons rose from the dome with a sudden flurry of wings. Three women stood up and walked across the flat roof to where their children were hitting the parapet with sticks. Mohyeddin ground out his cigarette on the parquet with the heel of his shoe and yawned. The children slid down the dome on their bellies and joined the women under an awning.

Mohyeddin gave a start as his P.A. appeared in the doorway and said, "They're marching past the Ministry now, coffins and all."

The women and children on the roof continued to crouch beneath their awning. The windows of the houses on the other side of the street were thronged with people. Shutters rattled in parts of the Ministry and a bird swooped across the courtyard. Mohyeddin straightened up with a jerk and flung open the window. The same rhythmical chanting came to his ears. He strode through the outer office and into the corridor, saying as he went, "Find my driver and tell him to stand by in the courtyard."

The funeral procession reached the Ministry of Information at about ten o'clock. Mohyeddin hurried downstairs, crossed the courtyard, and waited beside the sandbag barriers in the entrance until the first men came by, carrying poles adorned with wreaths for the dead.

There were four coffins draped with Egyptian flags. They swayed on their carrying-poles as the mob surged down the street toward the Kubbeh Palace. Youths running ahead of the coffins with palm fronds broke through the military police cordon a hundred yards west of the Ministry. The crowd divided as it met a jeep parked in the middle of the street, and flowed together again. Mohyeddin could hear the blare of the horn above the hubbub of the marchers and the wailing of the women who were accompanying the coffins. He stepped out onto the pavement and caught a man by the arm.

"Where do these people come from?"

"It was against the will of Allah." The man's eyes were half closed and his head rolled to and fro.

"Where do you come from?"

"It was against the will of Allah."

"I asked where you come from."

"Kharga, Kharga. It is our misfortune." The man broke away. A young fellah was carried past Mohyeddin, lying supine on a dozen hands which jutted above the heads of the crowd.

"The dam will destroy us all!" he cried. His arms thrashed the air and his right leg dangled above the heads of those who were carrying him.

"The dam will destroy us all!"

"The dam is our misfortune," chanted the people in the funeral procession.

"The dam is our misfortune!"

"It was against the will of Allah."

"The dam will destroy us all!"

Mohyeddin stared at the sweat-stained face. The boy's in a trance, he thought.

"It was against the will of Allah."

"We shall all die!"

"The dam is our misfortune!"

"Allah has spoken."

"The dam will destroy us all!"

"We shall all die, every one . . ."

.   .   .

That night, ten dummies in Egyptian officers' uniforms were set adrift in the Nile. Four lodged in the hawsers of boats anchored off the Nilometer on Roda Island, one was seen bobbing against the embankment at Gezira Island, and two were found next morning near the former German consulate by construction workers who had gone to light a fire in a tar barrel among the trees bordering Shari'al Nil. The two dummies were drifting along face downward with their arms splayed in a disjointed fashion. One of them was so low in the water that only an air bubble in the back of its uniform tunic kept it afloat.

The workmen ran along the quay, gesticulating. Two of them tried to stop a taxi but alarmed the driver so much that he accelerated away. Five hundred yards downstream, the men found a boat, rowed out, and towed the dummies to the embankment with boat hooks.

Another dummy was fished out of the water by the crew of a police launch as it floated past the Semiramis Hotel. The dripping figure was deposited on the engine cowling and left there until it began to steam. Then a young policeman took it by the legs and dumped it on the duckboards.

Yet another dummy became entangled with a buoy opposite the Coptic Museum and started to disintegrate. By the time it was recovered by some men of the 7th Division, the current had already torn off both feet and maize stalks and palm leaves were protruding from its sleeves.

The tenth dummy was carried under the Bridge of July 26th at about 9 a.m. A sentry threw a life belt after it and ran to inform his platoon commander.

That afternoon, by order of Defense Minister Nachram, the dummies were taken to a police barracks on the northern outskirts of Cairo. Attorney General Malom arrived an hour later, when Nachram's preliminary examination was complete.

The dummies, which were between five and six feet tall, consisted of straw, maize stalks, and palm leaves whipped with cord. The heads were bound with bast fiber and the officers' caps sewn on with fishing line. They wore obsolete Egyptian army summer uniforms, American lace-up boots, and underclothes bearing the label "Robinsons, Ltd., Birmingham." The two dummies found by the construction workers had bayonets driven through their chests. The hilts were kept in place by cords running crosswise round the figures' hips and shoulders, and it was the weight of the bayonets which had turned them face downward in the water. Five of the other dummies had nooses of half-inch rope around their necks.

The handkerchief stapled to the left-hand breast pocket of each uniform tunic bore the following inscription in indelible ink: "I, Anwar el Sadat, President of the United Arab Republic, tampered with this river and was destroyed by it. I dammed the waters of the Nile and was doomed to die before the flood came. But the Egyptian people will demolish the High Dam and live on. Have mercy on my remains. I met my death in the name of Allah and the nation. Signed: Sadat."

Defense Minister Nachram drove back to his Ministry at 6 p.m. and called for the file on the Israeli flags. The Attorney General telephoned a lecturer at the Botanical Institute, Cairo University, and instructed him to examine the sectional planes of the maize stalks and palm leaves used in the dummies.

By midnight, in an area extending sixty-five miles upstream from the center of Cairo, ninety-two members of the Moslem Brotherhood had been detained and conveyed to the capital in army trucks. Two of them, who slit a tarpaulin and tried to jump from the road bridge at Namib, were shot by their escort. A third escaped into a maize field.

The last radar report reached the Defense Ministry at 11 p.m. Like the rest, it confirmed that no unidentified aircraft had overflown Egyptian territory during the previous night. Nachram telephoned the Attorney General.

"I'm afraid it isn't just a repetition of the Aswan farce."

"You mean the flags?"

"I don't know what else I could be referring to."

"In other words, the dummies were launched from the riverbank."

"I doubt if they'd have survived a free fall from thirty thousand feet."

"Then it's mutiny."

"You could call it that."

"Any particular garrison in mind?"

"All, on principle."

"Then why round up the Moslem Brotherhood? In the name of Allah, I suppose."

"Quite so, just as it said on the handkerchiefs. This is merely a preventive measure designed to spread the word."

"In that case, you'd better detain some more categories tomorrow—all the brickmakers who've been short of Nile mud for the past six years, all those displaced Nubians from the upper reaches sitting around in camps, all the fishermen . . ."

"Of course. And you can interrogate every peasant who tries to lick salt off his fields in the Delta."

"Very funny. Whatever happens, we'd better get as much sleep as possible."

At the same time, officers of the military security service were interrogating their first army suspects at the camp of

El Saff, south of Cairo. In the laboratory of Cairo's Botanical Institute, a technician placed some straw in a dish of water so that he could measure the extent to which the stalks had swollen next morning.

A letter from the Food and Agriculture Organization was lying outside the door of Dr. Angelo's apartment. He saw the Swiss stamp and hesitated before tearing open the envelope, puzzled because he had sent his application to FAO headquarters in New York. The Geneva secretariat informed Dr. Angelo that Professor Ferguson's death had vacated a place on the list of speakers scheduled to address the 8th Congress on World Hunger in Khartoum. Dr. Angelo was advised to travel there several days in advance of his allotted time, because allowance must be made for changes of program.

T U E S D A Y

LAKE NASSER: LEVEL FALLING

Lake level: 515.34 ft. above sea level. Change: minus 1.27 ft. (Top water level: 597 ft.; crest of dam: 643 ft.)

PORE-WATER PRESSURE IN BODY OF DAM: DECREASING

Main piezometers	A	B	C	D	E
kg/cm^2	7.96	7.95	7.82	5.76	6.13
Change	-0.07	nil	-0.09	-0.03	-0.01

EARTH PRESSURE IN BODY OF DAM: DECREASING

Pressure gauges	A	B	C	D	E
kg/cm^2	17.81	16.59	17.37	6.49	12.00
Change	-0.06	-0.06	-0.04	-0.06	-0.05

SEEPAGE VELOCITY: INCREASING

In alluvium (subterranean)	(tolerance: 9 thousandths of a mm/sec)	
West bank 6.2 thousandths of a mm/sec	Valley center 6.1 thousandths of a mm/sec	East bank 5.9 thousandths of a mm/sec
Change +0.005	+0.006	+0.005
In apron of dam	(tolerance: 5 thousandths of a mm/sec)	
West section 3.9 thousandths of a mm/sec	Dam center 4.0 thousandths of a mm/sec	East section 3.9 thousandths of a mm/sec
Change +0.006	+0.005	+0.004

SEEPAGE OUTFLOW: INCREASING

Drain well A	3.3 l/sec	Drain well B	4.6 l/sec
Change	+0.1		+0.1

PARTICLES IN SEEPAGE (tolerance: 0.8mm). Fine sediment, granular diameter 0.001-0.006mm. First incidence of medium sediment with a granular diameter of 0.006-0.02mm.

The Botanical Institute at Cairo University estimated that the dummies in officers' uniforms had spent between six and ten hours in the water prior to recovery. "The stuffing consists of freshly cut maize stems and palm leaves, also wheat straw from last year's crop. Assuming that the dummies made of these materials were introduced into the water at once, the time of entry can be gauged with comparative

accuracy, because immersion retards the coagulative properties of the juices escaping from the surface of a cut. This
factor may be confirmed by comparison with the swelling of
the straw stems. If the Institute stipulates a margin of four
hours, it does so only because the dummies were recovered
from the Nile at different junctures and no attempt was
made to tag them at the time of recovery. It should nonetheless be possible, with the aid of the above figures and details
of the Nile's mean rate of flow, to narrow down the area in
which the dummies were put into the water."

Inquiries by the Egyptian commercial attaché in London
disclosed that Robinsons, Ltd., the Birmingham textile firm,
had been bought up in 1952 by Merlinghams of London.
Robinsons, Ltd., had got into difficulties following the can-
cellation of a series of government contracts. The report was
telexed to the Egyptian Foreign Ministry and conveyed to the
Ministry of Defense by messenger.

At midday, investigations by the military security service
were extended to cover units stationed in the El Minya-Asyut
area. The U.S. military attaché in Cairo received Pentagon
approval of his request for permission to supply the Egyptian
government with particulars of boots used by the U.S. army
until 1965, and the head of counterespionage, Ewal Hamid,
flew by helicopter to Asyut. President Sadat requested the
members of the Inner Revolutionary Council to assemble at
his country residence in Heliopolis.

Fifty miles north of Cairo, the crew of a dredger recovered
an eleventh dummy from the Nile. Sadat was informed of
the discovery two hours later.

.   .   .

43

ASWAN!

At Camp El Saff, two majors declined to submit to questioning by members of the military security service. Defense Minister Nachram, speaking from the President's country villa, ordered the transfer of two paratroop brigades from Asyut to Ismailia.

An interim report issued by the Defense Ministry confirmed that the summer uniforms in which the dummies were dressed had not been worn by the Egyptian army since 1962. "As for the boots and underclothes, these were obviously taken from consignments stored in Egypt by the British military authorities. In the case of the boots, it was possible to detect this from manufacturers' code numbers. Inquiries should be concentrated upon all depots formerly belonging to British military installations."

While being interrogated at Asyut, an Egyptian army corporal dived through a first-floor window into the barrack square. A sliver of glass severed the man's carotid artery as his head went through the pane. He was given several blood transfusions in hospital, recovered consciousness toward midnight, and tried to signal to the sentry at the door, who failed to notice, and died an hour later. The man in question was Mehmed Fuad, twenty-four years old, a native of Nag'Gudi in Aswan Province.

The meeting of the Inner Revolutionary Council at the President's country villa was attended by the following: Anwar el Sadat himself; Defense Minister Nachram; Minister of the Interior Gidaff; Generals Boghdadi and Shafai; Admiral of the Air Force Hassuni; Colonel Shuker, commanding the Asyut garrison; Yakoub Sidki, Secretary-General of the Socialist Union; and Professor Bahaeddin.

They assembled in the President's study, where aides had

44

arranged nine armchairs in a semicircle round the glass-topped table. Sentries of the 7th Division were posted at each corner of the rectangular garden, and plainclothesmen from the military security service patrolled the road outside. The pilot of the President's helicopter sat smoking in his cockpit until dawn. Shuker's helicopter had landed in the grounds of the Heliolido Sporting Club, only fifty yards from Shari'al Saud. Its crew spent the night on inflatable mattresses in one of the President's cellars.

Addressing the Knesset in Jerusalem, Premier Dayan announced that latest intelligence reports indicated that the condition of the High Dam was deteriorating daily. The volume of water escaping below ground had assumed such proportions that the dam itself might be washed away. Egypt was heading for a national disaster which only the most radical countermeasures could avert. Dayan emphasized that, given this state of affairs, Israel would practice the utmost military restraint, so that the Egyptian government could concentrate all its energies on saving the dam. It was thus in the interests of the United Arab Republic to desist from all provocative acts on the Suez front and in the Red Sea area.

Geoffrey Swinnerton, the BBC's correspondent in Jerusalem, compared Dayan's statement with the Israeli attitude during the Jordanian civil war of 1970. Jerusalem had made a great show of passivity at that time, not least because any Israeli move would have led to a reconciliation between King Hussein's troops and the Palestinian commandos.

In a recorded report broadcast on "The World at One" and "P.M.," Swinnerton said: "The very fact that Premier Dayan has made this formal announcement seems to indicate that events at Aswan have sparked off a struggle for power inside the Egyptian junta. The issue is between those who wish to restore the dam and those who look upon recent tragic events as a pretext for demolishing this mighty work of man. To judge by Dayan's note of urgency, a decision may be made within the next few days."

The meeting of the Inner Revolutionary Council at the President's country residence lasted—according to the tape-recorded minutes—for just under seven hours. Commenting on Sadat's remark that he wondered why the conspirators had not dressed the dummies in civilian clothes, General Shafai said:

"Because you've never really taken off your own uniform. To the people who did this thing, you've always been—like Nasser—a member of a junta whose only claim to fame was that it fired Naguib. You were a colonel in his day, if I remember rightly, and the colonel's image sticks. Personally, I couldn't care less who put those dummies in the water. You were only supposed to interpret them as a warning. These are people of 1952 vintage. Nasser could play them off against each other—you lack the stature and some of the drive. They want to remind Colonel Sadat that he can't take any decisions without consulting them first. That was the agreement after Nasser's death, and the agreement covered all decisions relating to the dam."

President Sadat: "I don't think we need discuss Freudian symbolism this evening."

General Boghdadi: "Why not? You've been obsessed by the dam ever since you learned to think. I can remember your discussing it with me at Military Academy. It fascinated you from the start. You wanted to build it even as a cadet. Your entire loyalty to Gamal stemmed from the fact that his ideas coincided with yours. You realized that he had greater ability, so you backed him—simply because of the dam. At the Academy, you talked about the human energy that was squandered in building the Pyramids. Then, when the first figures from Düsseldorf were lying on Nasser's desk, you rhapsodized about ten or twenty Great Pyramids being tipped into the neck of the valley at Aswan . . ."

President Sadat: "The night before last, eleven straw dummies were washed down the Nile. My name was pinned to their chests."

Colonel Shuker: "If it were only a question of your personal safety, Anwar, I wouldn't have left Asyut. There's something fundamental at stake here. We've all made errors in the past twenty years. Nasser and you because you wanted the dam, I because I didn't oppose the scheme strongly enough. Why didn't you and Nasser build a Great Wall of Egypt along the Libyan Desert to keep out sandstorms and fleas? Your High Dam is a monstrosity—it's unnatural in the truest sense of the word."

Defense Minister Nachram: "Why did you ever join the army, Shuker? You'd have made a fortune as a professional mourner."

Minister of the Interior Gidaff: "The President just talked of eleven dummies drifting down the Nile. No dummy that I know of ever swam against the stream. At least, nobody in the Revolutionary Council has produced any evidence to that effect. The general mood is hostile to the High Dam. Nasser would never have given it up. Sadat wants to keep it. So do I, and Nachram, and Mohyeddin. I don't know about you, Sidki, but I think you do, too. The opposition is banding together under the pretext that the dam must be demolished if Egypt is to survive. What they're really aiming at is a coup d'état, because the country went to sleep for the first six hours after Nasser's death. They're planning to revolt with the blessing of a nation that has succumbed to hysteria."

Admiral Hassuni: "Let's be practical. If the dummies had

been set adrift in the Sudan, they'd have put down roots on the way here or been pulverized by the turbines. Perhaps they were thrown into the river below Aswan. At Luxor or Asyut . . ."

Professor Bahaeddin: "They could have been put together at Alexandria and driven upriver in a truck. An army truck, mark you. The students are quite capable . . ."

Admiral Hassuni: "We're neglecting the possibility that they were dropped by Israeli aircraft. First flags, then dummies. The next thing you know, the Gahal Party may send a charter plane to Cairo and shower us with Moses' baskets."

President Sadat: "I recognize the challenge and I accept it. No one here can say I angled for this job. You all know perfectly well that Nasser offered me the succession after the June War. The day before he asked Mohyeddin."

Colonel Shuker: "And what a television show you put on! If my squadrons at Asyut hadn't taken off that night and dropped some practice bombs on Cairo, do you really think you could have lasted another week, Nasser and you? They'd have taken Nasser at his word. He might have been put out to grass by this time, but at least he'd be alive. Collecting stamps."

President Sadat: "I said I recognize the challenge and accept it. I'd gladly retire tonight, but I'm no fool to waste time wrangling over the dam with you and your cronies."

General Shafai: "No one wants to wrangle. The dam must go, do you hear? The dam must go. It must be demolished before it's swept away."

President Sadat: "By all means, let's dismantle it. Let's remove the apron stones from the cofferdams and drop them in the lake. We'll have a spillway blasted out of the crest— preferably by your engineers, Yussuf. The water will pour over the top. Congratulations! Pressure on the base of the dam and the lake bed decreases like magic. That's what we all want, isn't it? You'll be standing up there on the bank, laughing your head off because there's no more need to dig. The dam will disappear of its own accord, and next day Cairo will be swamped. No doubt you'll insure that your family camp on the roof of the Nile Hilton until it's all over. I envy them the view next morning . . ."

Secretary-General Sidki: "There are rumors about a directive you're supposed to have given your secretariat; namely, that when you die you're to be buried beside Nasser on the crest of the dam. Which brings us back to Freud—or, to be more precise, your Pharaonic ambitions."

General Shafai: "I'd like to put a few points on record. Let's start with the Delta. You can sit there in a deck chair and watch it contract. The coastline is receding because soil is being washed away by the westerly current and there's no new silt to take its place. Talk to the farmers in the Delta if you want to see a revolution in the making—as an observer, this time."

President Sadat: "The Russians have poured millions into the Aswan project and sent us two thousand engineers. Can you honestly see them allowing us to carry away the dam in wicker baskets? I can't—I've discussed it too often with the Soviet Ambassador in the past few months."

General Shafai: "To repeat, the Delta is disappearing and the remains are turning into a saltpan. Meanwhile, the mud which used to fertilize the land and supply its inhabitants with bricks is being trapped by Lake Nasser."

Minister Gidaff: "But we're gaining 1,300,000 feddan of land."

General Boghdadi: "True, and sluicing bilharzia into every last village through the new irrigation canals. How many generations does it take to build up some kind of immunity? A century from now, the descendants of these people will still be bleeding from the guts when they go on pilgrimage to the tomb of the Great Dam Builders—if it's still there."

Colonel Shuker: "I hadn't finished. In July, 1970, the twelfth turbine came into service. We shall eventually be getting a total of ten billion kilowatts out of that accursed lake."

President Sadat: "You can read that in any newspaper file."

Colonel Shuker: "What are you going to do with all that energy, roast a pigeon for supper every night?"

General Shafai: "I doubt if the current would stand it— the loss of power over the long-distance transmission line between Aswan and Cairo is too great."

President Sadat: "In fact, it's about ten percent, which means that our industry will have to make do with a paltry nine billion kilowatts. Anything else?"

Colonel Shuker: "We really need twin-core transmission lines, because there isn't enough ground water to act as a conductor. We also need two lines to each section, so we can switch them off alternately while the flower of our nation digs sand out of the insulators."

Minister Gidaff: "You're crazy, Shuker. I just told you— we're gaining 1,300,000 feddan of land. The evaporated moisture from the lake will change the climate. It won't be long before there's no desert left for you to play soldiers in."

Colonel Shuker: "What's the use of 1,300,000 feddan? Our peasant women will step up their pregnancy rate until the net gain is zero. Has anyone at least made sure that they can read the directions on a packet of pills? Visit us in the Kharga Depression and you'll see donkeys turning the water wheels as they used to three thousand years ago. One little diesel engine would be worth—"

President Sadat: "You come from a heaven on earth, Ahmed—you forget that sometimes. Three days ago on the way to Ismailia, I saw people sprinkling water on their tomato plants by hand."

General Shafai: "Watering tomatoes is high treason if it means neglecting our cotton plantations. After all, the government of the United Arab Republic has mortgaged our entire cotton crop to the Soviet Union until the turn of the century. Any peasant who fails in his duty is a saboteur, Anwar. You should lock him up with the brickmakers, the Moslem Brotherhood, and anyone else who has the effrontery to disagree with you."

President Sadat: "It occurred to me while Shuker was meditating on Kharga that the inquiry into the funeral processions has been concluded. The demonstrators and their dead came from Kharga. They were victims of the sudden flood."

General Shafai: "Everyone knew that on the day of the processions."

Minister Gidaff: "Of course, but it took a little time to reconstruct their route. They were flown to Cairo in army helicopters and an Ilyushin of Transport Command. After landing at the 7th Division airfield, they and their coffins were dumped in the city by truck and pointed in the direction of the Kubbeh Palace. They set off, promptly followed by the Cairo mob."

General Boghdadi: "Well?"

President Sadat: "I only mention it because I think they were shoddily treated. You might at least have flown them back to Kharga the same afternoon."

After the suicide of Corporal Mehmed Fuad, the board of inquiry set up by the military security service made four attempts to get in touch with Nachram. An aide at the Defense Ministry said that the Minister was probably at the

President's country residence, but the switchboard had strict instructions from Nachram not to divulge the President's secret number. Nachram himself was not available at the present time.

Ewal Hamid, chief of counterespionage, returned to the officers' mess after the second abortive phone call and asked Major Kudeiri, Shuker's second-in-command, for a ground plan of the garrison installations.

"Your men have had a hard day," Kudeiri said. "Why not inspect the buildings tomorrow morning?"

"You should have some photostats here. The originals are filed at the Ministry. Perhaps we could try your office . . ."

The stores depot was situated in an extension of the north wing which had, according to Kudeiri, been empty since 1967. The storerooms could be reached via the parade ground or the second inner courtyard.

"We don't even need a jeep," said Hamid. "Let's take a look now, shall we?"

Kudeiri phoned for four men to meet them in the square with flashlights. On the way downstairs, he vomited.

The bars over a window in the west wall of the depot had been sawed through and bent aside. Blinking in the torchlight, Hamid stirred the broken glass at the base of the wall with his toe, then swung round. "Worse and worse," he said dryly. "First high treason and now wanton damage to government property." One of Kudeiri's men dropped his torch. Hamid took a step toward Shuker's second-in-command. "No chance of finding the keys until tomorrow morning, I think you said?"

"I merely told you that the depot hadn't been used since the British withdrew."

"No, not until Monday night."

"I didn't say that."

Hamid pulled himself up by one of the bars until he could

kneel on the sill. He called for a light and dropped into the storeroom. Four members of the board of inquiry squeezed through the bars after him.

Eleven pairs of boots were missing from a shelf in Magazine No. 7. The soles had left clearly discernible outlines on the dusty plank. Hamid rejoined Kudeiri, who was standing silently outside the depot. Hamid said, "Although you're already under arrest, you have my permission to hand over current business to your next-in-command. That is, if he's not too busy making dummies out of straw and fishing line. We're just comparing shoe sizes—I mean, types of boot. A pure formality . . ."

"What makes you so certain that we won't arrest you instead?"

"I feel reasonably secure, particularly as I know where Colonel Shuker is spending the night."

As they walked back to Kudeiri's office through the second inner courtyard, Hamid said, "Strange, when you consider the history of those boots. Manufactured for GIs in the Korean War, passed on to the British as an item of U.S. military aid, stored in Egypt, and twenty years later sent floating down the Nile on feet made of straw."

Kudeiri vomited again, on the floor of his office.

At 3 a.m., the Defense Ministry switchboard rang to give Hamid the telex number of the President's country villa.

T H U R S D A Y

LAKE NASSER: LEVEL FALLING

Lake level: 506.02 ft. above sea level. Change: minus 1.54 ft. (Top water level: 597 ft.; crest of dam: 643 ft.)

ASWAN!

PORE-WATER PRESSURE IN BODY OF DAM: DECREASING

Main piezometers	A	B	C	D	E
kg/cm²	7.92	7.89	7.65	5.74	6.09
Change	-0.03	-0.02	-0.03	-0.03	-0.02

EARTH PRESSURE IN BODY OF DAM: DECREASING

Pressure gauges	A	B	C	D	E
kg/cm²	17.76	16.88	17.30	6.39	11.84
Change	-0.02	-0.02	-0.04	-0.03	-0.02

SEEPAGE VELOCITY: INCREASING

In alluvium (subterranean)   (tolerance: 9 thousandths of a mm/sec)

West bank	Valley center	East bank
6.5 thou-sandths of a mm/sec	6.4 thou-sandths of a mm/sec	6.5 thou-sandths of a mm/sec
Change +0.002	+0.004	+0.004

In apron of dam   (tolerance: 5 thousandths of a mm/sec)

West section	Dam center	East section
4.0 thou-sandths of a mm/sec	4.1 thou-sandths of a mm/sec	3.9 thou-sandths of a mm/sec
Change +0.003	+0.002	+0.004

SEEPAGE OUTFLOW: INCREASING

Drain well A	3.7 l/sec	Drain well B	4.9 l/sec
Change	+0.2		+0.7

PARTICLES IN SEEPAGE (tolerance: 0.8mm).
Medium sediment, granular diameter 0.006-
0.02mm.

According to the tape-recorded minutes of the meeting of the
Inner Revolutionary Council, President Anwar el Sadat said,
shortly after midnight:

"I consider this argument futile and valueless. For all that,
I propose we now take a vote, if only to show exactly where
we all stand."

Minister Gidaff: "We move that measures to stabilize and
preserve the High Dam should be pursued with all speed and
backed by an appeal to the international community. These
measures comprise, first, using nuclear charges to seal the fissures through which impounded water is escaping; secondly,
congealing the base of the dam with liquid ammonia; and,
thirdly, studying the practicability of inhibiting seepage by
injecting hydrophobic silicic acid. All other suggestions, from
demolishing the dam to evacuating the inhabitants of the Nile
Valley, are rejected. We recommend that international public-
relations firms be retained to propagate these schemes, that
teams of psychologists be dispatched to the Nile villages, that
drastic steps be taken to deal with all cases of alarmism."

President Sadat: "Thank you. And now the opposing
resolution."

General Shafai: "We propose no resolutions. We say that
the dam must go because it's an abortion—because it represents the most acute threat ever to confront the entire Egyptian people. It must be demolished—by mobilizing world
opinion, if you insist—because we can't afford to squander
any more resources on preserving a monumental blunder to
the detriment of local development projects. The fact that
Israel could simply drown our nation by bombarding the
dam, that we're pawns in the hands of the Israelis twenty-

four hours a day, is intolerable. We do not mind if the skeleton of the dam is salvaged—e.g., for those who insist on exclusive burial places. We do not object if the lake is lowered to a tolerable level. But we shall never accept a situation in which Egypt remains at the mercy of seepage rates or a few aerial torpedoes."

President Sadat: "In that case, I call for a show of hands. For the sake of fairness, abstentions will count as nays. Those in favor of demolition?"

Minister Gidaff: "Three—no, four votes."

President Sadat: "In favor of the first resolution?"

Minister Gidaff: "Four votes."

President Sadat: "Plus . . ."

Minister Gidaff: "Of course, your own. That makes five."

The vote was taken just before 4 a.m. At 3:15 a.m., the teleprinter in the secretariat of the President's country villa had sprung to life. The message consisted of two lines only. The final word was printed; the carriage came to an abrupt halt. The duty officer bent over the humming machine and tapped out the telex number of the garrison at Asyut.

"You forgot the code word, Hamid," he typed.

"Dummies," the message came back. "And give my regards to the President."

At 3:22 a.m., the duty officer entered the President's study and handed Sadat the message. He returned to the secretariat, removed a sealed envelope from his desk, and went to inspect the sentries in the garden. In the transparent dome of the President's helicopter, he could see the shadowy outline of the pilot and the glowing butt of a cigarette.

The members of the Inner Revolutionary Council left the President's villa at 4:30 a.m. General Shafai and Admiral

Hassuni returned to Cairo in an air force Chevrolet. Professor Bahaeddin and General Boghdadi drove to the airport. Defense Minister Nachram, Minister of the Interior Gidaff, and Secretary-General Sidki walked through the grounds to the guesthouse. When Shuker made a move to wake the two pilots in the cellar, Sadat, who had lingered on the veranda, said, "Let them sleep on. I'd like a word with you."

Shuker leaned against the handrail of the steps that led down into the garden. "Why not fly to Asyut with me? We could have breakfast in the mess."

"That won't be possible."

"Why not?"

"Because helicopters with defective fuel lines don't get far."

"I see."

"We could sit on the terrace instead."

The pilot of the President's helicopter jumped from the cabin, ground out his cigarette in the grass, circled the machine, and climbed inside again.

"Am I under arrest?" Shuker asked.

"Come, let's sit on the terrace." In the dawn light, they could see two soldiers beneath the trees with their backs to them.

"No, you aren't under arrest," said Sadat. "You're going for a ride."

"That's outdated. They didn't even bother to kill Khrushchev."

"You misunderstand me. I've chosen a villa for you, ninety miles east of here. A pleasant house on the outskirts of Ismailia. With an air-raid shelter. No doubt you'll appreciate that, after the Sharm el Sheikh episode."

"And you think you can solve your problems by putting me under house arrest? As long as the garrison commander of Asyut languishes in detention, the dam will hold. I admire your logic."

"At least no more dummies will come floating down the Nile. In the present climate of hysteria, that's worth a good deal."

"Was it the telex message just now?"

"That was merely confirmation. I didn't want to do you an injustice. At first, I thought your group was headed by General Sabri."

"I knew Kudeiri wouldn't stand up to a grilling by Hamid. I should have guessed it three months ago, when he started puking for no apparent reason. I had the same trouble myself, once."

"Yes, at Sharm el Sheikh in 1956. Don't worry, I felt my own gorge rise last night."

"In that case . . ."

"I know we've taken Freud's name in vain more than once in the past few hours, but I'd like to hear why you hate me."

"I don't hate you."

"You ridiculed me with those dummies."

"I meant to warn you, more than anything else. The dummies were a hint, Anwar. I'm afraid you still haven't got the message. If I'd chosen to drop some men on Heliopolis last night . . . Fifty paratroopers would have done the trick. Forty could have played halma in the Heliolido Sporting Club while a couple smashed up your communications center and the rest hung around waiting for you to pack your toothbrush."

"You never got over the death of your brother Alim, did you? I took another look at the files yesterday morning."

"My brother never wanted to become an engineer. He wanted to be a soldier."

"I'd sooner work on a construction site in Aswan than chase the Israelis out of Sinai."

"That's your problem."

"We were talking about your problems."

"We often discussed the matter at home. My brother used to say that our real enemy was the desert, not Israel."

"Why do you think Nasser and I built the dam? Those gibes about a tomb are idiotic. If I drop dead in two minutes' time, you can bury me beside the airport road—a sprinkling of sand will do. Water is all I care about. Empty a can of water into the sand. Do the same tomorrow, and by next day everything will be green."

"And the day after that you may be drowned by your own grandiose ideas. Water, water! My father dinned that word into me as soon as I could stand. He used to take us to Cairo every August. By coach to see the Nile Festival, when the flood came. I'll never forget it—all the sun ships and fountains. The High Dam has finished all that. Can't you sense how you've destroyed the natural rhythm of things? Today, when they throw the Bride of Arussa into the water—a sacrificial offering to a regulated river with artificial storage basins—it's prostitution."

"I beg to differ."

"You've no idea what goes on inside people, Anwar. Pay another visit to the Aswan housing developments for Nubian evacuees. You haven't been there for three years. At least, Nasser had the guts to talk to the poor devils. You ought to take another look at them, see how they sit around, how their children scratch about in the gravel, waiting until evening comes and they can carry their sheep up six floors to a one-room apartment. Have you ever watched the villages upstream as they slowly subside, as water laps over the threshold and the mud walls turn to slush? The houses don't even crash when they fall in. They just fold up on themselves. A heap of slush—and that was where they made their children and reared them. Until you started building your dam."

"Your brother went to Aswan of his own free will."

"Yes, and he did something else of his own free will. He joined a group of engineers who said it was a crime to build the dam in its present form."

"Was it the concrete apron?"

"They wanted to take all the borings down to virgin rock and not stop short somewhere in the middle of the gravel, halfway between riverbed and bedrock. If seepage washes out the detritus between the base of the dam and the bedrock, you might say that Alim will have been vindicated."

"Don't be hurt, but it won't come to that."

"A number of reputable engineers wanted to seal the water-bearing layers right down to the bedrock by filling the pores with injected material. My brother became their spokesman."

"With the result that he was transferred to the construction depot. I read all about it yesterday."

"Of course, you're always reading. You read instead of going out and about."

"Your brother—"

"My brother was crushed to death when a crane collapsed during loading operations at the depot. They were hoisting a defective bulldozer from a low loader when the jib gave way and it sank into the gravel. A steel cable caught Alim and sliced off the top of his skull. The bulldozer had arrived at midday and was supposed to be repaired within an hour. The foreman said they ought to reinforce the jib with some girders, but a Russian engineer shouted that the next convoy of trucks loaded with filling material was due at 2 p.m., so they couldn't spare the time. Then the crane collapsed. The convoy didn't arrive till 5 p.m. It was all a big mistake. My brother died because some bloody Russian didn't understand Arabic."

"Who was your *Putsch* aimed at? Me, or a system which

transfers an engineer to a construction depot when he criticizes his superiors?"

"You, because you've personified the system ever since Nasser's death. You and the dam . . ."

"We spent enough time discussing the dam last night. There are ways of preventing a flood without destroying one of the greatest man-made reservoirs in the history of the world. We told you—congealing with liquid ammonia, injections of silicic acid. We may even seal the fissures with nuclear charges."

"I often wonder how things look to you, Anwar. You sit there at your Presidential desk and decree experiments which have no bearing on reality. It's an eerie thought, the President of the United Arab Republic sitting beside his reading lamp, studying a paper on silicic acid—half a dozen pages, let's say. It takes you thirty minutes, an hour at most. You lay the file aside and pace up and down while the lobbyists in the outer office gnaw their nails. Some of them want to sell you ammonia, others want to save the Pyramids. You go to the lavatory, sit down at your desk again, smoke a cigarette, walk to the window and back, flick through the pages a second time. Another hour passes. During that hour, seepage has washed a billion grains of sand from the dam, maybe ten billion. Every time we draw breath on this veranda, the level of the lake falls a fraction of a millimeter. By the time you try to sleep tonight, it may have lost a centimeter. By tomorrow it may be two. Put me in front of a court-martial and it could be five. Why are you sitting here with me, anyway? You could have had me locked up in the cellars. Is it because you're afraid to go to bed and think? You don't want to think because you know you're suffering from an obsession."

"And you want power."

"I could have had it long ago—more cheaply, too."

"Were any of your relations drowned in the Kharga floods?"

"Why do you ask?"

"Because I'm temporarily more interested in the origins of your traumata than in grains of sand."

"One of my cousins died when he tried to rescue a sheep. Some men in the neighboring plantation called to him to cling to his house and climb on the roof. He was a fool. Do you really think I'd demolish the dam because of that?"

"Then I'll say it again—you wanted power. Shuker, the man destined to save Egypt from a second Flood, was planning to grab the Presidency."

"Don't you remember what I told you in 1957, when I was discharged from the hospital? Ever since I ran back into the dugout from that minefield at Sharm el Sheikh, while my men were crawling around outside on their stumps, one of them with yards of intestine trailing between his knees— ever since then, I've been finished. I told you, Anwar, and I told Nasser. He had to browbeat me into taking over the garrison at Asyut. I don't have any ambitions left."

"I believed that until two days ago, when the dummies turned up. As soon as I heard about the officers' uniforms, I knew you were behind this thing. I was puzzled by your motives at first, but not any more. You lost your nerve at Sharm el Sheikh and you've nursed that realization with all the persistence of a masochist. Now you want to assert yourself. If Hamid hadn't done such an efficient job at Asyut, Egypt would have had a neurotic for President by tomorrow."

"It has one already."

"And I thought you were merely suffering from a complex at first." The President paused. "You attended some maneuvers in Algeria five years ago, didn't you?"

"Yes."

"Foreign military observers were accommodated at a camp in Kabylia, I believe."

"That's right, in a dry riverbed."

"You were there when the rains came?"

"I was."

"Your jeep wouldn't start when the flash flood swept down the valley, would it? The driver ran away."

"He went to get help."

"He didn't come back, though. You scrambled onto the hood and clung to the windshield. The water swirled round the jeep and you didn't even get your feet wet. However, you were unconscious when they found you."

"You're misinformed," said Shuker.

"You've been through it all before, haven't you? Stuck in a valley and unable to escape because the banks are too steep, hearing water roar along the wadi, seeing birds take wing or a jackal dash past. You lie on your belly and cling to something, and then a yellow wall of water bears down on you. That's it, isn't it?"

"No."

"Later you hear that the High Dam is being undermined. You get hold of some statistics and become hysterical. You multiply your own private nightmare by the population of Egypt. You talk yourself into an insane belief that disaster is inevitable."

"It makes no ultimate difference whether one peasant family drowns at Kharga because of your error of judgment or a whole nation. It's the same horror on a larger scale."

Sadat rose and walked to the steps. His pilot was standing beside the helicopter, urinating against a wheel. The guards at the entrance stirred and turned their heads in the direction of the gate. The sound of approaching vehicles could be heard on the veranda.

"They've come to fetch you," Sadat said. "I will accompany you."

The column left Heliopolis at 8 a.m. President Sadat sat beside the driver of the second jeep. Colonel Shuker and a military policeman perched on the back seat with their knees drawn up. A machine gun was mounted on the roof of the fifth jeep. "Where's the Presidential pennant?" Shuker inquired as they got in. "What are you afraid of, Israeli hedge-hoppers or your own peasants?"

They took the road that ran along the north bank of the Ismailia Canal. The sentries, who had been warned in advance, waved the jeeps past various roadblocks. Twenty miles short of Bilbeis, the convoy was overtaken by a dark-colored Moskvitch sedan. Sadat watched Shuker's face in the rear-view mirror. The colonel was staring at the gaiassas with their terra-cotta sails. Pigeons soared from their mud-brick cotes on the south bank. Two men were walking an empty ferryboat across the canal by its steel cable. On the edge of Abu Hammad, a lorry had plunged over the embankment. Flour was seeping from a number of burst sacks and drifting along the surface of the water in pale slicks. A fire engine, its hood camouflaged with branches, was parked at the approaches to a bridge. Women crouched on the canal bank, drawing water in clay pitchers.

"What are you thinking about?" Sadat asked the colonel.

"I'm counting."

After another fifteen minutes, they caught a first glimpse of the squat turrets of some tanks dug in on high ground to the north. A helicopter flew over the convoy. Shuker sat back and asked for a cigarette. During the night, an Israeli Fouga Magister had crashed onto the road beside the goods yard, where burned-out wagons had been shunted into a long line.

. . .

Military policemen waved the column to a halt while a bull-dozer nudged fragments of the wrecked aircraft across the carriageway. Sadat left the jeep and walked to the verge. Soldiers had piled the handkerchief-sized scraps of metal beneath a tree. The President bent over one of them and made out the inscription "Pression d'...o.z kpz." In the mulberry trees three hundred yards away across the canal fluttered the remains of a parachute.

"Did you see the white flag over there?" Shuker asked when Sadat had resumed his seat beside the driver. The convoy was forced to turn around. It drove northeast along the road to El Qantara and then headed south.

"I've counted three tractors so far," remarked Shuker. The jeeps skirted the northern limits of Ismailia and drove through deserted streets to the Suez Canal. Looking in the rear-view mirror, Sadat could see Shuker staring at the shop fronts with their boarded windows. It was midday when the convoy pulled up outside the town hall. The President turned, one elbow resting on the back of his seat. "You ought to take another look at this place," he said to Shuker. "Get out."

They walked into the town hall. The drivers and escorts waited beside their vehicles. An officer who was lolling against the desk beside the main door sprang to his feet and saluted. Three firemen were standing by the stairs.

"I've visited Ismailia a dozen times since the evacuation," Shuker said. "What's the point?"

"I want you to look at it again."

On the wall of one abandoned office hung a 1967 calendar and a portrait of Nasser. The card index was overturned. Above the desk, a length of electric cord swung in the draft from a broken window.

"Look at that," said Sadat. He pointed to a poster on the door. Two MIG fighters were pursuing an Israeli aircraft.

A plume of smoke streamed from the Star of David on its fuselage.

"Printed by order of the army, early 1967. That was when you joined the General Staff."

"You're making a fool of yourself, Anwar."

They paused in front of some photographs which the Ministry of Information had mounted in the entrance hall for the benefit of visiting journalists. "They took most of these pictures in the napalm ward. You've never seen children with their hands charred solid, have you?"

The recorded voice of the muezzin rang out over the rooftops. Shuker turned and walked to the main door. The officer beside the desk saluted again. I forgot to remove his badges of rank, thought Sadat. Foxholes had been dug in the park across the road. Their covers lay on the grass. Visible through blossom-covered branches, the surface of the canal shimmered in the noon sun. Sadat said, "We could sit on the steps and watch all the activity. A few weeks ago, I counted three soldiers, a postman, an ambulance, a nut-vendor, two children, and a dozen dogs."

"Don't worry, if the dam breaks the Israelis will be strolling here as soon as the mud's dry enough to walk on."

"I'm driving back to Cairo now," said Sadat. "I just wanted to take another look at Ismailia. With you. I wanted you to see the lush gardens with no one to enjoy them, the shuttered windows with nobody behind them. The townspeople are still sending furniture vans to remove their things. The last time I was here, I saw three wing chairs being carried out of a bombed house. You may find that funny—who knows? In the north of the town, you can stand under an awning and buy Guinness from the stocks of the Pilots' Association. When I went to inspect the snipers in the tower of the Presbyterian church, there was a notice in the porch announcing a service for the same day, but nobody came. No town has ever depressed me as much as Ismailia since the evacuation. Even when they shot up the refineries at Port Suez and set them on fire . . ."

"I'd like to get some sleep," Shuker said.

In the view of a British parliamentary delegation which had spent a fortnight visiting Tel Aviv, Jerusalem, Beersheba, and the new fortified settlements of the Jordan Valley, events at Aswan had produced a swing in Israeli public opinion which would scarcely have been conceivable a few months earlier. The party's spokesman, a Sussex M.P. named Gerald Broadman, referred during a press conference to several young kibbutzniks who had spoken of a single great family of Semitic nations. A Save Egypt action committee had apparently been set up at Beersheba by Israeli nuclear physicists. Echoes of the same trend were perceptible in the army and even among the orthodox rabbinate. According to Broadman, dismay was particularly widespread among Orthodox Jews who felt that Isaiah's prophecies about Egypt—"And the waters shall fail from the sea, and the river shall be wasted and dried up"—were patently coming true.

Questioned about the motives underlying this change of mood, Broadman claimed the existence of a genuine urge for solidarity. Large sections of the population were now convinced that Israel had a duty to help, if only because of her technological and scientific knowledge. This state of affairs, which could lead to a breakthrough in the Arab-Israeli confrontation, must be recognized and exploited. It was a historic moment, Broadman said. Subconsciously, the people of Israel no doubt felt that they must make some form of moral atonement for their occupation of Arab territory.

ASWAN!

S A T U R D A Y

LAKE NASSER: LEVEL FALLING

    Lake level: 495.98 ft. above sea level.
Change: minus 2.39 ft. (Top water level: 597
ft.; crest of dam: 643 ft.)

PORE-WATER PRESSURE IN BODY OF DAM: DECREASING

EARTH PRESSURE IN BODY OF DAM: DECREASING

SEEPAGE VELOCITY: INCREASING

In alluvium (subterranean)	(tolerance: 9 thousandths of a mm/sec)	
West bank 6.8 thou- sandths of a mm/sec	Valley center 6.7 thou- sandths of a mm/sec	East bank 6.8 thou- sandths of a mm/sec
Change +0.005	+0.004	+0.005
In apron of dam	(tolerance: 5 thousandths of a mm/sec)	
West section 4.1 thou- sandths of a mm/sec	Dam center 4.2 thou- sandths of a mm/sec	East section 4.0 thou- sandths of a mm/sec
Change +0.003	+0.002	+0.003

SEEPAGE OUTFLOW: INCREASING

Drain well A	4.8 l/sec	Drain well B	5.7 l/sec
Change	+0.9		+0.6

PARTICLES IN SEEPAGE (tolerance: 0.8mm)

77.5% very fine sediment, granular diameter
       0.001-0.002mm.
  9%   fine sediment, granular diameter
       0.002-0.006mm.
 6.7% medium sediment, granular diameter
       0.006-0.02mm.
 4.8% coarse sediment, granular diameter
       0.02-0.6mm.

President Sadat received the news of Shuker's escape at 8:30 a.m., shortly after the Cabinet had assembled for a working breakfast. Ewal Hamid, head of counterespionage, informed the Presidential secretariat by radiotelephone.

Also missing were the two military policemen who had been patrolling the grounds of Shuker's villa in Ismailia during the night. A member of the military security service had been slugged and was found lying unconscious in some rhododendron bushes beside the south wall of the garden. Sentries on the Ismailia-Abu Hammad road stated that a Moskvitch sedan had passed them at dawn, heading for Cairo. It was followed, half an hour later, by a furniture van. Both vehicles were stopped and searched. The travel documents had been issued by headquarters at Bilbeis.

Questioned by military police investigators, a peasant family at Bahtit stated that a helicopter had landed near the Ismailia Canal that morning. It flew off in a southerly direction only a few minutes later. The peasants plucked their children out of bed and hid among the maize behind their hut, because their first thought was that the intruders were Israelis.

The investigators radioed this information to Hamid, who was in the basement of the military hospital at Ismailia, waiting for the injured security man to regain consciousness.

They then proceeded to search the fields for the helicopter's landing place. Shortly before Hamid joined them, they came across some footprints leading into a wheat field. Two minutes later, they reached a circular clearing which had been flattened by the helicopter's downdraft.

In a village northwest of Mit Hamal, police towed away a furniture van which had been obstructing traffic since morning. The driver had claimed that his steering was defective and had waited beside the road. According to a local peasant, he had been picked up by a dark-colored sedan traveling in the direction of Cairo.

The head of the Luxor section of the military security service informed headquarters in Cairo that Qena was alive with rumors about Colonel Shuker, one of them being that he had gone to ground in the guise of an agricultural assistant at a municipal crop research center. Defense Minister Nachram extended the search for Shuker to every military district in the country.

Commenting on the anniversary of Nasser's death, *Saika*, the official organ of Syria's Baath Party, closed with the words: "Perhaps his greatest failing was that he paid too much attention to the Israelis. Like his successor Sadat, he tried to fathom their mentality by reading the Old Testament at undue length and with undue frequency. In the course of time, he was overcome by a sort of Joseph syndrome, by delusions about seven fat and seven lean years. This was his motive for building the High Dam at Aswan, a reservoir in which, during rainy years, water could be stored against future years of drought . . ."

A military security service liaison officer attached to the garrison at Idfu reported in a coded signal to headquarters that he had seen Colonel Shuker leaving the officers' mess there. Shuker, who was wearing a uniform but no badges of rank, had been escorted to a jeep by Major Elassim, the local commander. He then drove off toward El Ridisiya with masked headlights.

Summoned to Cairo by the Ministry of Defense, Major Elassim drove to the military airfield at midday. His helicopter pilot reported for the last time as he was flying over Qena. At Idfu, a lieutenant and two corporals were found to be missing at evening roll call. They had left at noon on a routine patrol of the western highlands. Their jeep was discovered among some rocks, its tracks already obliterated by the wind. The spent cartridges of two green signal flares were lying on the passenger seat.

Security men investigating a break-in at the blockmaking department of the army printing works discovered that someone had stolen a portrait photograph of Shuker which was about to be reproduced on some "Wanted" posters. The Ministry of Defense increased the reward for Shuker's capture to fifty thousand dollars. Eighty agents were withdrawn from the Alexandria, Port Said, and Mansura sections of the military security service and distributed among the hotels and military establishments of the Aswan area. Garrison headquarters at Idfu reported by teleprinter that the lieutenant and two corporals were presumed to have stolen two machine guns, five rifles, and a quantity of rifle grenades.

Two air force officers boarded the night train from Cairo to Aswan at Idfu. They waited in the aisle of the dining car while the steward asked a party of Swedish tourists to vacate one of their tables and move up. The officers ordered tea. The

71

train wound its way through the darkness. The Swedes sat squashed together round a table beside the left-hand row of windows. The officers stared at their reflections in the glass, pistol holsters gently slapping their thighs to the rhythm of the swaying car. A curtain flapped in the breeze. There was a clatter as a white-jacketed Nubian boy piled some ashtrays on the serving counter.

The detonations followed each other at an interval of four or five seconds. The driver had already applied his brakes by the time they heard the first report. Everyone lurched as the locked wheels of the diesel locomotive squealed to a halt. Tea slopped across the tables. One of the Swedish women stifled a scream with the back of her hand.

The soldiers who had stopped the train with signal detonators and red lamps were combing a three-mile stretch of track for an unexploded fragmentation bomb. An Egyptian Sukhoi fighter had been forced to jettison it during a training flight that afternoon.

An hour later, the train continued its journey at a snail's pace. One of the officers passed the dining-car galley on his way to the lavatory. As he was returning to his table, the train accelerated round a bend and the door of the galley swung open.

The man who had been raking about in the charcoal grill raised his head and looked toward the door. The officer gave a start of recognition. The train raced into an opposing bend. Slices of meat splatted on the tiled floor and a glass fell out of a rack. The door swung to. The officer returned to his table.

"I've just seen Shuker. He's out there in the galley. I thought I was dreaming."

"Are you sure?"

"He was bending over the grill. The door swung open and

he looked up—stared straight at me. I think he recognized me."

"Anyone with him?"

"No one apart from the little Nubian who collects the ashtrays. And the steward, but he's outside in the corridor now, smoking."

"When do we get to Kom Ombo?"

Mirrored in the window beside them, their eyes met.

"No idea. Ten minutes, maybe."

"Not enough time. I haven't worked out what we ought to do."

"What about changing tables? You've got your back to the galley. If we moved up and sat beside the Swedes . . ."

"No, we'd take too long to reach the exit. Better stay where we are and dive through the window if he makes a dash for it. Are the MPs in the first coach?"

"Probably."

"What if he pulls the communication cord and jumps?"

"If I know Shuker, he won't meet his troubles halfway. So they were right about that business at Qena and Idfu. He's moving steadily southward. Now he's making for the High Dam."

The Nubian stood swaying on the junction plates between the dining car and the sleeping car, fingering the buttons on his white tunic.

"You could go to the lavatory and catch him unaware."

"Let's wait till the steward finishes his cigarette. He'll probably go back to his chair beside the serving hatch. We'll give him another five minutes."

They unbuttoned their holsters at the table and strode down the coconut matting to the galley. The first officer kicked open the door and sprang inside. Steam misted his glasses, but he raised his automatic and called into the haze:

"Colonel Shuker, you're under arrest. Hands up!"

The man was still crouching over the grill. He had been blowing on the embers and was breathing hard.

"Stand against the wall!"

The man fell to his knees on the tiled floor, shook his head, mouthed something unintelligible. His hand came up holding the poker, then dropped it with a crash against the grill, where a film of ash had already formed on the embers. He drew up one knee and lowered his hands until they lay clasped together on his white cap. Beads of moisture had gathered on the officer's glasses and were leaving tiny snail tracks on the lenses. He could see the outlines of the figure cowering in front of the stove.

"Get against that wall!" he shouted.

They knotted dish towels together and bound the man. He shook his head, gurgled, pursed his lips, gagged, fell forward on his face with his tongue protruding, and was eventually lifted onto the serving counter, where he sat swaying from side to side. The Nubian boy and the steward had vanished in the commotion.

"Why don't you say something, Shuker?" asked one of the officers. The man bared his teeth and shrugged.

"Look at the way he's sweating. It's enough to make you sick." They undid his neckerchief and looked for an identity disk.

The train drew into Aswan ninety minutes late. The diesel locomotive was uncoupled. A taxi and three horse-drawn carriages were waiting in the station yard. The cab horses had their heads buried in nose bags. Nubian women scattered like a flock of frightened birds as the officers propelled their prisoner onto the platform. The man stumbled and pitched forward into some bushes.

At 6 a.m., a jeep from Command Post Aswan East arrived and took the trio to headquarters.

The German dredger *Orion*, employed by the Sudanese government to pump sludge from mining excavations into the Red Sea, located a powerful fresh-water spring with its echo-sounder off the island of Mirear in Foul Bay. Its readings coincided with statements by local fishermen who had observed shoals of fish migrating from the bay. Isotopic measurements confirmed that water from Lake Nasser was subterraneously following the course of the Rahaba and Hodein valleys and only emerging from the impermeable strata east of Mirear where the coastal shelf ended. The outflow from the fresh-water spring in Foul Bay had an estimated volume of thirty-nine cubic yards per second, or three times that of the Kiveri spring in the Gulf of Argolis in southern Greece. The fresh water was welling from the seabed at a depth of forty fathoms.

Yussuf Alisan, formerly a pupil at the deaf-mute institute in Port Said and for six years employed as a chef by Egyptian State Railways, was interrogated at H.Q. Aswan East until late in the morning. He was then given a plate of lentils in the enlisted men's canteen and driven back to the station by jeep. He spent the afternoon squatting among the bushes on the edge of the station yard and left Aswan by the night train.

Just before 8 p.m., Minister of the Interior Gidaff telephoned President Sadat at his Heliopolis residence to inform him that the High Dam Authority had submitted its second set of readings in twelve hours. Seepage from the base of the dam had increased sharply during that period. Latest checks indicated a flow velocity of 6.9 thousandths of a millimeter per second. The volume of water passing through drain well

A had risen by 6 percent. A preliminary examination of samples taken from the settling tank confirmed that the proportion of sediment with a granular diameter of up to 0.05 millimeters had greatly increased.

The High Dam Authority further stated in its telex report that a new fissure must have opened in the vicinity of the dam and was accelerating the escape of water from the lake.

The crew of the machine-gun post on the west abutment of the High Dam informed their platoon commander that an officer resembling Colonel Shuker had appeared in front of their sandbag barrier at dawn. He offered them cigarettes and tried to engage them in conversation, then climbed back up the side of the gorge. Shortly afterward, they heard a helicopter take off. It was not until later that they noticed the resemblance between the unknown officer and the photograph on the "Wanted" poster in barracks. As soon as it struck them, they reported the incident. The colonel had asked them if there was any point in polishing a machine gun on the crest of the dam while its base was disintegrating under their backsides.

The Bavarian provincial government granted Hoffmannthal-Chemiewerke of Frankfurt permission to carry out trial borings in the gravel bed of the Isar south of Lenggries. The firm was working on a process designed to stabilize the subsoil of dams by injecting liquid ammonia. The research division of Hoffmannthal-Chemiewerke was proceeding on the principle that liquid ammonia absorbed so much thermal energy during its conversion into gas that the surrounding water would drop in temperature and the base of the dam become congealed.

The tests were financed by the Foreign Office. The Parliamentary Secretary at the Foreign Office summoned the representative of the Arab League in Bonn, Ambassador Haduni, and told him that if the High Dam could be saved by congelation with ammonia the Federal Republic would have made perhaps its most vital contribution toward strengthening the traditional ties of friendship between Egypt and Germany. The Federal Ministry of the Interior placed units of its Technical Advisory Service at the disposal of Hoffmannthal-Chemiewerke for the duration of the trial borings.

Dr. Angelo stopped at the vegetable stall outside the church door in the Campo S. Lio and bought a melon, some grapes, and a small crate of oranges. Recent experiments had suggested that the oil glands in the outer skin of citrus fruit tended to impair the preservative properties of perymethylene ether.

A spokesman for the Bavarian provincial government denied rumors of a threat to the Sylvenstein Dam in the upper reaches of the Isar Valley. The borings made south of Lenggries by Hoffmannthal-Chemiewerke were concerned solely with freezing experiments designed to help save the High Dam at Aswan and had nothing to do with rectifying faults in the blanket of the Sylvenstein Dam. The Isar Valley had been selected for this large-scale experiment simply because its geological conformation approximated that of the Nile Valley. This applied in particular to the incidence of gravel layers between the riverbed and the bedrock underlying it. The Bavarian radio service broadcast the communiqué as the first item in its midday news bulletin. Despite this formal disclaimer, the mass exodus of tourists from the Bavarian Oberland continued. According to a report from the Munich-Upper Bavaria tourist board, 85 percent of the holidaymakers had already abandoned the camping sites in the Isar Valley.

· · ·

77

That evening, a peasant family from Wegscheid took refuge on the Rauhmoosalm.

Police arrested a Seventh-Day Adventist named Andreas Mühl on the Isar Bridge in Bad Tölz after he had harangued pedestrians through a megaphone with excerpts from Revelation, among them: "And I stood upon the sand of the sea, and saw a beast rise up out of the sea, having seven heads and ten horns, and upon his heads the name of blasphemy."

The Munich-Upper Bavaria tourist board called upon the Bavarian provincial government to prohibit further trial borings by Hoffmannthal-Chemiewerke so as to allay fears of a threat to the Sylvenstein Dam.

A car driven by Adolf Berlett, a civil engineer who was returning to Bad Tölz from the test site, crashed into a fir tree which had been hauled across the road by a person or persons unknown. Berlett escaped unhurt.

According to estimates prepared by the Munich-Upper Bavaria tourist board, rumors that the Sylvenstein Dam was undermined and in danger of collapse had reduced commercial takings by DM7,000,000. Horst Röchting, a spokesman for the board, declared that the exodus of North German and foreign tourists from Bavaria had reached a climax when the ammonia-freezing experiments in the Isar Valley got under way.

The Bavarian provincial government announced that it would make good all losses from a special fund. An official communiqué stated: "Large-scale experiments designed to congeal the subsoil by injecting liquid ammonia have reached so promising a stage that it would be irresponsible to discontinue them at the present time. The Bavarian provincial government wishes again to emphasize, with all the force at its command, that these tests are aimed solely at stabilizing the High Dam at Aswan in the United Arab Republic. The importance of this international relief operation is such as to justify any temporary loss or inconvenience to our own people." The Bonn representative of the Bavarian provincial government received a teleprinted message from Munich instructing him to request the Foreign Office for compensation totaling at least half the estimated loss.

Two companies of mobile police sealed off Hoffmannthal-Chemiewerke's experimental site in the upper reaches of the Isar Valley after some laborers' huts had been set on fire by persons unknown.

Ambassador Haduni, the Arab League representative in Bonn, inspected Hoffmannthal-Chemiewerke's test site in the upper reaches of the Isar Valley and watched the fifth congelation experiment. Engineers employed by the Frankfurt firm pumped three tons of liquid ammonia into a borehole which led through the gravel of the riverbed to the solid rock beneath. Four hours later, using a core sampler, they recovered frozen chunks of gravel from a parallel shaft ten yards distant.

That evening, Haduni sent the Egyptian government a special-priority telegram containing full details of Hoffmannthal-Chemiewerke's experiments.

Meeting at Ravenna, the flood research committee appointed by the Western European Union to study methods of environmental protection requested the government of the United Arab Republic for permission to send a team of observers to Aswan.

After an all-night session, the Egyptian Cabinet decided to adopt the congelation system recommended by Hoffmannthal-Chemiewerke of Frankfurt. Ludwig Barms, the firm's managing director, flew to Cairo by executive jet.

In order to congeal the dam, five hundred boreholes were to be sunk from the crest to the virgin rock beneath the bed of the Nile. Work would begin on the west abutment of the dam, where seepage had attained its highest level in terms of volume and velocity. The Egyptians calculated that 270,-000 tons of liquid ammonia would initially be required to congeal the entire core of the High Dam. Thereafter, maintenance of the congelation process would entail the injection of three tons of liquid ammonia into each borehole every week.

The Secretary-General of the United Nations summoned all U.N. ambassadors and asked member countries to contribute liquid ammonia for use in Egypt. The *International Herald-Tribune*, in an article by its industrial correspondent, pointed out that this operation would lead to a decline in the world-wide output of chemical fertilizers because of insufficient stocks of ammonia. The shortage would exert an adverse effect on summer crops two years hence at latest.

In Trenton, New Jersey, creditors of Eastern United Chemicals resolved to defer bankruptcy proceedings. President Nixon ordered the dispatch of heavy drilling equipment to Egypt within forty-eight hours.

Eighty thousand tons of liquid ammonia were donated to Egypt by the Soviet Union. After consultation with the Federal German Ministry of Economic Cooperation, the Indian Cabinet offered Cairo seven shiploads of nitrate fertilizer as a basis for the extraction of ammonia. The freighters, at the time off Mozambique, were rerouted to Alexandria.

Having waited until midday Thursday for an insulated parcel of Lihama strawberries from Calabria, Dr. Angelo decided to confine his Fragaria test series to the varieties Georg Soltwedel, Regina, Senga Prescosa, Senga Sengana, and Madame Moutot. He removed the fruit from their freezing compartments, placed them in dishes on the window sill to thaw out, filled the pipettes with perymethylene ether, and preheated the dehydration chamber. It occurred to him while he was checking the thermometer that he had forgotten to repair a defective air vent.

While attempts were being made to convert an oil tanker for the transportation of liquid ammonia, an oxygen cylinder exploded in the dockyard at Odessa and killed three welders.

In response to an approach by the Egyptian Ambassador in Ankara, the Turkish Cabinet reversed its previous decision to bar the Dardanelles to foreign ships transporting liquid ammonia in bulk. At the same time, invoking the terms of the Montreux Convention, Ankara stipulated that tankers should negotiate the Dardanelles only if the wind did not exceed Beaufort Force 2, so that the population of Istanbul should not be endangered by clouds of gas in the event of a mishap.

Israel's Defense Minister, Mme. Meir, informed the press that the Israeli air force would suspend all operations while liquid ammonia was being transported across the Eastern Mediterranean and up the Nile Valley. Jerusalem nevertheless insisted that Soviet consignments of ammonia should be checked by a U.N. representative: "Shipments of mustard gas would strain our patience too far!"

Edvard Alsund, the Norwegian director-general of the world food organization FAO, resigned his post in protest against the international curtailment of chemical fertilizer production. The secretariat of the World Health Organization announced the same evening that the United Nations would subsidize deliveries of ammonia to Egypt only if producers took the precaution of mixing colorless ammonia with a conspicuous marker gas which could promptly be detected in the event of damage to a storage tank. The WHO recommended green oxalic acid gas for this purpose.

Young Israelis from Jerusalem and Haifa chained themselves to cypresses and olive trees in the Jewish cemetery on the Mount of Olives, and a girl buried the keys near the gates. Placards which the demonstrators had affixed to the cemetery wall bore slogans such as: "Egypt Needs Help—Jerusalem Can Give It," "Technicians to Aswan, Not Troops to the Canal," and "Reconciliation Now!"

Passers-by summoned a detachment of military police. The girl demonstrator informed them that her group was an activist wing of Chechdot, the religious youth movement which advocated a compromise with Egypt. The demonstrators in the cemetery would fast until the Israeli Cabinet offered to assist the Egyptian government in averting the disaster that threatened the Nile Valley.

By afternoon, several thousand people had gathered on the Mount of Olives. Chechdot helpers handed out hectographed leaflets bearing quotations from Proverbs: "Rejoice not when thine enemy falleth, and let not thine heart be glad when he stumbleth; lest the Lord see it, and it displease him, and he turn away his wrath from him. . . ."

The first two tanks of liquid ammonia were hoisted onto low loaders at Aswan station and driven along the crest of the dam to the west abutment. The mayor of Aswan proclaimed a curfew while the ammonia was in transit, and householders were ordered to seal their doors and windows with plastic sheets distributed for the purpose by parties of soldiers. Men of the 9th Medical Battalion maintained a state of readiness. Antoine Luwassi, the Congolese U.N. representative at Aswan, telephoned Sweden's Count Hengström in Cairo to confirm that the U.N. seals on the first two tanks of ammonia were intact.

During preliminary excavations for the first borehole through which liquid ammonia was to be pumped into the base of the dam, workmen employed by the High Dam Authority unearthed a skeleton five feet below the ashlars on the crest of the dam. The skull was encircled by an ornamented brass band and some bird's talons reposed on the rib cage. The Authority hinted in its report that Nubian laborers might have killed the unidentified man shortly before the dam's completion and buried him in the crest to propitiate the river gods.

The attempt on the life of President Anwar el Sadat took place at 3:12 p.m. The would-be assassins had no fixed schedule. Their timing was dependent on the wind.

The President's four-jet Tupolev landed at Aswan early that morning. Sadat, his personal secretary Ahmedi, and two bodyguards flew in an army helicopter to the New Cataract Hotel, where the chiefs of staff of the Luxor, Aswan, and Diwan districts were waiting in the first-floor dining room. Other members of Sadat's entourage traveled from the airfield in a convoy of cars and did not enter the room on the first floor until thirty minutes after the President, by which time he was already in conference.

At midday, Sadat emerged from the New Cataract Hotel and crossed the gravel path to the red sandstone knoll at the northern extremity of the garden. Ahmedi and his other advisers remained in the hotel foyer. The Luxor and Diwan chiefs of staff drove to the Nile City Hotel in a Moskvitch sedan. The two bodyguards hovered among the rhododendron bushes twenty yards from the sandstone outcrop.

Some Venetian blinds rattled on the fifth floor. In the foyer, Ahmedi pushed a slip of paper across the glass-topped reception desk and asked for a top-priority call to Cairo. Two moneychangers in the lounge locked their cashboxes and went to the window. On the roof of the old Cataract Hotel, half hidden by the white stone balls on the balustrade, stood three camouflage-suited sharpshooters of the 7th Division. Sadat climbed the worn stone steps to the summit of the knoll. He could feel the warmth of the rock through his soles.

The knoll culminated in a flat surface the size of a tabletop and was bounded to the west by a sheer drop to the Nile. A fishing boat was moored so close to the rock that its masthead was level with Sadat's eyes and only a few feet away.

The President craned forward and looked down at the white deck. The garboard timbers were painted pale blue. A man was squatting there, coiling ropes. Beyond the boat, Sadat could see a human shadow projected on the milky-emerald water. He lifted his arm and the shadow followed suit.

Of course it's me, he thought.

Beside the rhododendron bushes, a bodyguard turned and scrutinized the front of the New Cataract Hotel. Somebody at a window on the extreme right of the second floor removed his hand and let the curtain fall.

"You're through to Cairo," said the receptionist. Ahmedi opened the door at Booth No. 3 and picked up the phone. One of the snipers on the roof of the old Cataract Hotel leaned against a flagpole.

The President took a step forward and looked across at

the island of Elephantine. White-robed men were busy at the water's edge, filling cans with water and carrying them on their heads to a building site.

Nothing's really changed, thought Sadat.

Down in the boat, a young Nubian started to climb the red crosspieces that served as a ladder. Gripping the mast with his thighs, he proceeded to unfurl the sail.

"What's your name?" asked Sadat.

"Yussuf Nugal."

"You live in Aswan?"

"Yes, the government gave us a room in a stone house. We shall get land someday. Three feddan."

"How do you know?"

"My father says so."

"How does your father know?"

"The government told us before we left Diwan."

"Why did you leave—because of the dam?"

"Yes."

"What do you do for a living?"

"Fish. Yesterday we caught three fine perch."

"Good luck."

"Thank you, sir." A rope fell from the youth's hand and slapped the limp sail.

The sort of conversation dictators conduct with children, thought Sadat as he turned and made his way back to the rhododendron bushes.

The bodyguards signaled to the helicopter pilot in the hotel garden and rotor blades began to turn silently. Then the engine came to life. The President, his secretary, and the two bodyguards took off at 12:15 p.m. and flew to the officers' mess, Aswan East.

The first borehole was due to be injected with liquid ammonia at 3:30 p.m. The President's return flight to Aswan airport was scheduled for 5 p.m. On the west abutment of the dam, thirty yards from the borehole, the High Dam Authority had erected an awning-covered platform for Sadat and his entourage, its parapet draped with the Egyptian flag. The framework consisted of tubular scaffolding, and the plank floor rested on bearers eight feet from the ground. A flight of wooden steps ascended the structure on either side. The boring rods had been disconnected and were neatly stacked behind the platform. Employees of the High Dam Authority had marked out a landing place for the helicopter between Nasser's tomb and the two ammonia tanks on the crest of the dam—a rectangle measuring twenty feet by thirty. On the far side of the road stood a mast carrying a windsock to assist the pilot on landing and takeoff. On the road itself, parallel with the ammonia tanks, a strip of sand had been laid for the guard of honor.

As 2 p.m. approached, troops of the 19th Parachute Brigade took up their positions on the ridge overlooking the west abutment.

At 2:25 p.m., the President's helicopter passed over machine-gun post No. 2 on the crest of the dam, described an arc above the south cofferdam, and landed in front of the generating station. Sadat left the aircraft and walked along the asphalt road to the edge of the rock face which fell away in terraces to the stilling pond at the foot of the dam. Beside the parapet stood three soldiers armed with rifles and the lemonade-seller to whom the President had graciously spoken on his last trip to Aswan. The bottles were again lying in a plastic bucket among fist-sized chunks of ice.

Water spouted from the six outlets of the generating station in a gigantic ellipse which rose steeply before flattening out at the end of the basin. Swirling eddies of air wrested spray from the boiling cauldron and carried it up to the railings beside the road.

For the first time, Sadat was struck by the pale-green film that covered the rocky walls of the stilling pond. He wondered if Nasser had ever noticed that the spray was making vegetation grow on bare rock—they had never talked of it. Ten minutes later, the President's helicopter flew over the dam for a second time and landed on the crest.

While inspecting the guard of honor, Sadat started and took a pace backward. The major who was escorting him wavered. Sadat had paused in front of one of the men and was studying his face intently. The man stared straight ahead. Behind him, Sadat could hear a murmur from his entourage.

"Good afternoon, Shuker," Sadat said very softly. The soldier did not move, but a strange expression flitted across the impassive face. The escorting major cleared his throat. He said, "May I conduct you to the platform, sir?"

An instrument panel had been mounted on the rail. Mahmoud Fahlewi, the engineer in charge, explained the various dials. "They can be read off from the left as follows: Manometer 1, the pressure in the ammonia tanks—that gauge just below it records the temperature. Manometer 2, the pressure in the valve chambers. Manometers 3 and 4 enable us to check the supply pipes which lead to the borehole. We start by pumping the liquid ammonia to a depth of 246 feet —in other words, to a point still above the first sand layer. At that stage, the ammonia emerges from the pressure pipes, passes through decompression chambers, and becomes gas. Because the gas is under pressure, the column of air in the shaft is simultaneously forced upward. The ammonia now drops at a velocity of 6.5 feet per second . . ."

Sadat caught his secretary by the wrist. Ahmedi inclined his head.

"I thought I saw Shuker in the guard of honor," the President whispered. "Front rank, eighth man from the left —I was positive at first. If it weren't for the steel helmet . . . Something confused me."

Ahmedi leaned against the rail and stared.

"Impossible, sir. It can't be him."

"I'm probably imagining things . . ."

The engineer said, "Telethermometers have been installed from the 246-foot mark down to the base of the borehole—in other words, down to the granite bedrock. At intervals of thirty-two feet . . ."

"Shuker's taller," murmured Ahmedi.

"I wasn't talking about height. Don't forget I saw his face from two paces away."

"I'll have the bodyguards come forward to the rail and stand on either side of you."

"Thanks, Ahmedi. That won't be necessary."

The President glanced at his watch and thought, if they shoot me down here on the platform, Shuker will never allow me to be buried on the dam.

"The water in the core of the dam will freeze for a distance of thirty-two feet around the borehole," Fahlewi continued. "We're counting on a freezing time of ten to fifteen minutes at most. This congelation process, which will stabilize the base of the dam and prevent further undermining, can be followed on the lateral thermometers which have been installed around the borehole—Thermometer 1 at a distance of six feet, Thermometers 3 and 4 sixteen feet from the edge of the borehole. If one draws imaginary lines from these two thermometers to the center, the resulting angle measures fifty-nine degrees. Our object is to gauge the radiation effect in the lateral sections of the dam . . ."

The President stared across the shimmering surface of the lake. Two Nubian workmen were squatting on the face of the dam, tapping the ashlarwork with hammers. Shuker's first official act would be to rename Lake Nasser, thought Sadat. The windsock hung limp from its ring on the mast beside the landing place. The President could feel that his palms were moist.

"Do you have a cigarette?" he asked Ahmedi.

At the control post beside the platform, an engineer opened a wheel valve and liquid ammonia flowed into the valve chambers. It was 2:59 p.m. On the instrument panel, a red needle jumped abruptly and came to rest, quivering, on the figure 26.

Fahlewi said, "The ammonia is now flowing through the pressure pipe into the borehole." He shot his cuff and checked the time.

Just as the ammonia reached the decompression chambers, the breeze freshened. The red-and-white-striped windsock danced on its pole. The wind, which came from the southeast, played over the ammonia tanks and filled the awning above the platform.

The first shot missed. The men on the platform heard a crisp report and turned their heads to look.

"It came from up there!" shouted Ahmedi.

The second rifle grenade pierced the side of one of the tanks, the third mangled a junction valve six feet from the ground.

The guard of honor scattered. Some of the men had flung themselves to the ground at the first shot and were crawling across the asphalt. Their shouts were drowned by the hiss of escaping ammonia.

Gas swirled from the broken valve in a pale-green cloud. The moisture in the air froze and rained down on the dam. Carried by the breeze, green vapor drifted along the crest toward the platform.

"Stay up here!" screamed Fahlewi. "Whatever you do, stay up here! In this temperature, it's heavier than air."

The cloud of gas had reached the foot of the scaffolding. On the dam, a soldier rose to his feet, staggered toward the platform, threw up his arms, and collapsed across a heap of twitching bodies.

The gas was streaming perpendicularly from the valve in a thick jet. The deputy chief engineer was the first to vault the rail, one sleeve clamped over his nose and mouth. He headed for the helicopter but collapsed after a dozen paces. The men standing behind Sadat crowded forward to the rail. One of the President's bodyguards seized him by the shoulders and pulled him into a corner. Seconds later, the wooden rail broke and the flag ripped as Ahmedi and several officers tumbled into the glaucous fog below. On the steps facing east, a hunched figure sat spitting blood onto the wooden treads. The bodyguard wrenched off Sadat's jacket from behind, wound it round his head, and knotted the sleeves over his face. Beneath the platform, Ahmedi crawled onto some boring rods, retched, and died.

The hissing grew softer and the pale-green geyser above the valve dwindled. The needle of Manometer 1 returned to zero. The cloud of ammonia flowed under the platform, billowed over the north side of the dam, and sank to the river, where it dispersed. President Sadat boarded his helicopter at 6:03 p.m. and flew back to Aswan airport.

Attempts to congeal the base of the High Dam with injections of liquid ammonia were discontinued after the fifth boring. Government spokesman Quaruni justified this step at a press conference. "The method was correct in principle," he said. "The relevant sections of the dam were actually stabilized, but the results did not accord with our calculations. To put it another way, five times the estimated quantity of ammonia would have been required to keep the water in the core of the dam in a frozen condition, because the outflow of seepage absorbed too much gas—ammonia producers, please note. The considerations that have prompted us to drop the scheme are not in any way connected with finance, still less politics. We are governed solely by the fact that it would be impossible to transport such vast quantities of liquid ammonia to Aswan over a long period. The Egyptian government will seek and find other means of preserving the High Dam."

Replying to a question from a German industrial correspondent, Quaruni announced that the High Dam Authority had already tested a condensing process developed by Hamburger Holten AG. In this, ammonia gas from the core of the dam would be reliquefied by compressors and conveyed back to the crest. Being a closed-circuit system, this would certainly cut down the quantity of ammonia required. On the other hand, technological problems precluded its installation at Aswan for another two years at least.

According to a report from the Middle East correspondent of the London *Daily Telegraph,* Quaruni's denial that political considerations had played any part in the decision was indirect confirmation of the rumored attempt on President Sadat's life during the inaugural attempt to congeal the dam.

On the Paris, London, and New York stock exchanges, chemicals slumped by an average of twenty points within hours of the Cairo announcement. The industrial correspondent of *Le Soir* pointed out in the late Paris edition that precisely the same reaction would, in any case, have set in after the collapse of the High Dam. "The worldwide production of ammonia has been boosted to such an extent, thanks to the recent fit of international hysteria, that disastrous pressure on the chemical fertilizer sector is now inevitable."

Israel's Defense Minister declared that if squadrons of Egyptian MIGs persisted in raiding Israeli fortified settlements there would be little reason not to bomb the ammonia tanks at Alexandria. "After all, it ultimately makes no difference to the children of either nation whether they are mangled by fragmentation bombs or asphyxiated by ammonia gas."

The creditors of Eastern United Chemicals instituted bankruptcy proceedings against the company at Trenton, New Jersey. The Catholic priest of Wegscheid, Upper Bavaria, tried to persuade the peasant family on the Rauhmoosalm to return to their home in the valley.

The would-be assassins had fired on the ammonia tanks from a range of four hundred yards. Investigators found the three rifles from which the grenades had been projected behind a rocky outcrop overlooking the west abutment of the dam. To the south, the granite ridge fell away in three stages to the temple of Kalabsha. The dunes began a few paces away to the west.

The snipers had bent steel reinforcing rods into cradles, wedged the ends into fissures in the rock, and bound their weapons to these improvised bipods with wire. Each rifle still contained a spent cartridge.

No fingerprints were found on the rifles or cartridge cases. Lying in a dip beyond the firing position were three sleeping bags, a pair of binoculars, and two water bottles. The investigators also found, on the edge of the dunes, a charred copy of Monday's *Al Ahram* and a can opener. West of the first dune, jeep tracks led off into the desert.

. . .

A lieutenant and a corporal, who belonged to the paratroop unit which had been deployed below the rock with orders to cover the platform party, stated that they had spoken to the suspects during a routine tour of inspection. After studying photographs brought to the dam from H.Q. Aswan East, they identified Colonel Shuker, Major Elassim, and the two military policemen who had disappeared in Ismailia. The conversation took place thirty minutes before the attack on the President, by which time the rifles were already lying in their metal cradles. The lieutenant and the corporal admitted that they had not challenged Colonel Shuker, who was wearing a camouflage jacket adorned with badges of rank. The colonel forestalled them by explaining that his men belonged to a squad which had been detailed to cover the ammonia tests by the military security service. He offered them cigarettes and asked if every member of their unit had been carefully checked by counterespionage at the foot of the gorge. Shuker seemed quite calm, although it struck them in retrospect that he had remained lying behind his rifle throughout the conversation, even offering the cigarettes from a prone position. When they left the rock on their way to inspect the next outpost, someone—presumably Major Elassim—had called after them, "If one of your men makes a false move, he'll stop a bullet. We're responsible for the President's safety."

The three shots had rung out in quick succession, stated the corporal. It had been impossible to determine their source in the initial confusion. The men posted lower down the gorge had merely seen the guard of honor scatter and heard a babble of cries. Seconds later, clouds of greenish vapor rose from the ammonia tanks. There seemed no point in opening fire until a lance corporal shouted, "It was them, up there!" At the same moment, a grenade case came tumbling down the rocky slope. When they reached the cone of rock some minutes later, Shuker and the others had vanished.

In a note addressed to the Secretariat-General of the Arab League, the Sudanese government protested against the United Arab Republic's proposal to impound the fresh-water spring situated off the Red Sea island of Mirear and pump the outflow back to the Egyptian coast along floating pipelines. By employing Professor Sander of Karlsruhe to supervise this operation, the Egyptian Ministry of the Interior had committed an unfriendly act.

Sander had previously enclosed the Kiveri spring in the Gulf of Argolis by towing concrete caissons into position round it and sinking them to form a dam which prevented the intermixture of sea water and fresh water.

Replying to the Sudanese accusation, a government spokesman in Cairo claimed that the water escaping from the seabed off Mirear was the property of the United Arab Republic.

The unsuccessful assassins had followed the telegraph line which runs in a long curve through the Libyan Desert and rejoins the Nile Valley at Nag Dibtut. They were evidently compelled to change a wheel near the Wadi Kalabsha, because they left the rim and shredded tire lying among some loose stones; these remnants were found on the second day of the search and taken aboard by the crew of an M.S.S. helicopter. The jeep's tire tracks disappeared after eight miles into the scree of a side valley. On the third day, the co-pilot of a reconnaissance plane spotted some more tracks southeast of the Dunqul oasis.

. . .

The remains of the jeep lay on the edge of a dry riverbed. It had skidded, plunged down the rocky bank, and burned out. The metal framework of the windshield had pinned the driver to his seat.

Three military policemen extricated his body from the spiral seat springs. Charred fragments of cloth trickled onto their boots as they did so. They wrapped the corpse in a tarpaulin and towed it through the sand to their helicopter. Raking through the layer of ash on the floor of the jeep, they found an identity disk, the two halves of a belt buckle, and a revolver which had been exposed to intense heat.

The body was flown to the military hospital, Aswan East. Comparison of its teeth with dental record cards delivered to Aswan that evening by courier plane proved that the dead man was the lieutenant who had deserted from Idfu. At midnight, having been X-rayed for good measure, the body was placed on a handcart, trundled across the helicopter pad by three soldiers, and buried near the water tower. The tarpaulin was ceremonially burned on the barrack square next morning.

Ewal Hamid, head of counterespionage, dispatched nine search parties into the dunes round the wrecked jeep, each radiating outward on a different compass bearing. At midday, the party which had set off in a southeasterly direction announced by radio that it had found some shreds of cloth from an army-issue shirt adhering to a thorn bush. Spots of blood could be identified on the twigs, and there was a long drag mark in the sand nearby. Half an hour later, the party came upon three boot prints in the lee of a rock, and early that afternoon they found a human forearm which had evidently been mauled by jackals.

Colonel Ahmed Shuker had crawled to some rocks and died in their shade. He was sitting propped against a boulder with his left leg drawn up and his right leg extended. His outspread fingers were buried in the sand. There were two packets of cigarettes in his uniform tunic. The magazine of his automatic pistol was empty. An identity disk hung down his back on a thin chain.

The body had already swollen and subsided. In the opinion of the army medical officer who examined him, the colonel had been dead for three days. The skin, which was blackish brown, had dried out and lay taut across the withered muscles of the forearms. Wishing to recover the brass chain and identity disk, a soldier removed the uniform cap from Shuker's head. He stared at the bunches of hair in the crown and vomited.

Shuker's notebook had slid off his right thigh into the sand.

Submitting his report that evening, the commander of the search party stated: "The only strange feature was that we were unable to find his ball-point pen. Once we established that Shuker was writing up to the time of his death, we combed the ground for fifty feet around. We even lifted the body and sieved the sand between our fingers. Somebody must have been with him when he died, but it seems odd that he should have taken the pen and left the diary."

On Wednesday, Shuker had noted: "I thought I'd taken leave of my senses when the third flare failed to ignite as well. I can still hear the 'pfft' as the powder simply smoldered away. Red, green, red was the prearranged signal, but the helicopter flew so low over the valley that the crew should have seen us anyway. Hagal emptied his gun in the air, and this evening he asked if I'd give him any rounds I have left. Elassim flew into a rage afterward and tried to run away. He'd be dead by now if we hadn't knocked him out and tied him to the gasoline cans.

. "The helicopter business is beyond me. Even as we fired

the third grenade, though, I had a presentiment that Sadat would come out alive. I don't know why—I watched the windsock like a hawk and didn't give the order to fire until the breeze was right. Perhaps the clouds of ammonia weren't high enough to reach the platform. If Sadat were dead, they'd probably have sent every squadron at Asyut to get us out of here."

On Thursday, he wrote: "I knew the youngsters would crack first. I told Elassim I'd shoot him on the spot if he pissed against the tires again. The stones are bad enough— this morning I fell and gashed the palm of my left hand.

"Grotesque that the survival of an entire nation should depend on the quality of a tire case. If the canvas holds, we'll live to demolish the High Dam. If not, Sadat will go on playing with his ammonia until the flood comes."

The entry for Friday: "Late this morning, we heard the sound of a helicopter northeast of us. The flare was a good one this time—I knew it the moment I pulled the ignition toggle and heard it hiss. I jumped aside, only to hear Hagal shouting that it was white. I was stunned for a moment. It whooshed into the air and drifted down on its parachute. The plume of smoke was all that could be seen in the sunlight. We all fell on the cardboard container. It said red, all right. They probably mixed up the flare powder in the factory—I can't think of any other explanation. The helicopter had veered away by the time Elassim started to weep. The corporal tells me we forgot to bring the can opener with us . . ."

On Saturday, Shuker wrote: "We ought to have removed the lieutenant's identity disk. If Hamid can't identify him, so much the better . . . I think he was already dead when the gas tank went up. If I come through this, perhaps I'll adopt his children. This afternoon, Elassim complained that his water ration wasn't enough to die on, even. I make the men carrying the water walk ahead of me now, so I can keep an eye on them. It was probably a mistake to give Hagal all my rounds. Elassim may survive until this evening. If the night is very cool, he'll last till morning. In other words, one more water ration. I try to picture Fewa's expression when she hears I'm dead."

Saturday evening: "I'll never forget the way Elassim looked at me when I was doling out water. If I'd known he would be dead in eight hours' time, I might have given him some more. That rattle he made . . . He told me his tongue had swollen so that he couldn't breathe any more. It was like a ball of fire in his throat . . .

"We changed direction this afternoon. The chances of the helicopter reappearing are zero. Hamid has probably rounded up the whole network. We're trying to head back to the Nile. I put us on a level with El Diwan. Hagal says he'd welcome a court-martial after this. The dam . . . If I simply lie here and let the others take the water bottles . . .

"They say it bursts your lungs, the wall of air that races ahead of the flood wave, so I wouldn't even taste the water if I sat here and waited for the dam to break. Fewa would be alone. She'd be sitting on the roof with the boys when the flood came. Elassim has been dead for an hour—at least, his pupils didn't react. He'd be a little stiff already if it weren't for this heat . . ."

The spidery script undulated, the characters became larger.

On Sunday, Shuker wrote: "The night was good. I think the temperature must have dropped five or six degrees. I pulled off my shirt and lay on the sand in my trousers. If there's any dew, I told myself, the skin ought to absorb it somehow. I breathed very deeply. Hagal shot a jackal this morning. He left camp for half an hour, saying he must see if there were any others prowling around. I think he sampled the blood—there was a dark crust on his lips when he came back. I've been wondering whether to try my own urine. No good, probably, because of the salt, but it would be one way of recycling my body fluids. What I wouldn't give for a can of water . . . Anwar said, 'Empty a can of water into the sand two days running and it'll be green by nightfall.' That was in Ismailia. They'll come in—probably the children will be asleep by now—and tell Fewa I've died of thirst. One can, he said—that would mean thirty-six hours at most. Then I could munch the leaves . . ."

On Monday, in big sprawling characters: "Perhaps she'll only mind because of the children. Fewa has never been the same since I started vomiting after Sharm el Sheikh. I can tell from the way she averts her head and makes those exaggerated moaning noises. Her arms go limp, too—that's the clearest indication of all. It doesn't matter, though, except from the children's point of view. I know I must concentrate like mad now, because the hallucinations have started. They began this morning, really, but I recognized them in time. The dam. Perhaps the children won't take it too hard.

"The dam . . . If Gamal were still alive, he'd drown while I died of thirst. A bumpy ride he'll have when the water sweeps his tomb away. He wouldn't get beyond the old dam, not in a lead coffin. As soon as it went over the cataract . . . Actually, Fewa isn't like that any more. Bed doesn't mean so much to her. The water looks like a green glass wall. I should have shot Gamal when he started to build the dam. And Sadat. If Sadat had been the first President, he'd have done precisely the same. I could lie face downward now and drink. Take a mouthful, wait until it cools my gums, raise my head and swallow. Lie on my belly and dangle my tongue in it. The lake is 310 miles long. I told him so from the start. Gamal, I said, you'll never dodge paying the Sudanese an indemnity for the land you inundate. That's 310 miles, southward from Aswan. My father always came with the sun ships. I never liked traveling by coach. The boys can't have heard anything yet. As Gamal used to say at the Academy, one tomorrow and another the day after, and by evening it will all be green. I don't think the delusions have started yet—I can still picture the lake, after all. Hagal just came back. I'm almost certain he drank some more jackal's blood. I can picture the lake perfectly. Sadat is sitting up there on the crest beside the ammonia tanks, waving to me. I lie face down and drink. He gets furious because he's worried about his godforsaken lake. I carry on drinking. Do you understand, Fewa? I lie face down and drink from Lake Nasser. Hagal has probably gone off with the last water bottle. Then I crawl from the bank to the base of the dam and start gnawing through it. He gets belligerent, so I knock him down. I finish the channel, the water drains away, and we go to sleep. Sadat races up and down the crest, shouting like a madman. Elassim would be dead by now even if I'd poured all our water down his throat. I'm terribly afraid of delusions, that's why I'm writing. You and your can of water. How long before you understand? Quick as lightning, lungs exploded, a taste of water. How long before you understand? We could have demolished it a year ago . . . Concentrate. I can see it quite clearly.

"Make him give me a mouthful from his can. Help me, Fewa, he doesn't have to pour it all away into the sand. What worries me most is the thought of the jackals afterward. Crazy to reflect that the dam is still standing. If only I had a fat green leaf to suck. I'm so far gone I could drink the lake dry. What about the water, Fewa? What about all that greenery? Gamal lies in his lead box on the dam, laughing. I gnaw through the apron stones and the lake drains gently away. The water is like bottle glass. Cold. I'd never have believed water could be so cold. I've done it after all.

Nobody can say I'm dead. Nobody. You'll drown. Demolish it, I said. All right, I'm drinking. Too cold . . ."

The remains of Colonel Ahmed Shuker were stowed in a rubber sack and winched aboard helicopter M 1-234/1.

Part Two

INTERVENTION

THAT EVENING, an Israeli secret service agent in Berne reported by radio that Professor Ferdinand Schaller of Zurich had visited the embassy of the United Arab Republic. Schaller, who was a co-designer of the Auld Valley Dam near Los Angeles, had later lectured at California universities on the dynamic computation of shearing strength in dams subjected to seismic stress. He had originally concentrated on dynamic triaxial experiments aimed at determining the mechanical properties of granular materials. For the past three years, he had been engaged in geophysical field tests designed to ascertain shear-wave velocities, which in turn made it possible to predict oscillations in dams liable to damage by earthquake. According to the *Neue Zürcher Zeitung*, this procedure enabled scientists to compute the magnitude of the distortions to be expected in individual sections of a dam.

The same afternoon, Dr. Angelo resprayed two Green Hubbard pumpkins from the sixth experimental series with perymethylene ether, placed them in the dehydration chamber, and exposed them to a temperature of 116° Fahrenheit for four hours. Having pulverized the rind ready for weighting, he estimated the moisture loss at 1.01 percent.

According to information received from the Israeli agent in Berne, Professor Schaller left Switzerland on a Lebanese aircraft of Middle East Airlines. The plane had taken off from Zurich-Kloten at 9:23 a.m. and was scheduled to reach

Cairo-Heliopolis airport at 2:16 p.m. after an intermediate stop in Athens. A Greek informant of the Israeli secret service notified the Israeli military attaché that Schaller had remained on board at Athens. Headquarters in Tel Aviv waited until 7 p.m. for a routine message from Colonel Ramon, its agent in Heliopolis. At midnight, attempts to establish contact with Colonel Ramon on alternative frequencies 23 and 23a were abandoned.

President Sadat summoned the Soviet Ambassador in Cairo, Igor Vinyenev, and inquired if the government of the U.S.S.R. would supply nuclear explosives for the purpose of sealing the fissures between Lake Nasser and the Red Sea.

Undermining had attained such proportions that the use of conventional methods seemed pointless, Sadat said. Sonic depth measurements indicated that the cavities through which water was escaping had doubled in volume during the past three weeks.

The ambassador inclined his head. "You underestimate the Soviet Union's interest in the High Dam if you think you have to convince me by producing statistics. It goes without saying that we shall assist you in every possible way."

"Can you be more precise?"

"I refer to all practical methods of stopping these underground leakages without endangering the dam itself."

"Silicic acid, for example?"

"Precisely—we discussed that at our last meeting. We've developed a process which will allow direct injection into the base of the dam."

"You're as much of a layman as I am, but we're talking at cross-purposes. The erosion of the base is a secondary phenomenon. The moment we stop the outflow of water between Aswan and the Red Sea, not another particle will be washed out of the dam."

"And the moment you use atomic bombs to seal the fissures there won't be any dam left to worry about. That's the logical sequence of events."

"So you contend. We have prepared some figures of our own. They show that nuclear explosions in the vicinity of the lake need not overtax the dam's dynamic shearing strength—not by any means."

"Schaller's works are well known," Vinyenev said. "We even have them in the embassy library. You could have saved yourself the expense."

"We are asking your government a straight question, and we should appreciate—"

"I am empowered to inform you, on behalf of the Council of Ministers, that the Union of Soviet Socialist Republics cannot supply nuclear explosives for detonation outside Soviet territory. The decision was fundamentally a political one. In this particular case, however, technical considerations also militated against any such course of action."

"You already debated the matter?"

"Shortly after your last visit to Moscow."

"You aren't being fair."

"Because we won't blow up the dam?"

"No, because you and the Americans pledged yourselves, in the nuclear nonproliferation treaty, to give third countries which are also treaty signatories access to the benefits of nuclear research."

"But not to put them under water."

"Foreign Minister Riad will fly to Moscow tomorrow."

"I already told you—you could have saved Professor Schaller's fee."

At 7:47 p.m., the Presidential secretariat sent a radio message in cipher to the Egyptian Embassy in Moscow. The embassy radioed back that the Central Committee of the

107

Soviet Communist Party had that afternoon confirmed its refusal to supply the United Arab Republic with nuclear explosives for the purpose of sealing fissures between Lake Nasser and the Red Sea. The Central Committee had, on the other hand, decided that redoubled efforts should be made to stabilize the dam. A special commission headed by Anton Trotsky, the Minister responsible for hydroelectric engineering projects, would be flying to Cairo on Friday. Foreign Minister Riad had left the Soviet capital at 7 p.m.

Dr. Angelo sat reading in front of the equestrian statue in the Campo Ss. Giovanni e Paolo until darkness fell. Then he put a match to his newspaper, dropped it on the plinth, and walked across the bridge for a snack of rolled anchovies. He paused outside the windows of a bar for several minutes, watching the men at their cards and listening to the hum of the extractor fan in the transom, then walked down the steps to the door and leaned against the counter. The proprietor nodded to him and dipped a wooden skewer in the jar. He speared half a dozen rolled anchovies and scraped them off on the edge of the plate.

Dr. Angelo ate in silence, pushed the plate back, and said, "You're quite right to top up the jar, Antonio. Water is a great preservative."

"So you keep telling me, Doctor. That's why I always make sure it's full."

The secret note from the Egyptian government was submitted to President Nixon at 9 a.m. Nixon conferred for an hour with Henry Kissinger, his Presidential adviser for national security affairs, and Secretary of Defense Laird, welcomed a South Korean parliamentary delegation in the White House garden, and talked with Kissinger again at noon.

The U.A.R. chargé d'affaires in Washington was summoned to the White House at 2 p.m. Kissinger informed him that the United States government could not assume responsibility for detonating nuclear charges in order to seal fissures in the area of Lake Nasser. Apart from the technical considerations which had dictated this decision, there was the fact that Washington had pledged itself, under the terms of the nonproliferation treaty, not to introduce nuclear weapons or similar devices into politically sensitive areas, or to store them there.

Kissinger announced a special U.S. aid program for Egypt. Washington planned to make available $180,000,000 for the control of bilharzia and the establishment of agricultural research centers.

The United Arab Republic's representative at the International Atomic Energy Agency (IAEA) headquarters in Vienna requested that the board meet in special session at the earliest opportunity.

The specially chartered United Arab Airlines plane which was to transport diagrams and a model of the High Dam to Vienna could not land at Schwechat because of fog, and was diverted to Prague. The Director-General of the International Atomic Energy Agency, the Finnish diplomat Dr. Tuuksumen, postponed the special session of the governing board until that evening.

The ambassadors of the Soviet Union and the United States consulted in private at a neutral rendezvous.

At Prague airport, United Arab's Comet 4C received clearance for Vienna. An hour later, two squad cars from Vienna's municipal police headquarters conveyed the diagrams and model from Schwechat to the IAEA building in the Donaupark.

Shortly before midnight, Dr. Tuuksumen called upon

Riad to address the meeting in the boardroom. The Egyptian Foreign Minister illustrated the structure of the High Dam with the aid of cross-sections and traced the course of the fissures connecting Lake Nasser with the Red Sea. Red flags marked the position of the three largest fresh-water springs recently located on the seabed.

"Echograms covering the last four-week period are displayed on side tables and may be inspected at your leisure," Riad said. "The cavities are growing hourly, with the result that tectonic subsidence must be expected in the near future. The most alarming development of all concerns the water-bearing fissures which run due east from the abutment of the dam to Foul Bay, where the outflow of fresh water from the seabed is naturally greatest. In this case, the particles currently being dislodged have already attained a granular diameter of 0.5 millimeter. The material carried by the other fissures consists mainly of fine sediment, but it's only a matter of time."

The British delegate said, "Of course it's a matter of time. That's why I don't understand your feverish haste. According to my government's information, the fact that water is escaping from the lake bed and the base of the dam has been common knowledge for three years at least. After all, you've been constructing lateral aprons along the west bank since spring, 1969. At the level of Abu Hor, for example, if my memory serves me correctly. What puzzles me is your timing—especially when one views it against the political background that prevails in the Near East—"

Tuuksumen interrupted him. "This is a technical problem, Sir Richard—a nuclear problem, even if we're all alive to the political implications."

Riad said, "So Sir Richard is puzzled. Do you know what puzzles me? The ignorance which we sensed even during preliminary discussions. There's a flat refusal to recognize the disastrous interaction between progressive erosion and rising outflow. If undermining increases, more water escapes. If more water escapes, fissures are washed clear more rapidly. That is a formula which could drown an entire nation."

"Histrionics will get us nowhere," said the British delegate.

Tuuksumen leaned over the table. "I move that the remarks of Sir Richard and His Excellency the Foreign Minister be stricken from the record."

"And I should like to revert to the question of timing," said the British delegate. "Why now, I ask myself?"

"We relied on the judgment of experts, as any government must. It was originally envisaged that any seepage would carry suspended matter into the substructure and consolidate it. As it turns out . . ."

The Federal German delegate raised his hand. "A question, Your Excellency. What experts?"

"The engineers and hydrologists entrusted with the planning and execution of the High Dam project, if that's what you mean."

Riad saw the Soviet delegate reach for his pencil. He leaned forward with both hands on the top of the lectern and said, "If your shorthand isn't fast enough, I'll speak more slowly."

Tuuksumen rose. "I move that His Excellency's last remark, too, be stricken from the record."

The Indian representative said, "Why can't these fissures be sealed with conventional explosives?"

"Because we should have to feed two thousand tons of TNT into them through narrow boreholes. By the time we did, grass would probably be growing over the desert of mud called Egypt."

"May I draw the board's attention to one particular aspect of this matter?" inquired Sir Richard.

111

"Please do."

"The oceanic trench which extends across the Red Sea to the Indian Ocean is held to be one of the most sensitive tectonic zones in the world. I can well imagine that atomic explosions centered on the boundary between two continents would shed some light on the theory of continental drift. However, it would all depend on whether anyone survived to assess their effects."

"I now call upon His Excellency to formulate the proposal submitted by the United Arab Republic," said Tuuksumen.

Riad laid a sheet of typescript on the lectern.

"The government of the United Arab Republic formally requests the International Atomic Energy Agency in its capacity as an executive body provided for by the treaty relating to nonproliferation of nuclear weapons, urgently and with reference to the provisions of Article IV, Clause 2, of the said treaty, which guarantees all non-nuclear signatories access to the peaceful uses of atomic energy, to supply nuclear explosives from the stocks of the nuclear signatories for the purpose of sealing aquiferous fissures between Lake Nasser and the Red Sea. Preliminary studies indicate that the government of the United Arab Republic would require seven nuclear charges with a total equivalent capacity of between 1,800 and 2,000 tons of TNT. In all, the requested potential corresponds to one tenth of that possessed by the atomic bomb detonated over Hiroshima.

"The said preliminary studies further indicate that the seven charges should be detonated at depths of between 6,000 and 10,000 feet. It is envisaged that they should be laid in a horseshoe formation east of Lake Nasser and the Nile Valley, namely: in the Wadi el Allaqi, in the upper reaches of the lateral valleys of Umm'Ashira and Gabgaba; west of the oasis of Abu Hashim and at the point where the

Garara Valley intersects with longitude 34°E.; in the Nile Valley near the town of El Qattara, north of Aswan; in the Wadi Natash; and at the oasis of Bir el Gindi southwest of Mount Hidilawi.

"The government of the United Arab Republic would assume responsibility for the planning and technical preparation of this project in association with the International Atomic Energy Agency.

"The government of the United Arab Republic is prepared, on a temporary basis, to extraterritorialize the whole area between El Qattara and the Sudanese border, and, for such time as is required to lay and detonate the nuclear charges, to transfer to the International Atomic Energy Agency all rights of sovereignty with the exception of technical and military authority over the immediate area of the dam.

"The government of the United Arab Republic offers to defray all expenses incurred.

"The government of the United Arab Republic is cognizant of its full responsibility for this undertaking."

Director-General Tuuksumen reached for the bell. He said, "Gentlemen, I suggest we adjourn for fifteen minutes and reconvene at 3 a.m."

Foreign Minister Riad waited in the Director-General's office. A secretary brought him a cardboard cup of coffee from the automat in the corridor. Riad sat down in Tuuksumen's swivel chair and smoked. Reflected in the glass of a picture on the opposite wall, the traffic light beneath the chestnut trees glowed and died alternately. Like a beating heart, he thought.

At about 4 a.m., Tuuksumen came in to fetch a file from his desk. Riad stared out of the window. A girl in a pale mackintosh appeared and disappeared. A taxi pulled up on the other side of the road with its engine idling. The Minister crossed the room and paused in front of the picture. The yellow light flashed across a mountainscape, vanished, and returned. Riad saw chalets with stones weighting their roofs. A boy walking behind some goats. Apple trees. A spring beside the path. A woman with her hands on her hips, staring after the boy and the goats. A wood, some cliffs, a waterfall.

At 5 a.m., Riad was summoned to the boardroom. The curtains and shutters were open. Sir Richard had removed his jacket and was lighting a cigar. The German was leafing through a pamphlet. Riad knew, when the Indian delegate avoided his eye, that his proposal had been rejected. Tuuksumen stalked to the lectern and said:

"I am now able to announce the governing board's decision."

"Please proceed," said Riad. The girl who had brought him the cardboard cup pulled a chair across the carpet. He thought, the Finn's eyes are all bloodshot. In ten minutes, he'll go home and take a bath.

Tuuksumen said, "The governing board of the International Atomic Energy Agency, at its eleventh special session, has studied the United Arab Republic's proposal that it be supplied with nuclear explosives for the purpose of sealing underground fissures between Lake Nasser and the Red Sea and thereby preventing further outflow. The board regrets that this request cannot be granted . . ."

Sir Richard put his cigar in the ashtray and leaned back. The German fanned himself with a sheaf of papers. The Russian delegate chewed his pencil.

"Would it interest you to hear the board's reasons?" inquired Tuuksumen.

"I should be more interested to know exactly how the voting went," Riad said.

"The governing board is not obliged to disclose the number of votes cast for or against a resolution."

"Then state your reasons."

"The governing board of the International Atomic Energy Agency has come to the conclusion that—"

"Why don't you say, 'takes the uninformed view that'?" asked Riad.

"The governing board has come to the conclusion that it would be inexpedient to seal the fissures in the vicinity of Lake Nasser with nuclear explosives, not only for political but also, and predominantly, for technical reasons."

"What does that mean?"

"There is a danger that the dam's inherent frequencies would coincide with the shock frequencies which nuclear explosions in the immediate vicinity of the dam might be expected to produce, so that the two sets of frequencies would become superimposed and their effects correspondingly intensified."

"Is that all?" asked Riad.

"Some signatories to the treaty find it impossible to conclude with absolute certainty that nuclear explosions in the area of Lake Nasser would not conduce to precisely the opposite of the effect desired by the government of the United Arab Republic."

"In other words, the gentlemen in question are too cowardly."

"You asked the board to state its reasons," said Tuuksumen.

After consultations in the laboratory of the High Dam Authority at Aswan, Dr. Nuredin Nasser, assistant professor at the Hydrotechnical Institute, Cairo University, telephoned the section commander of the military security service and informed him that analysis of samples from the dam's settling tank had for the first time disclosed the presence of medium-sized grains of sand with a diameter of 0.6 millimeter.

"You know what that means?"

"No, I don't," replied the security man. "What's more, I don't know why you called me."

"If grains of this size are being washed out of the dam, it means that internal erosion may exceed the tolerance level at any moment."

"I still don't understand why you called me."

"It might interest you to know that the sample dish containing medium sediment has disappeared. To be blunt, someone has removed it."

"Do you know who?"

"Dr. Sabri. He was the only one who didn't visit the canteen this afternoon. He stayed behind in the laboratory."

"What does Dr. Sabri want with your grains of sand?"

"He wants to disguise the condition of the dam."

"Why?"

"Because it's in the interests of certain people—people who have an ax to grind."

"And Dr. Sabri is one of them?"

"Dr. Sabri is related to the director of our institute. That might interest you, too."

"I'm in conference now. Meet me at the laboratory in an hour's time."

The Israeli paper *Maariv,* in its report on the special session of the governing board of the International Atomic Energy Agency, claimed that the delegates of eighteen permanent member countries had voted in favor of using nuclear charges to seal the fissures between Lake Nasser and the Red Sea and thus stop the outflow of impounded water. Three delegates had abstained. The vote was taken again after protests from the Soviet and U.S. representatives because Director-General Tuuksumen had omitted to send a secretary out of the boardroom beforehand. During the second vote, the delegates of the Soviet Union and the United States of America had exercised their right of veto.

The correspondent's report from Vienna concluded with the words: "Painful as this decision may be for the government of the United Arab Republic, it has, from Israel's point of view, signally justified her own decision not to subscribe to the nuclear nonproliferation treaty. The two superpowers have demonstrated—and this is to a certain degree understandable, in face of a possible atomic apocalypse—that their interest in retaining control of nuclear explosives and leaving nothing to chance takes priority even over the vital interests of a third country."

In the morning, Dr. Angelo cleared out the dehydration chamber and washed down the racks on which the dishes stood. He took the record cards with the notes on the Fragaria test series and filed them in his card index, wrote out a check to the municipal electricity board, and cleaned the windows of the laboratory. Leaving the shutters open, he lay on his bed and tried to identify the postman's footsteps among the others that crossed the Ponte del Cristo.

At 10 a.m., Premier Moshe Dayan received the U.N. special representative Count Hengström, and informed him of the Israeli Cabinet's decision to offer the United Arab Republic nuclear explosives for the purpose of sealing fissures in the bed and vicinity of Lake Nasser.

"In my view," said the Swede, "reports on recent developments at the High Dam have been exaggerated. Even so, I discern a certain lack of taste . . ."

"I did not ask for your personal views, Count Hengström."

"Nevertheless, I consider it poor taste to play upon the hopes and fears of a nation which . . ."

Dayan clasped his hands behind his back and said quietly, "We asked for your services as an intermediary, nothing more. To repeat: we are prepared to assist the government of the United Arab Republic in sealing these fissures and preventing any further escape of water from the lake."

"At what price?" asked Hengström.

"For our own satisfaction, let's say. National self-respect demands that we make the offer."

"I came on behalf of the Mixed Commission, Prime Minister."

"Well?"

"It was agreed with your commanding general in the central canal sector that an absolute cease-fire should be observed while the three pilots were being handed over. As I told you on the phone, machine guns opened up as soon as the patrol boat carrying the coffins put out from Ismailia. The N.C.O. has since died. General Fachallah announced this morning that the next Israeli pilots to be shot down will be buried like dead dogs."

"Do you ever read *Achwal?*" Dayan asked.

"Sometimes. Translated excerpts only, of course."

"To quote a recent editorial, the Jewish people have brought enough suffering upon Egypt. The Lord turned the Nile to blood, and frogs crept into their bedchambers and bread ovens. Their cattle perished and their first-born were struck down. And the Lord said unto Moses, 'Stretch out thine hand over the land of Egypt for the locusts, that they may come up upon the land of Egypt, and eat every herb of the land, even all that the hail hath left.' "

"I do glance through the Old Testament from time to time."

"The east wind brought the locusts across the sea—we

118

had to use napalm for the first time in 1956. During the June War, there wasn't enough water on Sinai for the scattered Egyptian units. Later, we shot their Suez refineries to pieces."

"You're forgetting the fragmentation bombs on the school at El Baker in the Nile Valley. Spring, 1970, wasn't it?"

"The ninth of April, to be precise."

"Your self-assurance is only exceeded by your love of precision, Prime Minister."

"It was regrettable. Tell me, have you ever killed a snake?"

"Not that I'm aware."

"I trod on an adder when I was a boy. It wriggled and hissed at me. I was frightened because I knew the thing could be dangerous. I had a hammer in my hand—I was on my way to our playground at the time. The hammerhead was aluminum, I remember. My second blow caught the snake on the head. I smashed its skull, but I was so frightened that I went on hitting it. Then I dropped the hammer and ran off."

"A poor analogy, especially the last part."

"The last part? Perhaps. The fact remains that President Sadat is in our hands. The High Dam was still intact in Nasser's day. Our General Staff has worked out plans for bombing it, as Cairo well knows. As late as 1969, the dam's stability made it unassailable. Today, if we dispatched ten suicide planes loaded to the hatch covers with TNT, half of them would penetrate the SAM guided-missile cordon and blast it out of existence. You're familiar with the theory. We only have to crack the structure and the water will sweep it away. We're suspicious of Egypt. We're afraid, if you like—we have to be. I can see no way out, unless . . ."

"Unless what?"

"Our offer may be a monumental blunder. Let's assume

that Cairo agrees. We send teams of technicians and nuclear warheads to Aswan. Sadat interns our men, confiscates our bombs, and sends them back to Haifa by Ilyushin bomber. . . . I can't think of any comparable situation in history. Be that as it may, the Cabinet has made its decision. This is a unique state of affairs, a unique opportunity to reconcile our two peoples. We intend to exploit it for all it's worth."

"Is that how you wish me to put it to the President?"

"The Cabinet decision reads: 'The Israeli government is prepared to assist the United Arab Republic in combating seepage in the area of Lake Nasser by sealing subterranean fissures with nuclear explosives. There are no conditions attendant on this offer. We would simply supply nuclear charges and technical personnel. The time, location, and magnitude of the atomic explosions would be a matter for the government of the United Arab Republic to decide.' "

"Cairo would laugh me to scorn. In six weeks' time, I'd be back in Kristianstad, twiddling my thumbs."

"At least our little talk may have provided you with enough copy for one chapter of your memoirs."

That afternoon, Count Hengström flew by BOAC to Nicosia. He met the general officer commanding U.N. forces in Cyprus at the airport restaurant, conferred with him for an hour, and flew on to Cairo in a Boeing of Olympic Airways.

While flying over Cairo, the crew of an army helicopter noticed a yellow object on the roof of a house in the Bab esh Sha'ira quarter. The pilot banked, descended, and hovered thirty feet above the building.

A child darted across the flat roof and vanished through a trap door. Pigeons flew in all directions, alarmed by the whir of the rotor blades, and windows in neighboring houses slammed shut. Peering down, the pilot saw a rubber dinghy large enough to hold at least a dozen people.

That afternoon, a squad of security police arrested the Jewish shoemaker Shmol Bennoah at his home in Bab esh Sha'ira. Watched by wide-eyed children, they searched the house. Bennoah offered no resistance when detained and escorted outside. As he was climbing into the back of the jeep, he caught sight of two policemen on the roof and tried to break free. "It's only a Michelin dinghy!" he shouted.

According to a report received by Israeli intelligence, a Swedish Embassy car was waiting for Count Hengström outside the arrival hall at Heliopolis airport. The diplomat headed for Cairo but ordered the car to turn round just before the El Matariya road junction. While making a three-point turn, the sedan went over the edge of the asphalt and sank up to its rear axle in soft sand. At about 10 p.m., the crew of an army jeep pushed Hengström's car onto the road again. Hengström then drove to Sadat's villa in Heliopolis. He left the building shortly after midnight.

Austrian experts in dam construction, having visited Aswan at the invitation of the Egyptian Ministry of the Interior to study the readings for the previous thirty days, conferred with Minister Gidaff in Cairo and warned against any resort to drastic measures. No one would deny the need to reduce seepage in the alluvium and the dam itself, because internal erosion was developing at such a rate that it could only be a matter of weeks before the dam broke. On the other hand, if fissures in the immediate vicinity of Aswan were sealed, seepage would build up in the body of the dam. Water being incompressible, the result would be a huge increase of pressure in the filling material. As one hydrotechnician from Innsbruck put it, "The dam would virtually dissolve."

. . .

An Israeli intelligence report on the decisions reached by the Inner Revolutionary Council was handed to Premier Dayan before his own Cabinet met that afternoon. The Council had convened at President Sadat's villa in Heliopolis. Admiral of the Air Force Hassuni landed at Heliopolis by helicopter an hour after the meeting began. By that time, most members of the junta had already expressed their opposition to the Israeli offer.

Minister of the Interior Gidaff, who had earlier attended a third meeting with Professor Ferdinand Schaller, argued in favor of sealing the fissures around the lake with nuclear explosives on the ground that the peak acceleration of detonation waves on the crest of the dam would not necessarily correspond with oscillations in the argillaceous silt of the base. Although nuclear explosions near the bank and in the seepage outflow zone would exceed the dynamic shearing strength of the dam for some fractions of a second, it was improbable that shearing would occur in the face of the dam itself. Gidaff had prepared some diagrams relating to the behavior of dams under stress, but the Revolutionary Council waived the opportunity to inspect them.

An informant in the Presidential secretariat stated that General Boghdadi had cut Minister Gidaff short by remarking that, even under present circumstances, the Egyptian-Soviet relationship precluded any cooperation with Israel. Secretary-General Sidki insisted that nuclear explosives could not, in any case, be used without the express sanction of the Soviet Union. Any further discussion of Jerusalem's offer would strain the ties that existed between Cairo and Moscow. The only member of the Revolutionary Council to support Dayan's proposal, apart from Gidaff, was Professor Bahaeddin. There had evidently been a fierce argument between President Sadat and Admiral Hassuni, but no precise details of the altercation were known.

Colonel Ramon, who transmitted his coded message on Frequency 23a that evening, reported that exceptional security measures had been in force during the conference at the President's villa. Sharpshooters were posted on roofs in the neighborhood of his official residence ten minutes before Admiral Hassuni landed. For the first time in four weeks, too, the ambulance containing blood of the President's own group had parked in a side street north of the villa. Hassuni was the first to leave.

Shortly before midnight, Israeli secret service headquarters received a signal from Mansura to the effect that Ewal Hamid, head of Egyptian counterespionage, had visted Hassuni's headquarters that morning. There was some evidence to suggest that the admiral had been misinformed about the time of the conference at Heliopolis.

Speaking in a parliamentary debate on German cultural activities overseas, C.D.U. deputy Meichelbeck said, "All I really miss in the program under discussion is a suggestion that the federal government should, now that Lake Nasser is allegedly draining away, dismantle the temples of Abu Simbel and re-erect them on the banks of the Nile."

Count Hengström, U.N. special representative for the Near East, flew to Tel Aviv via Nicosia and reported to the Israeli Premier in Jerusalem that the government of the United Arab Republic had rejected Israel's offer to seal the fissures around Lake Nasser with nuclear explosives. Foreign Minister Riad had not, he said, given any reason for the decision.

"Nor did we expect one when we learned of the vote," said Dayan. He picked up a slim red file. "Nevertheless, my government would be much obliged to you if you could convey this explanation to President Sadat."

A sedan from the Israeli Foreign Ministry took Count Hengström back to Lod airport. The U.N. special representative landed in Nicosia at 3:30 p.m. and flew on to Cairo by the Olympic Airways evening flight.

President Sadat had flown from Heliopolis to Aswan that morning. He studied the past week's graphs in the boardroom of the High Dam Authority. Then, accompanied by the engineer Dr. Sabri, he took the lift from the crest of the dam to the central control station, walked through the dam to the west bank, and returned to the headquarters of the High Dam Authority by jeep after halting the vehicle for some minutes in front of the tomb of Gamal Abdel Nasser.

After lunch, the President paid an unescorted visit to the Aswan Museum and mingled with a party of schoolchildren who were inspecting the model of the dam under its plastic dome. They're all wearing leather shoes, Sadat thought. Shirts and trousers—that's a national victory, too.

The schoolchildren did not recognize him. The supervisor, who had been warned in advance, knew that the President wished to remain incognito and merely glanced up as he entered the hall. He indicated the plaster cross-section of the banks with his pointer. "The first question was whether to build a concrete wall or a rampart of earth. In resisting water pressure, a dam produces thrusts at either extremity. Solid abutments in the rocky banks would have been necessary to withstand them. Here above the cataract, this circumstance did not obtain—not, at least, on the west bank . . ."

They aren't listening at all, thought Sadat. The children were between twelve and fourteen years old. They stood around the circular table which supported the model. One of them was half crouching with his hands on his skinny knees, a few were leaning against the rail, and others were lounging against pillars staring at the ground.

"In addition, a concrete dam has certain disadvantages. You can't check what is going on inside the structure or what pressures are being exerted on the various sectors. If the worst happens, there's a sudden crack and everything falls apart. With an earth dam, you have time. You can measure the water pressure in the pores, the buoyancy of the filling material . . ."

Why are they so apathetic? Sadat wondered. Why don't they look at the model?

"Ever since summer, 1970, when the last turbine was installed . . ."

They hear nothing, feel nothing, Sadat told himself; they don't even ask questions. Either that or they don't understand. Apathy and ignorance . . . The bane of Egypt, not that Gamal would accept the fact. The idea of a diesel engine pumping water—that much they can understand.

An Irish officer of the U.N. Control Commission informed the authorities at Lod airport that a charter machine of Middle East Airlines, with Count Hengström on board, would take off from Heliopolis at 8 a.m. on Tuesday and fly direct to Tel Aviv. Transport Minister Sragil notified the head of Israeli counterespionage.

Hengström and Premier Dayan met at the Swedish Embassy in Jerusalem. Dayan said, "We stressed from the outset that we fully understand the misgivings of the United Arab Republic. Putting myself in President Sadat's place, however, I wonder if I would be quite as chary of offending the Soviet Union."

"His reservations are not only political."

"Let's get to the point. Have you read our explanation?"

"Minister Gidaff gave me a copy."

"Well?"

125

"As a special representative of the United Nations Organization, I can hardly participate in a scheme designed to hoodwink a permanent member of the Security Council. Also, I have no wish to spend the rest of my professional career smuggling messages back and forth between Cairo and Jerusalem."

"The Russians will be delighted if the dam remains intact."

"Nor am I employed to represent the interests of the Soviet Union."

"But you don't relish the prospect of provincial life in Kristianstad."

"I have other worries."

" So do we all, Your Excellency."

"I would emphasize yet again that your offer can never be kept secret from Egypt's Soviet advisers."

"Let Sadat worry about that later, when it's all over. I formally reiterate, here and now, our offer of technical cooperation. The nuclear warheads of our Rahab rockets, as Egyptian intelligence is aware . . ."

"I know."

"According to our calculations, we can make do with a bomb casing ten inches in diameter. It will therefore be sufficient to drill twelve-inch boreholes between Aswan and the Red Sea."

"It would be impossible to keep the drilling operations secret, let alone anything else."

"That's another of Sadat's problems. The transfer of nuclear charges to the United Arab Republic would take place as follows—I quote from our explanation: 'The scheduled United Arab Airlines flight from Teheran to Cairo simulates engine trouble or loss of power over Jordanian territory. The pilot radios Amman or Beirut but makes a forced landing here at Lod. Our security personnel impound the plane and escort the passengers to the transit area.' "

"Very cloak-and-dagger."

"Meanwhile, an Israeli Caravelle of the same series is waiting in a hangar at Lod. It carries Egyptian markings and the same registration number. With your assistance, Count, we match various items in advance—cabin carpets, ashtrays, curtains, and so on. Very well, the nuclear explosives are stowed away in the baggage compartment of our Caravelle, packed in special drums and inserted between the inner and outer skin. The hatches of the baggage compartment being too small, we shall have to cut away a section of the fuselage to get them into the aircraft—under normal circumstances, a forty-eight-hour job. That's why we can't simply load the explosives into the Egyptian Caravelle."

"Of course not. Well, what else?"

"The passengers wait in the transit lounge, leaving their hand luggage on board. The Egyptian Caravelle is towed into the hangar, ostensibly for repairs. Two hours later, the Israeli Caravelle, complete with Egyptian markings and a hidden consignment of bombs, is towed out of the same hangar. The passengers emerge from the transit lounge and board our aircraft. Their hand luggage is where they left it, their magazines and newspapers lying on the same seats. Once the plane reaches Heliopolis, Egyptian technicians will have plenty of time to extract the bombs from the baggage compartment. Our advisers would travel to Egypt in four or five parties— as tourists, congress delegates, anything you like. They would fly United Arab and board their planes in London or Rome."

"You don't imagine for one moment that the Soviet secret service will be taken in by your little ruse?"

"I'm an optimist, Count Hengström."

On Monday, Count Hengström informed Premier Dayan that the Egyptian Cabinet had reconsidered the Israeli offer at a special meeting and decided to accept it. Cairo was asking for seven nuclear charges with a total equivalent capacity of two thousand tons of TNT.

Radio Beirut reported that engine trouble had compelled a Caravelle belonging to United Arab Airlines to land at the Israeli airport of Lod. According to the Israeli authorities, the plane would be able to resume its flight to Cairo in two hours.

Ten minutes after the United Arab Caravelle had taken off from Lod, the passenger in seat No. 14 rang for service. "I'm sorry," he told the stewardess, "I must have dozed off just before the forced landing. I'm afraid my cigarette burned a hole in the arm of the seat."

"Please don't worry, sir."

"No, no, I'm very particular about these things. If your company would be good enough to send the bill to my secretary at the Soviet Embassy . . . Here's my card. The name is Dobranin."

"It really isn't worth bothering about."

"But I insist."

The girl leaned over the back of the seat. Her hair brushed the man's cheek.

"There's nothing there," she said.

"But I smelled it when the captain's voice woke me. A distinct smell of burning."

"I don't see anything."

"I could put my finger in the hole. I was rather preoccupied because of the emergency landing or I'd have mentioned it earlier."

"Perhaps you changed your seat."

"No, I left my newspaper here in the net. And there's my briefcase, right above me."

"I can't understand it," said the girl.

. . .

The captain of the Teheran-Cairo Caravelle simulated renewed loss of power in his port engine and called the control
tower at Heliopolis. Internal Flight No. 613, which was taxi-
ing to the central runway, received orders to wait. The
Caravelle lost height rapidly and swayed a little as it limped
to the edge of the runway. The starboard engine screamed.
Then the aircraft landed with a series of jolts which sent a
whiff of scorched rubber drifting across the tarmac.

Ten minutes later, the Caravelle was towed into a hangar.
Technicians of the military security service cut open the
outer skin of the aircraft and used forklift trucks to remove
the seven drums from the baggage compartment.

The hangar was guarded until dawn by members of the
military security service. Ewal Hamid, head of counterespionage, who had spent most of Monday sweeping sand
from tarmac runways in the guise of an airport employee,
supervised the night's activities from a canvas chair. Sharpshooters of the 7th Division were posted on the roof of the
airport resturant.

M O N D A Y

LAKE NASSER: LEVEL FALLING

     Lake level: 489.16 ft. above sea level.
Change: minus 2.19 ft. (Top water level: 597
ft.; crest of dam: 643 ft.)

PORE-WATER PRESSURE IN BODY OF DAM: DECREASING

Main piezometers	A	B	C	D	E
kg/cm^2	7.32	7.65	7.45	5.61	11.75
Change	-0.03	-0.04	-0.03	-0.02	-0.04

ASWAN!

EARTH PRESSURE IN BODY OF DAM: DECREASING

SEEPAGE VELOCITY: INCREASING

In alluvium (subterranean)	(tolerance: 9 thousandths of a mm/sec)	
West bank 6.8 thousandths of a mm/sec	Valley center 6.7 thousandths of a mm/sec	East bank 6.8 thousandths of a mm/sec
Change +0.004	+0.003	+0.004

In apron of dam	(tolerance: 5 thousandths of a mm/sec)	
West section 4.2 thousandths of a mm/sec	Dam center 4.4 thousandths of a mm/sec	East section 4.0 thousandths of a mm/sec
Change +0.003	+0.003	+0.003

SEEPAGE OUTFLOW: INCREASING

Drain well A	5.2 l/sec	Drain well B	6.1 l/sec
Change	+0.3		+0.4

PARTICLES IN SEEPAGE (tolerance: 0.8mm)
Proportion of coarse sediment, granular diameter 0.02-0.06mm, increases to 4.5 percent.
First incidence of fine sand, granular diameter 0.06-0.2mm.

Sadat was the first to leave the room after the Cabinet meeting. Ambassador Vinyenev patted his papers together until the edges were neatly aligned, and waited. He did not push his chair back until Fuwasi, the Minister of Power, had reached the door. Fuwasi paused.

"I was unable to support your request to my government," Vinyenev said.

"A pity. Every day counts."

"I can't understand your haste. Besides which, I hardly think your attitude will benefit current negotiations for a third moratorium on repayments."

"It was a collective decision by the Cabinet."

"I find that even harder to understand. Your crude-oil supplies are guaranteed."

"For the moment, yes. Until something untoward happens and your tankers fail to turn up. I'm afraid we must insist on these new drilling operations."

"But surely not in the immediate vicinity of the High Dam? I simply don't . . . ."

"In general, we're only taking our cue from previous surveys which indicated the presence of oil."

"Our experts conferred at the embassy last night. They say that any borehole, even if it's sunk twenty miles from the dam . . ."

"Your experts also said that the oil fields at Hurghada would supply us with at least—well, you're aware of the current level of output?"

"Of course. Thirty thousand tons."

"In other words, three-fifths of your original estimate. I'm sorry, we intend to start drilling by next week at latest. Equipment is already being transported from Aswan to the various sites at this moment."

"I know," said the ambassador. "You're starting at El Qattara. That's no more than twenty-five miles from the dam as the crow flies."

"Are you afraid the vibration of a drilling bit may cause the dam to collapse?"

"No, I'm not worried about that. My only fear is that you're wasting time and energy."

"We'll go down to ten thousand feet in the Wadi Natash. Then we'll drill at Bir el Gindi, in the Garara Valley, and at Abu Hashim. We'll go on until we strike oil."

"What puzzles me is the size of the boreholes—ten or eleven inches in diameter, so I hear. What do you hope to achieve?"

"A larger volume of oil."

"Your gushers may turn out to be river water."

"In that case, we'll stop."

"Another thing."

"Yes?"

"Colonel Kostyenko visited us at the embassy recently. He came from Teheran. You've met him?"

"Yes."

"He was on board the United Arab plane which had to make an emergency landing in Israel. So was First Secretary Dobranin."

"Sorry they were inconvenienced."

"Kostyenko said that although the port engine was supposed to have failed the captain banked to port as he approached the airfield."

"I'm a layman. For all I know, it may have been a piece of aeronautical wizardry."

"When Kostyenko reached the embassy that evening, he asked me if I thought an aircraft could be dematerialized—spirited away from under a passenger's backside, so to speak. Can you explain what he meant?"

"I'm afraid not."

"Nor can I. That's what worries me. Dobranin said he burned a hole in the arm of his seat just before the emergency landing."

"I'm sorry. For United Arab's sake."

"He said it wasn't there when the Caravelle took off again."

"Very interesting, but why tell me all this?"

"Because Dobranin isn't normally subject to delusions."

Security men detained a British guest in the dining room of the New Cataract Hotel, Aswan. Thomas Hall, fifty-seven, confirmed under interrogation that he had served as a navigator in one of the Royal Air Force planes which bombed the Eder Dam during World War II. He denied his daughter Elizabeth was married to an Israeli.

Reports of a sandstorm compelled the Ilyushin transport plane carrying the seven metal drums to make an intermediate landing at Luxor. The members of the Israeli team, who had traveled to Aswan by train, learned at the Kalabsha Hotel that it would be impossible to insert the nuclear charges in the boreholes before Friday. They were assured by an Egyptian liaison officer that the extra time would be devoted to isotopic measurements. Tests completed to date had confirmed that Borehole No. 1, northeast of the El Gindi oasis, had actually hit the main artery of escaping water. The outflow was so strong that Professor Schaller had recommended the placing of a second charge between Bir el Gindi and Aswan. In Schaller's view, it would be better to refrain from sealing the aquifers which led into the Libyan Desert from Nugu Tifa Gharb between the limestone plateau and the sandstone hills north of the High Dam, and to close them later by means of an injected apron. The seventh charge could then be detonated between Bir el Gindi and Aswan.

The leader of the Israeli team, Aba Mordach, rejected Schaller's proposal at an after-dinner meeting. He said that the original plan to lay nuclear charges in a horseshoe pattern enclosing the dam and the northern end of the lake was undoubtedly correct.

The liaison officer frowned. "It was agreed that all plans should be approved by the government of the United Arab Republic."

"Precisely. No one said anything about Professor Schaller."

Later that night, the Presidential secretariat confirmed by teleprinter that the original plan would stand.

The liaison officer walked into the hotel bar at 11 p.m. holding a strip of telex paper. "The cars will be waiting outside tomorrow morning, as arranged. If we leave by seven, the helicopters will be able to take off at eight. The Ilyushin carrying the special oil landed at Aswan an hour ago. I hope you have a good night's sleep."

"So do we," murmured Mordach.

Dr. Angelo caught the last ferry from Corte Albero to the Ponte della Libertà. He went into a bar, phoned for a taxi, and boarded the Trieste-Rome night express at Mestre Station.

By the time the Israeli engineers reached Aswan military airfield, the metal drums containing the nuclear charges had already been loaded into helicopters. Mordach and five members of his team were the first to leave. At 8:32 a.m., they took off for the borehole at Bir el Gindi. The radio communications center which was housed in a tent five hundred yards south of the drilling site reported at 9:55 a.m. that all teams had safely arrived at their respective boreholes.

The liaison officer, who had been bending over the radio, turned as Mordach ducked under the raised flaps of the tent. "If you manage to install those charges by tonight," he said, "we should be able to detonate just after sunrise tomorrow. Outflow has increased by over a hundred and fifty gallons per second in the past twenty-four hours—and that's only here at Bir el Gindi."

On Friday, when the seven nuclear charges were detonated, there were two hundred and sixty Israeli technicians in the vicinity of the High Dam. Seventy-six were camped near the boreholes themselves, a party led by Engineer Finkenstein was visiting the necropolis at Thebes in the guise of British tourists, thirty-two Israeli geohydrologists were helping Egyptian personnel to evaluate isotopic measurements at Aswan, and the rest were distributed between the seismographic station at Idfu, the Ministry of the Interior in Cairo, and Aswan airport.

The Nigerian Ambassador in Israel, Simon Awublu, had called on Premier Dayan the night before and intimated that President Sadat had ordered the military security service to confiscate all "containers."

"I see," said Dayan. "You got this tip from Cairo?"

"I was merely asked to pass the message on. I don't even know what it means."

"Can you pass one back?"

The Nigerian envoy nodded. "Of course."

"Then kindly inform President Sadat that we only supplied dummies in the first instance, to test his good faith."

"In the event of your replying in those or similar terms, I was to tell you that the message had no basis in fact. It was an attempt to test Israel's good faith."

"A hoax, in fact?"

"I can only quote what was told me."

"Then please say that my reply was also a hoax. Of course they can go ahead tomorrow morning."

"I don't quite follow."

"The President will," said Dayan.

. . .

135

At Bir el Gindi, soldiers winched the container out of the helicopter, pried open the end with cold chisels, and attacked the seam which ran along the cylinder with hammers. The sheet metal buckled and tore under their blows, the ragged edges curled outward as steel bit into steel. The whoosh of the rotor blades dwindled. Mordach pushed an empty beer bottle under the edge of the tent with his foot and stared at the patches of sweat blossoming on the soldiers' army-issue shirts. The officer hovered over the switchboard while his men continued to tear at the sheet metal. The helicopter's rotor blades gave a last gentle flup and came to a stop. Mordach glanced at his watch. The blades dropped, reminding him of withered leaves. The metal seam burst open and a hammer cartwheeled across the sand. The pilot switched off his landing light, the diaphragm of the public-address system crackled, cloth drew taut over the buttocks of a soldier as he bent to retrieve the hammer. Mordach turned away in quest of his briefcase and its cargo of bottles. It was standing at the entrance of the tent. He thought, If they've miscalculated, even by a hundred tons of TNT . . . He gashed his hand on the edge of a crate. The hammer clanged again. He could hear the sing-song voices of the soldiers as they wrenched at the cylinder, and felt the heat reflected from the framework of the derrick.

It isn't 3 p.m. yet, he told himself. He gripped the handle of his briefcase and felt for the neck of a bottle.

Mordach slipped inside the tent, clasping the briefcase to his chest with both forearms. He saw the green eye of the control light on the switchboard and heard again the sound of hammer blows on metal. A stench of oil from the helicopter's exhaust drifted through the tent. "Fourteen fifty-five hours, did you say? Many thanks," the loudspeaker said.

Some workmen left the derrick and headed for the tent. A final flurry of hammering and the last shreds of metal peeled away. A soldier embraced the steel capsule containing the nuclear charge with his arms. He swayed. Mordach could see veins swelling in his neck as other soldiers dragged away the shattered remains of the outer casing and left them lying in the sand. "That's it," said the loudspeaker. The officer pressed a transmission key and clouds of bluish-white vapor issued from the generator's exhaust.

Mordach sat splay-thighed on a crate just inside the tent. A jeep roared up to the entrance and braked to a halt. Soldiers manhandled the steel capsule into position across the back seat. The patches of sweat were bigger a few minutes ago, Mordach thought. "Half an hour gone," said the loudspeaker. "We'll hook up now." The jeep's wheels spun in the sand. "All set?" inquired the loudspeaker. The jeep plowed its way toward the derrick with the bomb perched uneasily on the back seat and two soldiers crouching on the gasoline cans behind. Mordach groped for a cigarette. A steel cable sang down from some pulleys at the apex of the derrick The officer coughed. A grabhook struck the sand with a thump. Mordach remembered that he had run out of matches and slid off the crate. Soldiers were gesticulating at the foot of the derrick. "No. 5 here," squawked the radio. Mordach heard the rattle of the grabhook. There was a scream from the winch as the gears meshed. I wonder if the officer has any, Mordach thought.

The diesel engine coughed and the exhaust emitted staccato puffs of bluish smoke. The cable drew taut and the bomb dangled above the soldiers' heads. They attached the high-tension leads to the charge, the capsule soared upward and swung gently beneath the pulley, the public-address system quacked instructions, the bomb glided down between the steel ribs of the derrick, the pulley hummed and cable snaked from the drum.

"Not so fast," Mordach called, and the officer raised his head. The bomb disappeared down the steel shaft.

"Three hundred and twenty-five feet . . ."

The drum spun on its bearings.

"Borehole No. 3 here. We now have oil."

Mordach chewed on his cigarette. The cable hissed.

"Do you have a light?"

The cable drum had become a blur.

"By all means."

The engine roared.

"Twenty-two hundred feet."

Mordach raised the microphone. "Start braking."

Two soldiers ran to the winch.

"Three thousand feet." Mordach's shoe mashed the cigarette.

"Thirty-five hundred feet."

"Another three seconds, starting now. Three, two, one . . ."

The locking lever swung hard over. There was a final scream from the cable.

"Bir el Gindi here," said the officer at the radio. "Of course it's still on. An hour after sunrise. We're reckoning with an outflow of one hundred gallons per second—initially, that is."

The last nuclear charge was installed in Borehole No. 6, Garara Valley, at 3:10 a.m. At 3:34 a.m., the Garara team switched to the frequency for remote firing from the communications center at Bir el Gindi, struck camp, and drove by jeep to their prepared shelter.

At 4 a.m., Mordach issued protective clothing and goggles to the Bir el Gindi team. He walked over to the generators and rechecked the voltage. Three soldiers shot out the spotlights on the derrick. Mordach winced as ricochets hummed through the framework.

The sun rose over the Jebel el Hidilawi. Mordach screwed up his eyes at the fiery disk above the rocky skyline. Two soldiers carried the radio set from the tent to a waiting jeep. Mordach shivered as the disk glided upward from the ridge. The soldiers returned and started to cut the guy ropes with axes.

"We'll leave everything as it is," Mordach told the officer.

Ten minutes later, the helicopter flew them from the borehole to their shelter. During the brief flight, Mordach asked for the latest readings from Aswan. The officer told him that Aswan had not reported since 2 a.m.

They lay face down behind a sandbag barrier. "Try them on Channel 2," Mordach said. "Perhaps the dam has gone already." The officer switched to Channel 2.

The BOAC plane which took Dr. Angelo from Rome to Cairo left Fiumicino at 2:36 p.m. and landed at Heliopolis at 6:20 p.m.

Dr. Angelo booked in at the airport hotel. He bought an armful of newspapers at the kiosk, killed a few hours in the restaurant, and went to bed just before midnight.

Mordach was sweating inside his protective suit. He jumped to his feet and almost tripped over one of the soldiers. They had flown into the wedge of shadow that fell across the dunes from the gorge. The red disk still stood a hand's breadth above the summit of Hidilawi. "We detonate in twenty-five minutes," Mordach said. He knelt in the sand beside the officer. "Please cross your arms and rest your head on them when the time comes. A purely theoretical precaution. The risk of retinal damage is remote—five-hundred-to-one against. Even so, your men should keep their goggles on."

The officer crouched against the sandbags. Mordach's goggles had misted over. "Do you know how Enrico Fermi tried to measure the blast of the first atomic explosion at Alamogordo in 1945?"

"No."

"He stood up inside the shelter, ten miles from the test tower, held a handful of shredded paper at chest height, and let go when the blast reached him. The distance traveled by the pieces of paper enabled him to gauge—"

"There's Aswan," whispered the officer, and pushed back his hood to put on the headphones. He turned on his side and propped his right shoulder against the sandbags. Mordach tapped the radio set with his knuckles. "What do they say?" he shouted. The officer shook his head and shrugged, still listening. Mordach tugged at the lead of the headset. "What's wrong?"

The officer turned on his stomach again. "Aswan says we must detonate at once. If not, firing will have to be postponed for twenty-four hours."

Mordach swung the lever once and shouted, "All lie down! Cross your arms!" The green light went out and the countdown began. A succession of numerals flicked across the control panel.

129 seconds: Mordach dug holes in the sand with his toes. He propped himself on his elbows so that he could watch the screen, and thought, I ought to pull the goggle elastic over my hood.

117 seconds: Mordach glanced across at the officer, who was lying huddled beside the sandbags. He tensed his stomach muscles and drew up his knees.

108 seconds: a soldier's head lightly brushed the soles of Mordach's shoes.

95 seconds: Mordach heard the droning sound for the first time. He grabbed the officer by the shoulder and shouted, "There's something wrong with the generators!"

87 seconds: the officer looked up, tugging at his hood. Mordach yelled at him to lie flat.

84 seconds: the officer said, "That isn't the generators. We couldn't hear them at all before."

75 seconds: Mordach crawled over to the officer's bag and opened the zip fastener with his teeth. "I need your binoculars. Where are the bloody things?" Packets of cigarettes slithered into the sand. Mordach seized the leather strap and wrenched the binoculars from their case.

68 seconds: Mordach leaned over the sandbag barrier, grasping the binoculars in plastic-mittened hands. He saw a helicopter swooping low over the dunes.

61 seconds: Mordach flopped down behind the sandbags. "Do you have any signal flares?" The officer did not reply.

58 seconds: the binoculars slid off the sandbags and landed on the back of the officer's neck.

55 seconds: Mordach gripped the strap in his teeth and pulled the binoculars toward him.

45 seconds: Mordach remembered that he had left his briefcase in the tent.

40 seconds: Mordach pinned his right mitten between chin and left forearm and withdrew his hand.

35 seconds: Mordach rattled the key of the transmitter which would detonate the charges.

29 seconds: the helicopter came lower.

25 seconds: Mordach threw himself on his back and drummed his heels against the transmitter.

18 seconds: the helicopter was hovering a hundred feet above the tent.

15 seconds: a soldier spat in the sand.

10 seconds: the pilot of the helicopter dropped a smoke bomb.

9 seconds: Mordach thought, I must find those toe holes; he turned on his stomach again.

8 seconds: the smoke bomb landed near the generators.

7 seconds: Mordach shoveled sand beneath his right forearm with the plastic mitten on his left hand.

5 seconds: the helicopter descended toward the tent.

4 seconds: "What if we fire into the transmitter?" Mordach whispered to himself.

3 seconds: orange-red smoke swirled over the tent.

2 seconds: the soldier behind Mordach choked.

1 second: My briefcase, thought Mordach.

Zero.

Zero plus 1: the derrick swayed. The explosion propelled knee-high fountains of sand into the air. Far below the surface, the cable melted.

Zero plus 2: the helicopter lurched in the sudden turbulence. Its tail rotor fell off and spun through the air. The aircraft gyrated, turned over, and hit the ground.

Zero plus 5: fuel gushed from a fracture in the helicopter's main tank, flowed over the transparent cupola, dripped onto the engine housing, and caught fire.

Dr. Angelo sent a porter to fetch the black bag containing perymethylene ether from his room. He lost his way while making for the transit lounge and found himself in a hall full of Bedouin women sitting on cardboard boxes surrounded by children and plastic toys. He went back to the buffet under the stairway leading to the hotel rooms and ordered a glass of tea. When his name was called over the loudspeaker, he asked a stewardess to take him to the desk. The Cairo-Khartoum Ilyushin took off at 7:12 a.m., banked left over Cairo, and flew southward across the Libyan Desert. The plane changed course at Girga on instructions from Aswan control tower and crossed the Nile Valley. Dr. Angelo woke up when the pilot throttled back his engines, and looked out of the window. The man in the next seat said, "From this height, the Nile looks like a length of green gut." At 8:55 a.m., Luxor ground control gave clearance for an intermediate landing.

The shock waves set off by the nuclear explosions reached the High Dam at intervals of 0.75 second, 0.98 second, 1.02 seconds, 1.08 seconds, 2.10 seconds and 2.19 seconds. The most critical phases occurred between the second and third and the fifth and sixth shocks. The computer at the High Dam Authority's headquarters, into which accelerations, velocities, and displacements were fed from twenty-seven different levels between crest and bedrock, recorded extreme oscillations during both these phases. In the west section of the crest, acceleration exceeded the critical amount which had been determined in the course of stability computations, and threatened to shear the dam horizontally. Oscillations in the base of the dam diminished two seconds after the final shock wave. Vibrations in the crest flattened out later.

Between 6:23 a.m. and 6:32 a.m., the seismographic stations at Addis Ababa, Nicosia, and Odessa registered an earthquake whose epicenter was estimated to be somewhere between the Red Sea coast and the Egyptian limestone plateau, on a level with latitude 25°N. Its strength was approximately 1.5 degrees on the Richter scale.

A Soviet liaison officer stationed at Command Post Aswan East reported to his embassy in Cairo that the destruction of reconnaissance helicopter AS 327 was probably attributable to metal fatigue. The bodies of Pilot Abramov, Co-Pilot Gergeyev, and Flight Engineers Solzhenitsyn and Beryav were transferred to the municipal morgue at Idfu.

The first build-up of water in the blocked subterranean fissures was recorded fifty minutes after the explosions by a chain of piezometers at El Qattara in the Nile Valley, north of the High Dam.

The passengers on board the Cairo-Khartoum Ilyushin which had been compelled to make an unscheduled stop at Luxor were informed that, for technical reasons, they could not resume their flight until that evening. Dr. Angelo and some of his fellow-passengers spent the morning in deck chairs in the shade of a tarpaulin. When a party of Arabs on the terrace of the airport building were called for the flight to El Kharga, he moved to their table under the awning and ordered some mint tea.

Three Soviet soldiers and the co-pilot of the medical corps helicopter which had retrieved the bodies from the wrecked helicopter at Bir el Gindi were admitted to the Soviet military hospital at Aswan. They had cutaneous burns on their forearms, necks, and faces, and complained of nausea. Doctors detected a sharp fall in their blood count. By evening, all four patients were suffering from severe loss of hair. Their blood count deteriorated rapidly.

All the piezometers which had been installed between the boreholes, the dam, and the shores of Lake Nasser were now registering back pressure in the subterranean fissures. By evening, so much water had accumulated in these cavities that the build-up extended as far as Aswan.

There was a concomitant decline in the velocity of seepage through the alluvium underlying the base of the dam.

The Ilyushin 18 resumed its flight to Khartoum but changed course a hundred and twenty miles short of the Egyptian-Sudanese border and landed at Aswan. The passengers were taken by coach to the New Cataract Hotel.

By 10 p.m., pore-water pressure in the base of the dam had risen by an average of 14 milligrams per square centimeter. Having concluded its evaluation of seismographic readings, the High Dam Authority stated in a third telex report to the Ministry of the Interior in Cairo: "The pulsating shock waves generated by the explosions imposed a heavier load than stability computations had let us to expect. Although the Authority took it for granted that the dam is not a rigid structure subject to equal acceleration in all sections between base and crest, and that the crest was bound to oscillate more severely than the bedrock beneath, phase displacements temporarily created a critical situation. On the other hand, the plastic properties of the dam are so pronounced that no evidence of consequential damage has been observed. It may also be assumed that the dam would not have held if dynamic loads during the explosions had been supplemented by an excessively high static load attributable to the pressure of a fully charged lake."

During dinner in a room off the main restaurant of the New Cataract Hotel, a spokesman for United Arab informed passengers that the Ilyushin had been forced to fly back to Aswan because strong Israeli fighter formations had been reported over the Red Sea. The flight to Khartoum would be resumed at about 1 p.m. next day.

After dinner, Dr. Angelo strolled through the grounds until, through the bushes, he caught sight of some red-robed Nubian hotel staff shooing away children from the peasant village on the far side of the wall. He returned to the gravel path, crossed the asphalt road to the Nile promenade, slipped in some fruit-bat ordure beneath the mulberry trees on the bank, and limped back to the hotel.

He changed fifteen thousand lire into Egyptian pounds,

paused in the bar corridor to inspect a photograph of a belly dancer balancing a walking stick horizontally on her breasts, sat down beside a flower urn on the terrace, tried to decipher the babble of conversation that rose from women lounging near him in wicker chairs, snapped his fingers at a passing waiter and ordered a cigar, heard the jingle of tambourine and bangles through the half-open glass door, ground his cigar into the soil between the flowers, remembered the photograph in the corridor, asked a waiter in English for a bottle of Tears of Ptolemy, limped to the door, glass in hand, and limped back to his seat beside the flower urn when the flutes and drums struck up. He sat and waited for the rattle of the tambourine. The women in the wicker chairs looked up as he accidentally knocked his glass off the table. His first thought was to take refuge in the grounds, but he paused at the top of the three steps and walked back to the door.

The girl was dancing in a pool of light the size of a hip-bath. Dr. Angelo hovered just inside the curtain and stared at the breasts twitching beneath the tambourine in her raised hands. He saw the sweat that coursed down the girl's neck, over her bare shoulders and jutting collarbones, to the hem of her spangled bodice, and sheepishly told the man in the dinner jacket who approached him that he already had a table. He walked back across the terrace, took the lift to the third floor, got a Nubian waiter to bring the bottle to his room, and went to bed drunk.

That night, seepage velocity in the alluvial filling of the crest decreased to between 8.3 and 8.5 thousandths of a millimeter per second. Readings in the apron of the dam averaged 4.4 thousandths. By morning, pore-water pressure in the base of the dam had risen to between 36 and 39 milligrams per square centimeter. Aba Mordach, who had returned to Aswan airport by jeep just before midnight, said over a celebration drink in the canteen of the High Dam Authority, "It's like a sponge which had water flowing through it. Now the sponge is filling again."

The United Arab office at Aswan had hired a coach to take passengers to the Aga Khan's mausoleum overlooking the west bank of the Nile. Dr. Angelo left the party after breakfast and went to the marketplace to buy a chessboard. He accosted some stallkeepers in an alley and inquired in sign language when their tomatoes and artichokes had been picked, pocketed a handful of horse beans for processing with perymethylene ether, bit a piece of peel out of an orange and squeezed the essential oils from its pores, lingered in front of some bamboo poles laden with live chickens, and then came upon a fish-vendor who was crouching beside a horse-drawn carriage, massaging the gills of a bichir with his thumb and forefinger.

Dr. Angelo bent over the aluminum bowl containing the dead fish and saw, when the man withdrew his hand, how the blood flooded back into the pale gills and restored their color. They faded again after a few minutes, so the man repeated the treatment. It's the fluid, of course, Dr. Angelo reflected as he walked back to his hotel. Osmotic pressure forces blood into the tissue, and there it ought to stay. He wondered why he had never treated animal tissue with perymethylene ether.

Geiger-counter tests confirmed that the four patients in the Soviet military hospital at Aswan had radioactive contamination. A special Soviet air force plane flew them to Cairo and from there to Kiev. Also on board were the victims of Bir el Gindi, stowed in coffins lined with lead plates taken from old tank batteries. Officials from the Ministry of the Interior sealed the morgue at Idfu.

·　·　·

ASWAN!

During a reception held by the Rumanian Ambassador in Cairo to mark his country's national day, Soviet Ambassador Vinyenev left the room just as Foreign Minister Riad was walking over to him, and drove back to his official residence. All Soviet diplomats in Cairo were instructed to assemble at the embassy that evening. General Mortchov flew back to Aswan from Alexandria. Units of the 3rd Eskadra cut short their routine patrol off the Israeli coast and sailed for the Nile Delta at dawn. Israeli intelligence noted exceptionally heavy radio traffic between Moscow and the Soviet Embassy in Cairo.

The Ilyushin 18 took off from Aswan at 1 p.m., flew across the High Dam, followed Lake Nasser for a hundred and twenty miles, left the Nile Valley at El Diwan, veered gently to port, and headed across the Nubian Desert to Khartoum. It landed there at 4:18 p.m.

Dr. Angelo took a taxi to the Bahr el Azraq Hotel on the banks of the Nile. He surrendered his passport at the reception desk and by 5:32 p.m. was installed in Room 138 on the third floor. He draped his white coverall across the basin and locked the bag containing the two flasks of perymethylene ether in the wardrobe.

At this time, seepage velocity in the alluvium of the High Dam at Aswan had decreased to between 8.1 and 8.3 thousandths of a millimeter per second. Pore-water pressure in the base of the dam showed a renewed increase and was now beginning to rise in the apron as well. Outflow from the two drain wells on the downstream side of the dam continued to fall steadily.

At 6 p.m., only an hour before Ambassador Vinyenev was due to call on him at the Foreign Ministry, Riad was notified by First Secretary Dobranin that Vinyenev would be unable to keep the appointment. Three hours later, the Egyptian broadcasting service interrupted its program to transmit a statement recorded by President Anwar el Sadat before he left by air for 7th Division Headquarters.

"Rumors that subterranean fissures presented a threat to the High Dam were temporarily and partially in accordance with the facts. Fissures of this kind did manifest themselves in the vicinity of Lake Nasser and beneath the base of the dam. In the long term, the outflow of impounded water from such fissures might have undermined the dam itself. As soon as the first symptoms of erosion became apparent, the government of the United Arab Republic took countermeasures. It has now managed to seal the said fissures and check the flow of water through them. The High Dam remains a symbol of our national future, just as Lake Nasser remains our national font of life. At the same time, the government of the United Arab Republic has entered upon a new phase of international cooperation."

Toward midnight, President Sadat flew back to Cairo from 7th Division Headquarters and drove to the Nasser Mosque with Defense Minister Nachram and Minister of the Interior Gidaff. General Boghdadi ordered the release of three hundred and twenty members of the Moslem Brotherhood currently detained for questioning. At 2:15 a.m., Count Hengström called on Sadat at the Presidential palace in his capacity as U.N. special representative. At Aswan, General Mortchov issued orders to reinforce the sentries guarding his command post at the military base of El Shallal. Pilots at Talc, the MIG base in the mountains east of Aswan, were ordered to stand by.

The conversation between President Sadat and Ambassador Vinyenev at the Kubbeh Palace lasted one and a half minutes.

Sadat walked up to Vinyenev, who was standing beneath the bust of Nasser in the Presidential study, and said, "I suppose I owe you an explanation . . ."

"As the chief representative of a sovereign state? Certainly not. I, on the other hand, have a declaration to make."

"A formal declaration?" asked Sadat.

"In view of the so-called new phase in international cooperation which you saw fit to mention last night, the government of the Union of Soviet Socialist Republics finds itself obliged to review the relations between our two countries. That is all."

Israeli agents in Cairo reported that the Soviet Ambassador drove straight from the Presidential palace to Heliopolis airport, where he conferred with General Mortchov at a military barracks.

The Israeli newspaper *Haaretz* brought out an extra midday edition in Jerusalem, Haifa, and Tel Aviv. The headline: "ISRAEL SAVES THE HIGH DAM."

The Bulgarian Ambassador in Tel Aviv suffered a nervous breakdown while awaiting a call from Moscow. In Jerusalem, Orthodox Jews gathered in front of the Wailing Wall for a protest march.

According to the report in *Haaretz*, Dayan's Cabinet had imposed no conditions before supplying the Egyptian government with nuclear explosives to seal the fissures in the area of Lake Nasser. Their prime concern had been to prevent the greatest potential disaster in the history of mankind. By taking this step, Israel had also ushered in an era of reconciliation between the two countries. It was already an incontrovertible fact that, as the President of the United Arab Republic had expressed it in his broadcast to the Egyptian people, international cooperation had entered upon a new phase in the Near East.

In a specially expanded evening edition, *Haaretz* published photographs which showed drilling operations in progress at the boreholes in the Wadi Natash and near the oasis of Abu Hashim. There were also pictures of Israeli engineers taking isotopic measurements at Bir el Gindi.

Foreign Minister Bar Lev stated at a press conference that the reports in *Haaretz* were based on an indiscretion.

"In other words," said a journalist, "you're not officially denying—"

"I used the word 'indiscretion.'"

"Thank you, Minister. That's all we wanted to hear."

W E D N E S D A Y

LAKE NASSER: LEVEL RISING

        Lake level: 504.35 ft. above sea level.
Change: plus 0.75 ft. (Top water level: 597
ft.; crest of dam: 643 ft.)

PORE-WATER PRESSURE IN BODY OF DAM: INCREASING

Main piezometers	A	B	C	D	E
kg/cm^2	7.91	7.88	7.64	5.73	6.00
Change	+0.02	+0.02	+0.01	+0.02	+0.02

EARTH PRESSURE IN BODY OF DAM: INCREASING

Pressure gauges	A	B	C	D	E
kg/cm^2	17.74	16.86	17.28	6.37	11.82
Change	+0.02	+0.02	+0.01	+0.02	+0.01

ASWAN!

SEEPAGE VELOCITY: DECREASING

In alluvium   (tolerance: 9 thousandths
(subterranean)   of a mm/ sec)

West bank	Valley center	East bank
6.5 thou-	6.4 thou-	6.5 thou-
sandths of a	sandths of a	sandths of a
mm/sec	mm/sec	mm/sec

Change		
-0.002	-0.004	-0.004

In apron   (tolerance: 5 thousandths
of dam   of a mm/sec)

West section	Dam center	East section
4.0 thou-	4.1 thou-	4.0 thou-
sandths of a	sandths of a	sandths of a
mm/sec	mm/sec	mm/sec

Change		
-0.003	-0.002	-0.003

SEEPAGE OUTFLOW: DECREASING

Drain well A	3.6	Drain well B	4.9
	l/sec		l/sec
Change	-0.2		-0.6

PARTICLES IN SEEPAGE (tolerance: 0.8mm).
Proportion of fine sand, granular diameter
0.006-0.2mm, falls to 2.1 percent of each
100gm of elutriated matter.

At the Hilton Hotel in Athens, George Papadopoulos, the
Greek Premier, opened the second plenary session of Inter-
Mediterranes, the association of countries bordering the Mediterranean. The delegates voted in favor of admitting Libya
and Cyprus to full membership. Chairman Rojas of Barcelona
and Vice-Chairmen Christophorakis and Sunay of Athens

and Ankara, respectively, were confirmed in office. A resolution urging that the conference should renew its offer of membership to Egypt was moved by the Italian representative and duly carried. The conference instructed Christophorakis and Sunay to get in touch with Cairo.

Funds for the hydrographic observation stations in the Eastern Mediterranean were increased from fifteen to twenty million dollars annually. Chairman Rojas informed the conference that the Egyptian Cabinet had agreed to the stationing of a United Nations research vessel inside Egyptian territorial waters and had recommended an anchorage on longitude 32°E.

The conference approved the text of a communication addressed to President Sadat and the U.N. Secretary-General. It read:

"In its growing concern for the maintenance of ecological balance in the Mediterranean, Inter-Mediterranes appeals to the government of the United Arab Republic, working in concert with the United Nations and UNESCO in particular, to take vigorous steps to restore environmental conditions in the Mediterranean area. The widely feared effects upon the Mediterranean of the High Dam and Lake Nasser can no longer be ignored. It was long ago pointed out to the government of the United Arab Republic that the impounding of 5,780 billion cubic feet of Nile water would entail disastrous consequences for an inland sea which has a surface area of 970,231 square miles but is now fed only by the Maritsa, Vardar, Tiber, Po, and Ebro.

"1. Since the completion of the High Dam at Aswan, the average salt content of the Mediterranean in sea areas east of Crete has already risen from 3.8 to 4.1 percent, and readings of 4.3 and even 4.4 percent have been recorded at isolated points. The tolerance level is drawing closer.

"2. Every year over 143,000,000 cubic yards of alluvial

and suspended matter are deposited in, and trapped by, the artificial lake which the government of the United Arab Republic has created in the upper reaches of the Nile Valley. The High Dam is thus inhibiting the supply of nitrogen and phosphorous compounds which are essential to the healthy growth of all marine fauna and flora. The effects on fishing grounds in the Eastern Mediterranean have been disastrous. Crab fishing has already been abandoned along the Israeli coastline and will shortly become impossible along that of Lebanon. There is alarming evidence of malnutrition among tuna fish and sardines, and symptoms of degeneration are multiplying.

"3. Furthermore, the retention in Lake Nasser of alluvial matter normally carried down by the waters of the Nile is accelerating the erosion of coastal formations, a process which, by reason of the strong west-to-east drift, is far from confined to the Nile Delta and already shows signs of affecting the Israeli and Lebanese coasts.

"The member countries of Inter-Mediterranes appeal to the government of the United Arab Republic to return by stages to traditional methods of regulating the Nile so as to prevent disastrous ecological changes throughout the Eastern Mediterranean. As an immediate step, they call for the discharging of a higher percentage of impounded water.

"The re-establishment of natural conditions being in the interests of all Mediterranean countries, and thus of the United Arab Republic itself, the second phase of such re-establishment should comprise steps toward the release of alluvial and suspended matter currently trapped in the Aswan reservoir, which will by the year 2000 have attained a volume of almost 40,000,000,000 cubic yards.

"The signatories of this resolution are sensible that the United Arab Republic will not forgo the High Dam altogether. They are, however, unanimous in their view that agricultural expansion in the United Arab Republic and a sixfold increase in Egypt's output of electrical power should not be attained at the expense of transforming the Mediterranean into a desert."

The Libyan, Syrian, and Algerian delegations voted against the resolution. The representatives of France and Israel abstained.

T U E S D A Y

LAKE NASSER: LEVEL RISING

Lake level: 512.26 ft. above sea level. Change: plus 2.52 ft. (Top water level: 597 ft.; crest of dam: 643 ft.)

PORE-WATER PRESSURE IN BODY OF DAM: INCREASING

EARTH PRESSURE IN BODY OF DAM: INCREASING

SEEPAGE VELOCITY: DECREASING

In apron   (tolerance: 5 thousandths
of dam   of a mm/sec)

West section	Dam center	East section
3.4 thou-	3.4 thou-	3.3 thou-
sandths of a	sandths of a	sandths of a
mm/sec	mm/sec	mm/sec

Change
-0.006   -0.006   -0.005

SEEPAGE OUTFLOW: DECREASING

Drain well A   3.0   Drain well B   4.1
                l/sec   l/sec
Change   -0.2   -0.5

PARTICLES IN SEEPAGE (tolerance: 0.8mm).
Very fine sediment, granular diameter 0.001-

ASWAN!

```
0.002mm.   Fine sediment, granular diameter
0.002-0.006mm.   Medium sediment, granular
diameter 0.006-0.02mm.
```

The Egyptian Ambassador in Moscow withdrew the United Arab Republic's request for an extension of the third moratorium. He announced that the tenth and eleventh installments to be set against the 1970 development loan would be paid out of Egypt's foreign exchange reserves by Thursday.

A twenty-three-year-old sergeant in the Egyptian army was killed during a scuffle between Soviet pilots and Egyptian ground staff at the MIG base east of Aswan. Colonel Naguil canceled his acceptance of an invitation to dine at the officers' mess in the Soviet military camp at El Shallal. The Ministry of Tourism in Cairo denied reports in the French press that two Israeli merchant banks had taken over the financing of hotel developments at Ras el Barr, Luxor, and Hurghada. The Soviet army newspaper *Red Star* reported that eight hundred Israeli advisers were stationed at Aswan alone. "Since the nuclear explosions which Israel recently engineered on Egyptian territory with the connivance of President Sadat and his government, the number of Israeli nationals in the United Arab Republic has risen by 200 percent."

Hurled over the railings by a pedestrian, a gasoline bomb exploded in the car park of the Soviet Embassy in Cairo, setting fire to a Moskvitch sedan. Minister of the Interior Gidaff requested Tass correspondent Adzhubei to leave the country within thirty-six hours. Adzhubei had reported that the establishment of diplomatic relations between Cairo and Jerusalem was imminent and that the former chairman of the Gahal Party, Shaim Begin, had accepted an appointment as Israeli chargé d'affaires in the United Arab Republic. Ewal Hamid, head of counterespionage, informed Defense Minister Nachram that two of the eighteen demonstrators responsible for breaking windows at the Aeroflot office in Cairo had been identified as Soviet exchange students.

Dr. Angelo complained in writing to the secretariat of the 8th Congress on World Hunger that his lecture did not appear in the official program. He went to the local office of the Food and Agriculture Organization, handed in his letter of complaint, and told the receptionist at the Bahr el Azraq Hotel that he would be available in the garden all day.

No one had called him by 5 p.m., so he took a taxi to the conference hall. He waited on the steps until FAO President Bühlmann and a secretary left the building, trailed them to the car park, and headed them off by climbing over the bumpers of two cars. He walked up to Bühlmann and said, "I'm sorry about Professor Ferguson, but he's dead. Having come to Khartoum in his place, I really think you might let me give my lecture on perymethylene ether."

The girl said, "So it was you who wrote the letter."

"God Almighty—of course I wrote it!"

She turned to Bühlmann. "This is the gentleman from Venice."

Bühlmann reached for the car door. "Quite so, quite so. Good evening, Doctor. I'll have someone phone you tomorrow morning."

The Egyptian Ambassador to the United Nations, Anwar Hussan, informed the General Assembly in New York that the danger at Aswan had been averted. The sealing of fissures with nuclear explosives had reduced outflow through subterranean channels to one thousandth of its former volume. The escape of water from the lake into the Libyan Desert had been completely stopped. Some Nile water was still flowing into the Red Sea, but only through lateral fissures at the level of Nag'Gudi and Nag'Khafir.

Hussan stated that several sections of the dam had been damaged by erosion at its base. In areas where filling material had subsided into cavities, the body of the dam had settled. These subsidences were currently being rectified by injection.

The envoy's concluding remarks were as follows: "If I have gone into some technical detail, it is because this organization has a right to know how things stand at Aswan. On behalf of the government of the United Arab Republic, I should like to express my gratitude to all countries and international bodies whose offers of advice, financial resources, and technical assistance have furthered our efforts to deal with an ominous development. The flood did not take place. My country has been spared the eleventh plague, to quote my colleague Mr. Malik. May what has happened at Aswan become a milestone on the road that leads us to the realization that, above and beyond any political differences of opinion, there must exist an ultimate solidarity which unites the members of the human race. I refer to the solidarity which all mortal creatures ought to feel. I refer to solidarity in the face of death."

Twenty-one Israeli agricultural experts arrived in Luxor by the night train. A Lebanese Boeing-747 of Middle East Airlines opened a scheduled service between Cairo and Jerusalem. Israeli archaeologists embarked on excavations in the ruins of Berenice and on Philadelphus Point in Foul Bay. Ambassador Vinyenev concluded his talks in Moscow and flew back to Cairo. A MIG-21 fighter which had taken off from its base at Talc made a forced landing on a sand strip at El Diwan. The Soviet pilot told the local Egyptian commander that his rudder assembly was defective. Closer inspection revealed that someone had sawed through a tube in the hydraulic system.

The Secretariat of the 8th Congress on World Hunger informed Dr. Angelo that his address relating to evaporation-inhibiting substances and their effect on agricultural products was scheduled for Thursday. The paper would be delivered at 11 a.m., after a film about insecticides sponsored by the Pontreux paint-manufacturing company. Time allowed: 45 minutes.

The Soviet Union urged Cairo to prevent the infiltration of Egypt by Israeli agents. The note handed to Foreign Minister Riad by Ambassador Vinyenev on the morning after his return from Moscow contained the following words: "The Communist Party and Supreme Soviet of the Union of Soviet Socialist Republics have, with extreme concern, been observing the United Arab Republic's endeavors to join the ranks of the imperialist-Zionist front. Recent developments in Cairo and attacks on Soviet citizens and property give rise to the gravest misgivings."

When Riad had taken the document, Vinyenev said, "May I venture an observation?"

"I should be grateful for any suggestions you have to offer."

"It's a purely personal one. I'm worried about the dam."

"A creditable sentiment, if rather belated."

"Can you guess why I'm worried about the dam?"

"Now that we've stopped the water escaping—no, not really."

"I wonder if . . . As I say, this is a personal observation only."

"Please go on."

"I wonder if the dam will stand up to the vibrations."

"What vibrations?"

"In view of the Jewish invasion, the ones your late President will make when he starts turning in his grave on the crest. I trust I've conveyed the metaphor correctly in Arabic?"

"I regret to say you have."

The three-year-old-son of a schoolteacher was reported missing from a village south of Luxor. A search of the surrounding fields and irrigation ditches disclosed nothing and was called off at nightfall. Next morning, military policemen found the boy's woolen cap. The rumor spread that he had been kidnapped and slaughtered by Jews who were working in the agricultural research centers on the west bank. Angry fellaheen thronged the ferry, and the military commander at Luxor sent a detachment of MPs to protect the Israeli advisers.

Chaim Begin, the newly appointed Israeli chargé d'affaires in Cairo, presented his credentials to President Sadat.

A cylinder of propane gas exploded in the laboratories of the High Dam Authority at Aswan, killing two Egyptians who had been drying samples of mud from the dam's settling tank. A technician from Ismailia alleged that the Israeli engineer Finkenstein had tampered with the outlet valve and then left the laboratory.

The missing child was found sleeping among some bales of straw on the outskirts of the village.

Egyptian technicians at Aswan refused to eat with their Israeli advisers and loitered in the corridors until the Israelis had left the canteen. Returning to their hut at nightfall, Finkenstein and his colleagues found the forelegs of a pig nailed crosswise above the door.

Tass correspondent Adzhubei visited the International Press Club in Cairo for the first time since his expulsion order was rescinded by the Egyptian Ministry of the Interior. In Alexandria, the offices of Hidrama, the Israeli construction company, were raided by demonstrators. Radio Kol Israel spoke in its evening broadcast of a mounting reign of terror in Egypt. Isaac Rodenski, a commentator noted for his caustic turn of phrase, said in a postscript to the news: "No student of animal behavior will be unduly surprised by this development. Rats which have been saved from drowning after an hour-long struggle for survival comport themselves in an extremely peaceable and cooperative manner—and not solely by reason of physical exhaustion. As soon as their fur dries out, their aggressive instincts revive."

Defense Minister Nachram sent tanks to protect the Israeli Embassy. The members of the Israeli team at El Minya were transported to the Hotel Nefertiti in army jeeps and spent the night slumped over their suitcases on the third floor. At Foul Bay, an Israeli gunboat took the two parties of archaeologists on board.

On the coast road between Marsa Alam and Quseir, Egyptian laborers speared an Israeli technician to death with steel surveyor's poles. At Fayum, three Israeli architects were lynched by fellaheen as they crossed the bridge to their bungalows on the heights above the canal. Defense Minister Nachram telephoned Chargé d'Affaires Begin to assure him that the army had been instructed to do everything possible to protect Israeli nationals. These outbreaks of mass hysteria among the population had been entirely unexpected. The only explanation was that the pent-up fears of the past few months were now, with the lessening of tension, venting themselves in random acts of aggression.

Radio Kol Israel called upon Israelis in Egypt to maintain a listening watch on their short-wave radios throughout the night.

ASWAN!

At dawn, military policemen who had been posted on the balconies and sun roof of the Hotel Nefertiti at El Minya used tear gas to repel a howling mob which tried to storm the building. In Suez, an Israeli geologist and his secretary were drowned in an oil tank by persons unknown.

Dr. Angelo entered the conference hall at 10:45 a.m., while the insecticide film was still in progress. On the screen, a pear midge was being eaten away by some corrosive fluid. The beetle's tridental proboscis quivered as, in magnified close-up, the substance crept over its wing cases and brought minute bubbles frothing from the chitinous plates. The sound track said: "Copper preparations may also be added, of course, but not in a ratio of more than five grams per twenty-five gallons of spray, or the fruit will suffer."

Dr. Angelo sat down on a folding chair beside the main aisle with the black case containing the flasks of perymethylene ether clasped between his knees. The sound track said: "It all depends, of course, on how deeply it penetrates the bark." The proboscis of the pear midge drooped like a rubber hose and its hind legs paddled the air. The wing cases shimmered with the colors of verdigris. Dr. Angelo had grown accustomed to the gloom in the hall. He estimated that there were still between a hundred and fifty and two hundred delegates sitting in the rows of seats. In an attempt to read his watch, he raised his arm and tilted it toward the beam of light which issued fanwise from the projector. The legs of the pear midge were still quivering.

At 11 a.m., the lights went up. Fifty or sixty delegates headed for the buffet in the anteroom. Dr. Angelo's ears rang with the clatter of seats springing up as they were vacated. There was an all-pervading hum from the blowers in the ceiling, and an amplified voice said, "Dr. Mario Angelo, Venice,

Italy . . . perymethylene ether and its capacity for inhibiting the dehydration process in agricultural products."

Dr. Angelo grasped the handle of the case. He walked down the central aisle to the platform, patting his jacket to make sure that the sheaf of manuscript was still in his breast pocket. A Sudanese attendant standing beside the lectern adjusted the microphone. Dr. Angelo pushed the bag between the uprights of the lectern and laid his hands flat on the polished top, thumbs spread inward. He lowered his head until he could only see the first row of seats, tapped the neck of the microphone with the knuckles of his right hand, and said: "To begin on a seemingly exaggerated note, ladies and gentlemen, this is a momentous hour in the history of the United Nations Food and Agriculture Organization."

He paused, doing his best to breathe deeply. "I should like to acquaint you with a phenomenon which is capable of suspending the process of evaporation. Equally, I should like to draw your attention to the bearing which this mechanism could have on international efforts to preserve agricultural products. I do so not least with an eye to the problems of the developing countries." The man sitting immediately in front of Dr. Angelo leaned back and stared at the platform.

"Let us proceed upon the assumption that an agricultural product becomes spoiled when its tissue fluid evaporates." Just as Dr. Angelo had delivered this sentence, the blowers fell silent. He gave a slight start and felt for the sheaf of manuscript in his breast pocket. "I have no doubt, ladies and gentlemen, that you must be wondering what an authority on surface tension in fluids can possibly say to interest a body consisting of agricultural and nutrition experts."

The man in front of him crossed his arms.

"We all agree, I take it, that the main problem is not so

much the production of foodstuffs as the worldwide distribution of agricultural surpluses—in other words, that the nub of the problem is preservation."

The man in front of him produced a handkerchief from his pocket and breathed on his glasses. Dr. Angelo thought, For God's sake, if the simultaneous translation system isn't functioning . . . He stooped and ran his fingers along the lip of the black bag. "Vegetable products can be preserved by the extraction of fluid, that is to say, by dehydration. But vegetable products can also be preserved if one retains the full fluid content of the fruit, wheat, leguminous plant, et cetera, by inhibiting the evaporation of tissue fluid. To employ a graphic illustration, if the rind of a cucumber—and this would be an extreme case, in view of its high water content—could be, as it were, hermetically sealed by a film of some sort, the cucumber would retain its original freshness indefinitely. To repeat . . ."

Dr. Angelo broke off as a folding seat swung shut with a crash. He pulled the manuscript out of his pocket. "It was while studying the surface tension of fluids—I worked at Ispra until four years ago—that I first stumbled upon the special properties of perymethylene ether. This substance affects the molecular structure of water by boosting surface tension. To put it another way, it reinforces the linkage between the molecules on the surface and the molecules that underlie them. They can be detached only by a greatly increased application of external energy, by greater expenditure of effort. In other words, the water does not evaporate as rapidly."

A delegate in the second row of seats raised his hand. The overhead lights dazzled Dr. Angelo as he looked up. He could not make out the man's face.

"Yes?" he said, bending over the lectern. "I'm sorry, I can't understand you."

The amplified voice said, "Dr. Angelo, kindly put on your headphones."

The interpreter whispered, "The gentleman was inquiring about the structure of perymethylene ether."

Dr. Angelo pulled off his headphones. "Many thanks, I'll come back to your question in a minute. The method of preserving a fruit by enclosing it in a water-repellent second skin—by wrapping it, as it were, in a film which—"

"You're being a bit ambitious, aren't you?" someone called in English. The man who had raised his hand laughed. Another seat banged. Dr. Angelo stooped and lifted the black bag onto the lectern. He moved aside so as to keep the first row of seats in view.

"We find this principle demonstrated in nature. Take the cactus, for example." The Sudanese attendant stepped silently up to the lectern and bent the neck of the microphone to the left, where Dr. Angelo was standing. "As I said, we find this principle demonstrated in nature. Take cacti . . ."

"What about groundnuts?" asked someone.

"Take the cactus, for example. The cactus protects itself against dehydration by means of a waxlike film. This coats its leaves and inhibits the process of evaporation."

A delegate stood up in the center aisle. Dr. Angelo saw the man rise and heard the clatter of his seat. He spoke a few words in French which drew laughter from the audience. Dr. Angelo put on his headphones again.

"Dr. Chambrelle says, in that case the conference ought to recommend Almighty God for the next Nobel Prize, preferably a double award in chemistry and physics." Even the woman interpreter sounded amused. Dr. Angelo looked around for her and decided that she must be in the glass booth above the projection aperture. He said, forgetting to remove his headphones, "I see little to laugh at." Then he dodged back behind the lectern and snapped open the catches of his black bag. "I have here two flasks of perymethylene ether—roughly five gallons. Perymethylene ether can be extracted from cactus preparations by a cracking process. Alternatively, it could be produced by synthetic means. What matters is the ability of perymethylene ether to diffuse itself over huge expanses of liquid in an extremely dilute state. Perymethylene ether forms a monomolecular film; that is to say, a film of the magnitude of a single molecule. Consequently, one teaspoonful of the substance could cover a vast area. Perymethylene ether remains effective in a solution of one to ten million. Theoretically, the contents of these two flasks would be enough to treat the surface of an entire world crop, because wherever there is an incidence of perymethylene ether the process of evaporation is inhibited. One could, for example, store the world's grain harvest in the Gobi Desert."

"What about groundnuts?" came the voice.

"And your confounded groundnuts, too!" shouted Dr. Angelo.

"But there isn't any fluid in groundnuts."

Laughter buzzed in Dr. Angelo's ears. His voice broke when he tried to reply. The blowers came on again and three seats swung back in quick succession. Dr. Angelo swallowed hard. "Of course there's fluid in groundnuts," he said. "Grains of wheat also contain a certain amount."

"Dr. Chambrelle would like to put a question," said the interpreter. Dr. Angelo lowered his head and adjusted the earphones. "Dr. Chambrelle wants to know, as a matter of extreme urgency, how the human organism reacts to agricultural products which have been treated with perymethylene ether. He wonders if the gastrointestinal tract is capable of digesting such food."

Dr. Angelo had guessed that someone would ask this question. To gain time, he said, "What does he mean by 'as a matter of extreme urgency'?"

"Dr. Chambrelle says, because he's dying for his lunch."

Laughter filled the hall. The blowers roared and the lights seemed to sway before Dr. Angelo's eyes. The man who was sitting immediately in front of the platform rose, unbuttoned his jacket, hitched up his trousers, and sauntered to the door. Dr. Angelo grabbed the black bag. Shouldering the Sudanese aside, he stumbled off the platform to the floor of the hall and strode down the center aisle to the main exit.

A taxi took him back to his hotel.

At Heliopolis, Defense Minister Nachram and General Saphir of the Israeli air force met to organize an airlift for the evacuation of Israeli nationals from the United Arab Republic. Nachram agreed that Egyptian troops should escort the Israelis to assembly points at Aswan, Luxor, and Heliopolis airports.

Dr. Angelo asked the receptionist to prepare his bill. He went back to his room, rang for the floor waiter, and ordered some writing paper and a bottle of mineral water. Then he wrote to the Secretary-General of the United Nations.

The first Hercules transport planes of the Israeli air force landed at Aswan, Luxor, and Heliopolis just before midday. Israeli paratroopers stood guard over them while convoys of Egyptian trucks transported refugees across the tarmac.

The jeep which was taking the Israeli engineers Mordach and Finkenstein and an interpreter from Shepheard's Hotel to Heliopolis found its route barred by an abandoned truck. The N.C.O. at the wheel backed away from the obstruction and turned down a side street which led to the bus depot, hoping to rejoin the airport road from there. "We're on the list," Mordach said. "They're bound to wait for us."

Finkenstein shrugged. "Provided we get to Heliopolis in time and the Egyptian army doesn't lose control of the runways."

The jeep braked to a halt in front of the depot. Derelict buses had been pushed together into an untidy line. A dog darted from behind a stack of old tires and crawled under a rusty chassis. The driver turned and muttered something to the interpreter.

"He says he must get out and ask at the office for directions," explained the interpreter.

"So I gather," said Mordach. "All right, let him, but I'd appreciate it if he left his pistol behind."

The Egyptian N.C.O. hesitated for a moment, then unbuckled his belt. He climbed out of the jeep and walked diagonally across the depot yard. Just before he reached the buses, he broke into a trot. Mordach got in behind the wheel and laid the belt and holster across his thigh. "We'll give him five minutes."

"Five minutes too long, if you ask me," said the interpreter. "I don't like the look of this place. It's much too quiet."

Mordach sensed that the other two were, like him, staring at some threads of smoke rising from an oil drum which had been converted into a makeshift stove. The dog slunk back to its stack of tires as Mordach climbed out.

There were ten wrecked buses in all. Rust stains ran from the empty window frames and fanned out over the blistered paintwork. One door had been wrenched off its hinges and hung at an angle across the driver's seat. On the roofs of the buses, ventilators revolved silently in the breeze. When Mordach returned to the jeep, Finkenstein said from the back seat, "He took the ignition key with him."

They pulled out the leads under the steering column and short-circuited the electrical system. Mordach forgot to depress the clutch and stalled the engine. Just as he started up for a second time, the bus workers who had been concealed in the derelicts leaped out of the windows and rushed at the jeep, which took off with a squeal of tires.

After two miles, they hit the road leading to the airport. Finkenstein crawled into the passenger seat. "Whew!" he exclaimed. "I never thought they'd actually try and lynch us." He pulled the pistol out of its holster and threw the belt away.

"We're not out of the woods yet," Mordach shouted back. "They're coming after us in a truck—I've had them in the mirror for the past two minutes."

The road curved gently to the right as it left the outskirts of the city and ran through an expanse of sand to the plateau above the Nile Valley. As soon as Mordach caught sight of the carts blocking the road, he instinctively took his foot off the accelerator. The engine braked the jeep so sharply that the interpreter lurched against the back of the driver's seat. At this stage, they were three hundred yards short of the improvised roadblock.

Peasants armed with sticks were waiting for them on the banks of a field. They had pushed three vegetable carts across the road. Mordach depressed the clutch and let the vehicle roll to a standstill. His eyes took in the baskets piled high above the big wooden wheels, the projecting shafts, the bundles of sugar cane hanging down on either side, a man hastily whipping a donkey onto the verge. Then he gripped the steering wheel tightly in both hands, trod on the accelerator, and averted his head as the jeep rocketed into the carts. The windshield shattered, chickens flew in all directions, and the peasants hurled their first volley of stones. The jeep skidded, veered toward the right-hand bank on two wheels, teetered for a moment, righted itself, and finally overturned after another two hundred yards when the near-side front tire burst.

Finkenstein's first reaction after the crash was to search for the pistol. The interpreter was lying beside a telegraph pole with his legs at a strange angle. Mordach tugged Finkenstein's sleeve. "Over there!" he gasped. "We must hide!"

The cemetery lay east of the road leading from Cairo to the airport. A strip of sand three hundred yards wide separated the road from the perimeter wall. Dominating the scene were a minaret, three domed buildings with openwork walls, and, on the south side, five acacia trees. The gravestones were painted white, ocher, and rusty brown. Beyond the cemetery, the ground rose in a series of undulations to the desert plateau.

Finkenstein was cut down by the peasants before he reached the perimeter wall. A stick caught him behind the right ear and he pitched forward into the sand without a word.

Mordach ran to the yellow wall and clawed his way up it, kicking out at the hands which tried to pluck him back. He heaved himself onto the top of the wall and lay there panting, then rolled sidewise and dropped into the cemetery.

He heard the yells of the men beyond the wall, crawled up the steps of a tomb on his hands and knees, dragged himself across the stone roof, and sank back against a buttress with his legs drawn up and his arms clasping his knees.

He tried to think about his wife.

Then the men scrambled over the wall and stoned him to death.

Part Three

TOO MUCH

IN ROOM 138 on the third floor of the Bahr el Azraq Hotel, Dr. Angelo removed his dinner jacket from the wardrobe and packed it in his pale leather suitcase. He stuffed his dirty linen into the wastepaper basket, tore up the notes on his latest series of experiments, threw the pieces into the lavatory bowl, and pushed his shoes under the bed. Taking the envelope addressed to the U.N. Secretary-General, he added a list of instructions to the hotel management and, using the ashtray as a paperweight, placed them on the desk.

Dr. Angelo signed some traveler's checks to the value of seventy-five thousand lire and pinned them to the hotel bill. He divided his ready cash into three piles, placed them on sheets of paper marked "For the switchboard operator," "For room service," "For the porters," and arranged them side by side on the bedspread. As an afterthought, he printed the words "PLEASE TRANSFER" in English on the book of traveler's checks and inserted it in his passport.

Dr. Angelo drew the curtains. He switched on the overhead light, took seven ties from the rod on the wardrobe door, knotted them together, and twisted them into a rope. Propping a chair against the window sill, he pulled the curtains a few inches apart to enable him to open the fanlights, tied his improvised rope to the upright, and fashioned the other end into a noose.

Dr. Mario Angelo's last act was to walk over to the washbasin, remove the two flasks of perymethylene ether from the black bag, and place them beside the bottle of mineral water. He put the bag on the floor and tied a label with the inscription "For the page boy" to one of the fasteners.

Dr. Angelo climbed onto the window sill by way of the chair, took the rope of ties from the crack between the curtains, and arranged the noose round his neck.

He pivoted as he jumped, hitting his right eye on the window catch. A ball of flame burst inside his head and expanded with infinite rapidity. He just had time to think, God, what have I done . . .

Dr. Angelo's suicide was discovered by the hotel watchman when darkness fell and his body was silhouetted against the curtains by the overhead light. The floor waiter locked the door of Room 138 in the presence of the manager.

Dr. Angelo was laid out in the morgue of the former British Hospital in Khartoum.

The page boy assigned to the third floor of the Bahr el Azraq Hotel helped to strip the bed in Room 138, unknotted the seven ties, and, at 11:12 p.m. local time, tipped the contents of the two flasks into the washbasin.

Five gallons of perymethylene ether gurgled down the plughole and along the cast-iron waste pipe situated beneath the corridor, gushed into the hopper head on the west wall of the hotel, dropped vertically into the sewers, negotiated the concrete tunnel underlying Freedom Square and the flower beds of the promenade, and finally trickled into the Nile.

WEDNESDAY

LAKE NASSER: LEVEL RISING

     Lake level: 567.12 ft. above sea level. Change: plus 3.34 ft. (Top water level: 597 ft.; crest of dam: 643 ft.)

```
PORE-WATER PRESSURE IN BODY OF DAM: INCREASING

EARTH PRESSURE IN BODY OF DAM: INCREASING

SEEPAGE VELOCITY: APPROXIMATELY CONSTANT

PARTICLES IN SEEPAGE (tolerance 0.8mm)
Very fine sediment, granular diameter 0.001-
0.002mm.  Fine sediment, granular diameter
0.002-0.006mm.
```

According to a report compiled by the Ministry of Justice in Jerusalem, twenty-seven Israeli advisers and private individuals met their deaths during the Egyptian pogrom. Thirteen Israelis were missing and sixty-one had yet to be discharged from civilian or military hospitals at Aswan, Luxor, Cairo, Alexandria, Idfu, Quseir, and Port Said. A total of six hundred and eighteen Israeli citizens had been successfully evacuated. The largest single group of fatalities occurred when the mob set fire to an army coach which was taking a party of agricultural experts from the Nile Hilton assembly point to Heliopolis. Fifteen passengers were burned to death behind the wire mesh which had been put there to protect them from flying stones. Another three Israelis were dragged from their jeep and trampled to death by workmen while driving through the grounds of the Helwan steelworks. Six more, including two women, had been hanged from lampposts and bridges at Aswan, Asyut, and Alexandria. One Israeli fugitive from the Kharga Depression had expired of thirst in the Libyan Desert. Five Israelis were stoned to death and two deliberately drowned. In the remaining cases, the cause of death had not been established.

Addressing an emergency session of the U.N. General Assembly, the senior Israeli delegate stated: "There is definite evidence to suggest that the massacre took place in defiance of the wishes of the Egyptian authorities. I should like to state that firmly and unequivocally. On the other hand, it seems improbable that such atrocities occurred spontaneously and then became transmitted into a wave of mass hysteria sufficient to engulf an entire nation. Of the many factors which militate against this theory, one is, for example, that it took rioters only twenty minutes to round up an Israeli geological team whose members were staying at five different hotels in Ras el Barr.

"It is, in the last analysis, idle to speculate on the question of spontaneity or deliberate intent. The fact remains that two Near Eastern countries, which were brought together by an imminent threat to the High Dam and availed themselves of a historic opportunity for reconciliation, have now, by barbaric acts, been thrust back into an age of barbarism."

Sweden, Iran, New Zealand, and the Federal German Republic sponsored a resolution condemning the United Arab Republic for having tolerated the pogrom, but it was rejected by eighty-two votes to twenty-five. Israel abstained. President Anwar el Sadat decreed seven days' public mourning for those who had died.

THURSDAY

LAKE NASSER: LEVEL RISING

     Lake level: 567.94 ft. above sea level.
Change: plus 0.82 ft. (Top water level: 597
ft.; crest of dam: 643 ft.)

PORE-WATER PRESSURE IN BODY OF DAM: INCREASING

The management of Sudan Airways informed the secretary of the former British Hospital in Khartoum that the cost of conveying Dr. Mario Angelo's body to Venice could not be guaranteed. No witness had been present when Dr. Angelo signed the traveler's checks appended to his list of instructions to the hotel management. A telex message to the local branch of the Banco del Santo Spirito in Venice, inquiring if the checks would be honored, had so far elicited no response.

Egypt accepted a renewed invitation to join Inter-Mediterranes, the association of Mediterranean countries. The representative from Cairo was elected chairman of the committee for coastal preservation.

The film of perymethylene ether on the Nile reached the town of Dongola, two hundred miles south of the Egyptian-Sudanese border.

An Anglo-Egyptian archaeological team resumed its quest for cat tombs in the gorges of Debeirae.

The meteorological station in the Seshia Mountains of Ethiopia recorded a rainfall of 3.5 inches in twenty-four hours.

Dr. Angelo's body was deposited in a zinc coffin soldered together by technicians in the hospital workshop.

The High Dam Authority used sonic depth finders to locate areas where filling had been washed out by seepage before the fissures were sealed.

Speaking on Radio Stockholm's current events program "Review of the Month," a commentator declared that recent developments at Aswan had indeed constituted a danger of the first magnitude. With due deference to the risks involved, however, it had been a symptom of worldwide hysteria to talk in terms of national extinction. "To place matters in their proper perspective, it should be remembered that the Nile's flow at Aswan—318,000 cubic feet per second and an annual mean flow of 76,000 cubic feet per second—is far exceeded by the Río de la Plata, with a mean flow of 883,000 cubic feet per second, and the Mississippi, with a mean flow of 636,000 cubic feet per second."

The control station at Nag'Azgirga notified the High Dam Authority at Aswan that the level of the lake had risen 9.44 inches since Thursday night. A rise of 6.69 inches was recorded at El Diwan. The main gauge at Aswan registered 3.14 inches plus.

In pursuance of an agreement between the management of Sudan Airways and the director of the former British Hospital at Khartoum, Dr. Angelo's coffin was deposited in a storage depot at the airport.

In the southern reaches of Lake Nasser, as far north as Abu Simbel, catches of fish doubled within a week. Nubian fishermen reported that shoals were avoiding the lake bed and congregating at depths of twelve to fifteen feet.

The lake level topped the 575-foot mark on the main gauge at Aswan. President Sadat flew there with Ambassador Vinyenev for a tour of the hydroelectric installations.

The gauge at Nag'Azgirga recorded a further rise of 9.44 inches within a single twenty-four-hour period.

Returning from a routine trip to the Nag'el Gami–Nag'el Hagar sector of Lake Nasser, the commander of an Egyptian army patrol boat reported that his vessel had run into a shoal of fish and almost capsized. "We saw the foam and the dark backs of the fish churning the surface before we reached them, and I immediately put the boat into neutral. The shoal headed straight for us, however, apparently attracted by the sound of the engines, and we were right in the middle of them before we knew it. They crowded round the boat with their mouths gaping. I hit out at them with a rifle butt, but they continued to break surface, goggling at us."

In the storage depot at Khartoum airport, a forklift truck backed into Dr. Angelo's coffin and overturned it.

For the first time, the gauges at Nag'Azgirga, El Diwan, and Aswan recorded an equal rise in the level of the lake. Minister of the Interior Gidaff instructed the High Dam Authority to submit readings to Cairo twice a day. The hygrometers at the dam site, which had been registering a steady decrease in humidity, were assumed to be defective and replaced.

South of Debeirae, the rising water washed some mummified cats adorned with scarab necklaces out of a cleft in the rocks. The Anglo-Egyptian archaeological team found that no water had penetrated the cats' carcasses and hinted at the discovery of an embalming process effected with the aid of hitherto unknown essential oils.

Lake Nasser had risen another 8.66 inches by Friday night. The High Dam Authority requested the Ethiopian Ministry of the Interior for a summary of all rainfall measurements in the catchment area of the Blue Nile. President Sadat flew to Aswan for the second time in ten days. Four hundred ampules containing water samples from every part of Lake

Nasser were transported by helicopter to the Marine Research Institute at Mansura. Preliminary experiments confirmed that the water had ceased to evaporate.

In response to a request from Sudan Airways, the Italian Embassy in Khartoum cabled the Venice branch of the Banco del Santo Spirito to inquire whether traveler's checks in the name of Dr. Mario Angelo would be honored.

Accredited journalists were summoned to a press conference at the Kubbeh Palace in Cairo. President Sadat entered the hall an hour after his return from Heliopolis airport. He was accompanied by Minister of the Interior Gidaff, Defense Minister Nachram, and Professor Saber. His prepared statement read as follows:

"I have an announcement to make. The surface of Lake Nasser has become subject to a phenomenon which is producing a rapid rise in water level. The water is, in fact, rising more rapidly than it did before fissures opened up between the shores of the lake and the Red Sea. This proves, first, that the process cannot be attributed to nuclear explosions or any consequential changes in the lake bed. Secondly, no doubt exists that the water is rising more rapidly than the present rate of summer rainfall in Ethiopia would warrant.

"We have reason to believe that evaporation has ceased throughout the lake, and that a factor which normally plays a vital part in regulating the level of impounded water has therefore become inoperative. The six penstocks which feed the Aswan generating station can only discharge a limited volume of water. In view of these circumstances, and of the danger that the Nile's flow will exceed the dam's maximum outlet capacity, thus raising the surface of the lake to a critical level, the United Arab Republic solicits aid from the scientists of all nations."

After the President had delivered his statement, Minister of the Interior Gidaff and Professor Saber answered journalists' questions. Gidaff said that, with day temperatures in the 104°–122°F. range, the average rate of evaporation was five–six millimeters daily. "To give you some idea of the dimensions and magnitudes involved, one cubic centimeter of water weighs one gram, and the water in a basin one meter square and five millimeters deep weighs five kilograms. In other words, every square meter of lake surface loses five or six kilograms of water a day by evaporation. Lake Nasser has a total surface area of 1,158 square miles, or about 3,588,000,000 square yards. Multiply that by 1.32 gallons for every day that passes, gentlemen . . . I should, at the same time, like to make the qualification that we don't yet know for certain if this phenomenon—nonevaporation—is currently affecting the entire surface of the lake."

Professor Saber amplified Gidaff's remarks by pointing out that evaporation could be considerably affected by wind conditions. Strong currents of air tended to accelerate the process of evaporation because they carried water vapor away.

From what Saber had said, evaporation was being inhibited by a sort of film resting on the surface of the lake.

Uproar broke out at the International Geological Congress in Evian, Switzerland, when the French delegation walked out in protest. The Austrian geophysicist Franz Buchprunner, in a paper entitled "New Geodesic Survey Methods Relating to Halperin's Theory of Continental Drift," had unexpectedly accused Professor Deniaux of plagiarism. In an open letter published in the May issue of *Mid-East Survey,* Deniaux had called upon the Egyptian government to divert the waters of Lake Nasser into the Red Sea through the river valley which had originally carried the Nile eastward from Aswan prior to the breaching of the rhyolitic barrier.

Buchprunner claimed that he had already, as long ago as 1934, recommended in *Orientalische Monatshefte* that the Red Sea should be sealed off from the Indian Ocean by an earth dam situated on a line with Cape Bab el Mandeb, and that engineers should, by redirecting the Nile along its original bed, gradually transform this inland sea into a gigantic fresh-water reservoir for the then British protectorates of Egypt and the Sudan, together with Saudi Arabia, Yemen, and Ethiopia.

The elderly Austrian scientist collapsed as he left the speaker's rostrum, but not before he had delivered his parting shot: "There have always been hyenas in the world of science, small-minded men whose sole response to the advent of a national disaster is to offer their services as advisers by exploiting the discoveries and intellectual achievements of others. M. Deniaux is one such."

The meeting was adjourned. The chairman of the International Geological Congress, Professor Malpatto of Turin, invited Deniaux and Buchprunner to a private exchange of views, but the French delegates insisted on a public apology and left Evian that evening.

A party of British engineers who had been commissioned by UNESCO to measure the salinity of soil in the Nile Delta were stoned by fellaheen at a village near Fuwa, east of the Rosetta Nile. They had been taking core samples from depths of six, twelve, and eighteen feet on the edge of a barley field, and did not hear anyone approaching above the noise of the diesel engine which powered their drilling equipment. Unobserved by them, peasants had gathered on the embankment of a nearby irrigation ditch and were staring at the intruders.

The engineers had just opened the hollow bit and placed

their last core sample in a plastic bag when one of the fellaheen jumped to his feet and shouted. There was a metallic
clank as the first stone hit the drilling rig. Ducking low to
avoid the hail of stones that followed, the party waded
hastily through the barley and tried to reach the road by a
roundabout route. A dozen peasants raced to cut them off
while the rest yelled imprecations from the embankment.

By the time the British reached their car, the chief mechanic was bleeding from a gash in the forehead. They piled
in and locked the doors while the peasants crowded round
and drummed on the bodywork. Blobs of spittle oozed down
the windshield. The mob drew back when the engine revved
but pressed forward again as the car pulled away, horn blaring. A stone shattered the rear windows. Above the drilling
site, clouds of oily black smoke rose from diesel fuel which
the peasants had poured over the engine.

That evening, an official from the Egyptian Ministry of the
Interior called on the leader of the party, Jack Lowell, at
his Alexandria hotel. Lowell had been drinking for three
hours.

"We regret this morning's incident, Mr. Lowell. The Governor has ordered an inquiry. We have reason to believe that
agitators were to blame."

"I doubt it," retorted Lowell. "My guess is, the sight of
their fields sent them around the bend. If salinity increases
at the present rate, all they'll grow next year will be bul-
rushes. I've seldom seen such a pathetic crop of corn as the
one between Birimbal and Mutubis. Mature pumpkins the
size of a baby's head, too. The brackish water is killing off
their cattle. And then we come along and tamper with their
fields . . ."

"It isn't as bad near the Damietta Nile. We have an
extreme situation here, politically as well—the two aspects

tend to overlap. In any case, the Governor has given orders that every survey party will be escorted by a detachment of troops from tomorrow morning onward. Once again, my Ministry would like to extend its sincere apologies."

"I'll pass that on to the rest of my team. As far as I'm concerned, the subject's closed. One question, though. Is it true that the peasants have been scraping salt off their fields and eating it in a sort of hysterical frenzy?"

"A mere rumor, my dear sir."

"I heard it from the Swedes who are taking soil and water samples in the east of the Delta. A few days ago, I heard it again at Damanhur. They eat the salt because they think it's a symbolic act which will purify their polluted land. Sympathetic magic, or something of the kind."

"Ever since 1963, Mr. Lowell, when the Nile last flooded and the High Dam enabled us to switch to all-year-round irrigation, we've had to contend with a very complex situation here in the Delta. Everyone is up in arms, from brick manufacturers to students. The peasants find it hard to accept such a change. They're chary of chemical fertilizers and want their mud back. Now the soil is being contaminated by salt. What do you think happens if we bring a load of artificial manure into a village? Or potash? The locals refuse to scatter it on their fields. They say the sacks are full of salt and the government wants to poison them because they produce too many children."

"Sounds logical in a crazy kind of way."

"Last October, they lynched a truck driver. That was in a village on the coast. They dragged him out of his cab and hanged him from a tree with some telephone wire. They claimed he'd been dumping salt."

"You said something about agitators."

"Yes. There are certain groups of people who go around telling villagers that we're deliberately salting their land."

"As a geohydrologist, I'd find it hard to refute that."
Lowell belched and fell asleep at the table.

T U E S D A Y

LAKE NASSER: LEVEL RISING

     Lake level: 580.60 ft. above sea level.
Change: plus 3.44 ft. (Top water level: 597
ft.; crest of dam: 643 ft.)

EARTH PRESSURE IN BODY OF DAM: INCREASING

Pressure gauges	A	B	C	D	E
kg/cm²	19.13	17.92	18.80	9.17	13.01
Change	+0.05	+0.04	+0.07	+0.05	+0.02

SEEPAGE VELOCITY: CONSTANT

Mahmoud Hassam, commercial attaché at the Egyptian Embassy in London, went to the reading room of the British Museum library and placed two orders, one for the May issue of *Mid-East Survey* and the other for *Orientalische Monatshefte*, 1934. At 5:10 p.m., the two blue order forms were inserted in a metal capsule and sent to the storeroom by Lansen tube. Hassam walked over to the reading stands and flicked through a newspaper, glancing repeatedly at his watch. At 6:05 p.m., an attendant placed the periodicals on table No. 127 in the reading room. Hassam announced that he had to take them to the Egyptian Embassy. The assistant librarian drew his attention to the regulations governing the issue of books and started to remove them. Readers at neighboring tables clicked their tongues as the attaché caught him by the sleeve.

"You filled out a blue order form," said the attendant

crossly. "Anyone who wants to remove books from the premises can fill out a yellow one, but not after 6 p.m."

The reading-room superintendent hurried over to table No. 127.

"Get me the Principal Keeper," said Hassam, clasping the volumes to his chest. "I must speak to him. There are human lives at stake."

The superintendent, with the assistant librarian in tow, went off to call Mr. Evans, the Principal Keeper. A secretary informed him that Mr. Evans had washed his hands and left the office a few minutes before. By the time the two men returned, Hassam had taken the periodicals and vanished. They found a visiting card with the scribbled message: "Please apply to the Embassy."

Hassam walked swiftly out of the British Museum and crossed Great Russell Street. By 6:22 p.m., he was sitting between two West Indian women in a Piccadilly Line tube train with the volumes on his knee. He changed to the District Line at Earl's Court and took a taxi from Station Hill Gate to London airport. A messenger met him at the main Departures entrance and handed him his ticket. Passengers traveling to Cairo by United Arab Flight No. 232 were called twelve minutes later.

A special UNESCO report transmitted to the Egyptian government by Count Hengström confirmed that the reduced flow of water to the two arms of the Nile was accelerating the seepage of sea water into the base of the Delta. The soil was already impregnated with salt as far inland as a line drawn between Damanhur, Kafr el Sheikh, and Shirbin. Even in the cotton fields of Aryamun, or more than twenty-five miles from the Mediterranean coast, the salt content of ground water six feet below the surface had increased from 2.3 to 2.9 grams per liter. If the Delta continued to be starved of Nile water for the sake of increased electricity output and land reclamation in the interior, the entire area would be contaminated within five years. Now that it was no longer opposed by a counterflow of fresh water, seawater was percolating the far-from-porous sinter and silt deposits of the Nile Delta at such a rate that it would ultimately threaten the Fayum depression, which was situated below sea level, together with the depressions of Sitra, Bahrein, and Siwa. Another twelve years at most, and plant life would become extinct in the suburbs of Cairo itself.

As alternatives to lowering the level of Lake Nasser, the UNESCO study recommended the construction of desalinization plants, either employing the electrodialytic principle or based on a system of reverse osmosis (hyperfiltration). These plants would have to be installed in the form of a barrier running laterally across the Delta.

In this context, the scientific division of UNESCO drew attention to work being carried out at the sea-water research center at Weir Westgarth, Scotland. This establishment had developed a cellular system for the desalinization of brackish water by electrodialysis, using an ideal combination of anodes, cathodes, and cell membranes. Expenditure of energy would decrease in inverse proportion to the size of the plant. The second process was based on semi-permeable membranes which allowed water to penetrate but retained salts. As the study put it: "In this technique, a balance must be achieved between high flow velocity (which reduces polarization of the concentration of salts on the membrane but is accompanied by high pressure loss) and decreased flow velocity (which results in smaller pressure loss but greater concentration on the membrane surface)." In view of variations in

187

the seepage velocity of the salt water infiltrating the base of the Delta, preference was given to the electrodialytic process.

Minister of the Interior Gidaff walked over to the map table and gestured to the Nubian beside the door. Two lights went on over the table and the Nubian scurried out.

It was Gidaff's habit to don and remove his glasses alternately while speaking. After two or three sentences, his left hand shot up. His thumb and forefinger closed on the cross-piece between the two lenses and swept the glasses off the bridge of his nose.

"It gives me particular pleasure to note that, today for the first time, Professor Deniaux of Lyons is present at a meeting of our coordinating committee. I need hardly add that Professor Deniaux is enjoined to absolute secrecy. Thank you, Professor. I should like to introduce General Fachallal, commanding the reconnaissance wing of the Egyptian air force, also Major Ahmodi of Luxor District, and Professor Anwar Heikal of the Geophysical Institute, Mansura University."

"Thank you, Your Excellency," said Deniaux. "Professor Heikal and I are already acquainted. Good morning, Heikal."

The Egyptian stared at his shoes. Deniaux shrugged irritably. At that moment, Gidaff removed his glasses again. He peered across the heads of the committee members at the paneling on the opposite wall. "We only established contact with Professor Deniaux by chance, though a copy of his open letter is probably lying around somewhere in the Ministry of Information. If one of our attachés in London hadn't read of an uproar at Evian in the *Neue Zürcher Zeitung,* we might never have . . ."

"I gather, gentlemen," said General Fachallal, "that you plan to divert the Nile."

"As an assistant professor at Bordeaux, I once made a

special cartographic study of the area between the Nile Valley and the Red Sea." Deniaux spoke without notes, apart from a sheet of paper on which he had jotted down some place names. "Our aim was to devote the long vacation to an expedition by motorcycle from the coast to the Saharan plateau via the Etbai Mountains. We started out by regarding it as something of an adventure, I suppose. Later, while studying old maps, I became fascinated by references to ancient mines in the area—the copper mines of Samiuki, for example. The presence of sheiks' tombs was enough in itself to alert me . . ."

"All very interesting, Professor," said General Fachallal. "If you thought you had something of value to impart, why didn't you contact the Egyptian government sooner?"

The Frenchman rounded on him. "I didn't push my ideas, for God's sake—you invited me, otherwise I should no doubt be in Brittany this afternoon, dabbling my feet in the sea."

Gidaff whipped his glasses off the bridge of his nose in a single abrupt movement. He inclined his head slightly. "A little misunderstanding, Professor. I think you were about to tell us how you discovered the original course of the Nile."

"I never discovered it as such. I simply recalled the subject when I heard that Lake Nasser was in danger of flooding the whole of Egypt. Any decent contour map will show you where the valley branches off. As I say, the original course of the Nile merely came to my notice when we were looking for a route which would take us across the coastal range to the Nile from a point on the Red Sea south of Quseir. We didn't want to ride our machines up six thousand feet unless we had to."

"And while you were at it you came across the original bed of the Nile."

"I can't say for certain. Being a cartographer and geologist, I instinctively selected a route which the water would have taken. It led inland from Sharm Luli through the Gimal valley. We should have come to water at least three times before reaching the ruins of Apollonos, kept below twenty-two hundred feet the whole way, and eventually gained access to Aswan via the Wadi Natash."

"And so reached your Saharan plateau," said General Fachallal. "One question, just for the record. This expedition never took place, did it?"

"No."

"Another interesting point," said Fachallal.

Major Ahmodi raised his hand. "I should like to ask Professor Deniaux if he considers the Wadi Natash to be the bed of the Nile as it existed up to the Pleistocene. That is all that matters."

"The only certainty is that above the Aswan cataract a large valley branches off to the east, eight hundred feet below the present level of the Nile Valley. Secondly, there is gravel on the shoulders of the Nile Valley. Taken in conjunction, these two facts strongly suggest that the river once followed a different course. Anything more would be pure speculation."

"For all that, Professor, do you think it conceivable that before it broke through the fundamental complex of the Nubian cataracts, the Nile used to flow into the Red Sea, and that it may have done so by way of the dry valley which branches off at Aswan—possibly through the wadis Natash and Gimal?

"In other words, Professor Deniaux, do you see any chance of discharging Lake Nasser into the Red Sea before it overflows?"

"Yes, there is a chance . . ."

"And what does it depend on?"

"On tracing the original course of the river within the next four weeks."

Major Ahmodi stood up and flexed his legs. "Very well, we'll send our recruits chasing through the desert armed with divining rods. Even if the scheme fails, at least it'll provide someone with enough material for a thesis."

"So that's your attitude," said the Frenchman. "Yours, too, General?"

"Professor Deniaux is right. We'll start in the dry valley at Aswan. We'll check every square mile of the area with geophones. What's the difference in altitude between Aswan and the gorge near the Apollonos ruins? Nine hundred feet? Twelve hundred?"

"You can't possibly use seismographic methods to trace the original course of the Nile," said Deniaux. "There just isn't time to sink hundreds of boreholes for explosive charges. What's more, it would be madness to detonate them in the neighborhood of such an unstable dam merely because you want to record sound waves. Displace a single underground watercourse and you might bring about the destruction of Egypt. One touch on a button . . ."

"We're not here to speculate, Professor."

"Of course not, your fee wouldn't cover it. I was thinking of satellite photography—the possibility of charting the area between Aswan and the Red Sea with infrared film. At night, when warmth is radiating from the ground. There must be a difference in chromatic value between the massive bedrock and the gravel which has filled the original bed of the Nile. You simply develop the film and send for bulldozers to clear it."

"Ah, yes," said Gidaff, "bulldozers. It all fits so neatly."

"What do you mean?"

"I'll tell you later."

"The first step would be to clear a narrow channel in the original bed. It would help, in the first instance, if you got rid of only about six million cubic feet of water a day. The water would then carry the gravel away and flood the valley."

Major Ahmodi said, "Then we can demolish the High Dam, redivert the river, and sustain ourselves on the handful of tomatoes which the fellaheen irrigate to the eternal rhythm of the unfettered Nile—after manuring them with their own dung, of course. It's as simple as that."

"You may find your remarks amusing, Major Ahmodi. Personally, I find them a bore." Deniaux shrugged. "All right, if the Israelis don't shoot you down like pigeons over the Etbai Mountains you can take your reconnaissance planes and look for the original riverbed yourself. Good morning."

Gidaff accompanied Deniaux to the door. The Nubian had scurried back into the room.

"The Cabinet will study your recommendations tomorrow, Professor. We also have to decide on Nazareth Iron's survival-tower scheme. You've heard of it?"

"Vaguely."

"We'll meet again on Friday, then."

Deniaux stumbled against a box of fire-fighting sand as he emerged into the corridor. His eyes took a few seconds to readjust themselves to the light.

"One moment, Professor!"

Gidaff was still standing in the doorway, swinging his glasses on the second joint of his left forefinger.

"Yes, what is it? Have I reduced General Fachallal to tears?"

"I completely forgot. Hampton was here earlier. He asked me to tell you eight-thirty this evening, if you can manage it. In the roof restaurant of the Nile Hilton. Hampton will be there on time. I shall join you a little later."

"Who the devil is Hampton?"

"Gerald Hampton, Patton Corporation. Eight-thirty it is, then. I'll look in later, as I said."

"There must be some mistake—I don't know the man. Good morning."

Gidaff's forefinger came to rest. Automatically, he caught the swinging glasses and put them on, then gripped Deniaux by the shoulder.

"Forget it, Professor, I was merely testing you. I hope you don't mind, but the Patton Corporation has been pestering us ever since we got in touch with you. The Americans also came up with the idea of diverting the Nile, except that they propose to send it westward across the limestone plateau. They don't care if we drown every last rat in the oases of Kharga, Dakhla, and Farafra, as long as we dig outlet channels. Using their bulldozers, of course."

"What is Hampton after?"

"He wants us to lease ten thousand items of earth-moving machinery from the Patton Corporation. Conveyor belts, scrapers, excavators, trucks, dumpers—you name it, they've got it."

"Very pretty, the leasing scheme," said Deniaux. "Live now, pay later."

"An original twist to an old idea, I admit."

"Why are you so anxious for me to meet Hampton this evening?"

"I told you to forget it, Professor. I simply wanted to see your reaction to his name. We estimate that Hampton has bought himself at least fifteen assorted experts, all of whom recommend the construction of an emergency channel by mechanical means and advise against the use of explosives because of unstable subsoil conditions. Hampton's latest acquisition is Professor Mathes of Montreal."

"I know Mathes. Anyone could buy him for five thousand dollars."

"You yourself would have been the tenth, reckoned from the time you fired off your open letter to *Mid-East Survey*. In case you're interested, *Mid-East Survey* is subsidized by Mink Petroleum, and Mink is a wholly-owned subsidiary of . . ."

"I'm flying back to Lyons tomorrow morning. You can forward my fee. I'll pay my own hotel bill."

"No, Professor, you must stay. We need you to help us find the original bed of the Nile."

Israeli troops stationed in the Gulf of Aqaba surprised some Arabs during a night patrol of the agricultural research establishment directed by Hugo Boyko, the agronomist. The three intruders, who came from Elath, were caught in the act of digging up melons, tomato plants, and sea grass and packing them in plastic bags. They offered no resistance when detained but refused to answer questions. Asked by the presiding magistrate at Elath if he had been prompted by hunger, Yussuf Mahali, aged twenty-three, retorted, "Yes, but not for Israeli melons."

The three Arabs were released but kept under surveillance by agents of the Israeli secret service. During a sandstorm on the fourth day after their appearance in court, they crossed the Jordanian border six miles north of Elath, walked up to an army post, and were taken by jeep to Aqaba the same evening.

WEDNESDAY

LAKE NASSER: LEVEL RISING

Lake level: 588.34 ft. above sea level. Change: plus 0.68 ft. (Top water level: 597 ft.; crest of dam: 643 ft.)

```
PORE-WATER PRESSURE IN BODY OF DAM: INCREASING

EARTH PRESSURE IN BODY OF DAM: INCREASING
```

Pressure gauges kg/cm²	A	B	C	D	E
	19.27	18.03	18.84	9.22	13.17
Change	+0.03	+0.03	+0.02	+0.02	+0.01

```
SEEPAGE VELOCITY: SLIGHTLY INCREASING

PARTICLES IN SEEPAGE (tolerance: 0.8mm)

Very fine sediment, granular diameter 0.001-
0.002mm. Fine sediment, granular diameter
0.002-0.006mm.
```

According to a report published in the *Neue Zürcher Zeitung,* the Egyptian citizen Shmol Bennoah, a member of Cairo's Jewish community, was sentenced by the district court at Bab esh Sha'ira to three years' hard labor for violating the security of the United Arab Republic.

A rubber dinghy of French manufacture had been discovered on the roof of the accused man's home. The public prosecutor claimed that Bennoah had acted in the interests of a foreign power by deliberately siting the boat, which was a conspicuous shade of yellow, so that its longitudinal axis was aligned with Cairo's main station and central post office, thus enabling enemy aircraft to check their bearings. The stocks of food and drinking water found on board were dismissed as an attempt to camouflage Bennoah's real intentions.

Bennoah defended himself to the court by predicting that the Lord would again cause it to rain for forty days and forty nights. Ever since sustaining a head injury some years before, he had repeatedly heard voices telling him that everything on earth would perish. These voices were not uncommon in his family. His father, who was drowned by a flood in Algeria, had heard them too. The accused claimed that he owed it to his family to make at least some attempt to save them from a watery death. He had acquired the rubber dinghy from a French tourist four years earlier. Pressed by the public prosecutor to state whether he had any particular flood in mind and whether it would come from the north or the south, Bennoah flatly refused to commit himself. He further vowed that he had never discussed the matter with any other member of the Jewish community.

Deniaux did not see the girl at first. He walked from the reception desk in Shepheard's Hotel to the breakfast room and sought out a niche beneath the Moorish arches. Like a badger, he thought. I always like to feel there's something overhead.

As he was negotiating the fountain, he knocked a handbag off the table with his bundle of newspapers. He stooped and saw her upturned face. It occurred to him that she had been breakfasting at the same table for the past four or five days. He murmured an apology and hung the bag on the arm of her chair. "That's how it all begins in novelettes," he said quietly in English. He couldn't tell if she had understood.

Deniaux stared at her from his niche. He smoked a cigarette and waited for the familiar tug at the pit of his stomach. The big Nubian waiter who was leaning against the scrollwork of the partition, his skin dissected into whorls of light and shade by the intricate tracery, was also staring at the girl. Deniaux calculated that a line connecting the girl's head, the waiter's eyes, and his own would produce an isosceles triangle.

He guessed that she was twenty—Egyptian, too, probably. She was wearing a white costume and had her hair tied up at her neck. Deniaux leaned forward but could not see her legs. Her hands were lying motionless on the tablecloth.

She's very beautiful, Deniaux told himself. He tried to picture her in five years' time, wondering if she would run to fat. If she stops at the kiosk afterward, I'll speak to her. Perhaps she'll sleep with me tonight.

Israel's ambassador to the United Nations called on the director of the FAO's Mediterranean section and asked him to convey an offer of help from Jerusalem to the United Arab Republic. It being virtually impossible to prevent the Nile Delta from becoming contaminated with salt, the Israeli Cabinet announced its willingness to supply Cairo with full details of research carried out by the Israeli agronomist Hugo Boyko. At his experimental farm near Elath, Boyko had grown one hundred and eighty varieties of edible plants which could be irrigated with salt water. In so doing, he had taken advantage of the phenomenon whereby readily soluble sodium chloride sinks rapidly into porous, sandy soil. The water vapor retained in the pores of such soil became condensed during the cold desert nights and the salt-water film on the hair roots of the plants cracked by reason of its lower viscosity, enabling salt-free water condensate to reach the roots. Thus, the Boyko process offered means of saving the Nile Delta. Israel was advancing this proposal in a further attempt to reduce current tensions in the Near East.

The envoy added that Boyko's experiments in crossing the sea grass *Agropyrum junceum* with cereals were so far advanced that it would be quite possible to launch a large-scale pilot scheme in areas of the Nile Delta which were already contaminated.

Twenty-two members of the Egyptian Cabinet voted in favor of Gidaff's proposal to ask NASA, the U.S. space agency, to take infrared photographs of the Arabian Desert. The opponents of the scheme—seven Ministers and five junior Ministers led by General of the Air Force Fachallal—walked out immediately after the vote was taken.

The controversy was sparked off by Fachallal himself, who had strongly urged that a similar request be made to the Soviet space association, Intersputnik.

"There is a line between trying to avert national disaster and political prostitution. My own feeling is that we crossed it a long time ago. I can see no good reason why this project shouldn't be entrusted to Intersputnik. Raise doubts about the quality of Soviet reconnaissance satellites today and you may lose faith in our MIG fighters tomorrow. What would we do then—buy Phantom aircraft for Egyptian cotton? So much for one argument. Here's another. The Russians know all about our radar stations and SAM batteries in the Etbai Mountains. So do the Americans, no doubt, but that doesn't mean the Pentagon submits every last close-up to the White House. If we order these photographs from NASA, it will be an act of supreme political significance. The Nixon administration will swing into action. The President's right-hand man is a Jew. So is Mr. Ehrlichman. If the Meir woman wants to get hold of these photographs, she need only phone one of them."

Sadat picked up a quartz paperweight and brought it crashing down on the tabletop. Pink splinters flew in all directions. "Stop talking drivel, Hussein," he shouted. "The lake is on the point of overflowing, didn't you hear? Listen, for a change, or I'll fire you like Shuker." The last words were spoken quite softly: "We need those satellite pictures at once. From NASA, what's more."

Sadat shook hands with Gidaff after the meeting and walked to the lift. He was limping slightly this morning. General Fachallal, who had lingered outside in the corridor, turned away when he heard the dragging footsteps. He did not turn round again until he saw Gidaff approaching, mirrored in a pane of glass.

"I wanted to tell you something . . ."

"I suppose you left some more Jews off your list—Goldberg, for instance."

"No, not Goldberg. My friends have been taking a closer look at that professor of yours. Could you swear to it that Deniaux isn't a Jew?"

Premier Dayan was attending a reception at the Uruguayan Embassy in Jerusalem. He turned to the ambassador, Felipe Rosario, and said, "I believe you wanted to speak to me, Your Excellency."

"Yes, though it makes me feel rather like some character in a James Bond thriller. I have a message for you."

"Your balcony gives a wonderful view of Mount Scopus," said Dayan. "I'd never noticed before. Do you smoke?"

The French windows were ajar. Dayan leaned against the balustrade.

"Last night," whispered the ambassador, "we received a cable from Montevideo."

"Your cigarette's out," Dayan said. "Let me give you another light."

"The ambassador of the United Arab Republic called at our Foreign Ministry yesterday afternoon."

"Really?"

"I'm to tell you that the soil isn't porous enough."

"Not porous enough?"

"I'm quoting. It consists of silt deposits which display no evaporation effect, not sand."

"Is that all?"

"No. The ambassador says you can keep your sea grass."

"Many thanks for the information. And now, Your Excellency, that cigarette of yours . . ."

Foreign Minister Riad summoned the U.S. Ambassador in Cairo to his office at 1 p.m. and told him of the Egyptian government's intention to ask NASA for infrared satellite photographs of the Arabian Desert.

An hour later, Professor Deniaux and the girl returned from Gezira by way of the Altahrir Bridge. By the time they reached the far end, Deniaux had bought her a silver bracelet set with green scarabs. "Here," he said, putting it on her wrist, "take the thing," and tried to calculate as they walked on how many francs he had been cheated of by the dealer, who shuffled backward across the bridge in front of them, an exotic figure in his gaily colored robes and tinkling glass beads.

They went straight to his room when they reached Shepheard's. Deniaux tossed their keys onto the bedspread and went to draw the curtains. He was breathing hard. I shouldn't have drunk those two bottles of beer in the Andalos Gardens, he thought. It could be the heat as well, of course.

Down below in a side street off the Shara Elamy, he could see the Egyptian car-park attendant and his son shunting a car in and out of the gap. Deniaux had observed them every evening since his arrival. Whenever he wanted to think, he would go to the window and prop his elbows on the flaking white paint of the sill, where he could watch them push the car aside to make room for would-be parkers. Coins flashed through the air and the boy caught them one-handed. A plum job by Egyptian standards, Deniaux reflected. They support an entire family by producing parking space which already exists. Merely by shuttling a car to and fro they make enough to keep themselves in mutton, onions, and vine leaves. When the dam breaks, the whole thing will be over . . . No more

Nubian page boys hanging around in the corridors like velvet-eyed puppies. Everyone will be dead, including that man who just rode past on his bicycle with a sheep's carcass draped over the carrier, the butcher's registration number stamped in violet on its leg.

And the vendor who cheated him on the bridge . . .

The girl behind him stripped off her stockings. He heard a rustling sound and was involuntarily reminded of a snake shedding its skin.

What if a floating tree trunk caught the girl—in the temple, perhaps? No, the atmospheric pressure would get her first, inflate her lungs and burst them like seaweed bladders. And her skin was so warm, too . . . **Gidaff**, with the frightful raw bridge to his nose, would also die, doubtless on the roof of some imposing villa in Heliopolis. He would await the flood clinging to his television aerial amid a clutter of deck chairs . . .

Deniaux's room was on the third floor. He calculated the drop from the window sill to the street. The flood wave would still be forty feet high when it hit Cairo, so the Swiss newspaper estimated. Forty feet. That meant he could sleep with the girl till the boats arrived, always provided the hotel didn't collapse first. When the water had subsided a little, sailors would lay alongside a first-floor window and moor their boat to a drainpipe. Then he and the girl would descend the muddy stairs and wade along the corridor to meet their rescuers.

Maybe I'll carry her, he thought. The rooms would probably be full of dead sheep and bloated children. He'd say to her, "Close your eyes, *chérie*, I'll carry you to the boat."

Her skin had been quite warm yesterday. He had known it would be. His only surprise had come when he tore open the last button of her blouse. Her breasts had hung heavy on her belly as she sat cross-legged on the mattress. He might have guessed it when he saw her sitting at the breakfast table, but her breasts felt so cool that he had instinctively withdrawn his hand.

She had caught him by the forearm and replaced his hand between her breasts. He could still feel the skin grow taut under his palm. She had cried out once, a short, sharp cry. It would be terrible if the flood came. We must find the original bed of the Nile, Deniaux thought. He couldn't even remember what her nipples looked like.

From behind him, the girl said, "Has my professor discovered a new bauxite formation in the Shara Elamy?" She was lying naked on the bedspread. He could see her reflected in the slanting fanlight.

"What made you think of bauxite?" he asked without turning round.

"You're a geologist, aren't you? It was the first thing that occurred to me. Will you do me a favor?"

There was a gnawing sensation in his stomach. It must have been three hours since his last cigarette.

"What sort of favor?"

"Take me south to the Etbai Mountains."

"What for?"

"Find me the Queen of Sheba's emeralds. And some myrrh and coffee beans. I'd adore an espresso."

"What about an expert opinion on the Wadi Natash?" He slammed the window shut. "Anyway, who told you what my job was?"

"I asked at reception."

"Why bother when you could have looked me up in Hampton's card index? Well, what's the word from Hampton?"

"Why all this talk of Hampton?"

"Because you're spying for him. You're supposed to find out my price. And I thought you were . . ."

"You must be crazy!"

He grabbed her wrists and jerked her off the bed. Releasing her, he fumbled for his key on the bedspread, unlocked the door, and pushed her into the corridor. "Why don't you sleep with the Patton Corporation?" he shouted as he threw her dress and stockings after her.

M O N D A Y

LAKE NASSER: LEVEL RISING

Lake level: 589.71 ft. above sea level. Change: plus 1.47 ft. (Top water level: 597 ft.; crest of dam 643 ft.)

Speaking at the third symposium on flooding held at Grenoble under the auspices of the European Committee for Environmental Conservation, Professor Antoine Lefèvre, who had just returned from Aswan, declared that recent developments at Lake Nasser defied explanation. That the surface of a lake should cease to evaporate was a phenomenon unique in his experience. The rate at which the level was rising bore no relation to current inflow. "Hitherto," he said, "the annual flooding of the Nile has been occasioned by winter rainfall in the catchment area of the White Nile—that is to say, the area of the Great Lakes—and by summer rainfall in the highlands of Ethiopia, where the Blue Nile rises. According to Schiffers, the rising waters—commonly known as the 'green' waters—reach the White Nile at Khartoum early in April and the Aswan area at the beginning of June. The so-called 'red' waters of the Blue Nile arrive during July, and in mid-July both flood waves join forces in

203

the lower reaches of the Nile. Gauges in the Aswan area normally record a rise of thirty-two feet between June and September, or over a period of approximately one hundred days. Prior to regulation by the High Dam, the figure for Cairo was twenty-six feet. To quote Schiffers once more, the Nile's flow in the Aswan section increases from 18,360 cubic feet per second to 297,000 cubic feet per second. At the end of September, the flow begins to diminish.

"These phases and the relation between flow and gauge readings have now, for the first time in recorded history, been completely disrupted. The waters of Lake Nasser are rising at such an alarming rate that consideration should be given to methods of evacuating the entire population of Egypt."

A merger between the tire firms of Pirdello, Schweitzer, and Manieu was signed in Milan. The *Times* referred to the new company as one of the largest and most powerful combines in the Common Market. Earlier moves toward a merger of the three companies had been dropped in 1970 because Pirdello insisted on retaining its centrifugal molding process. It was a conversation with the U.N. Secretary-General which had prompted Antoine Grosset, managing director of Manieu, to invite his opposite numbers in Schweitzer AG and Pirdello to resume negotiations at Montreux.

Grosset explained: "We have a unique opportunity, by standardizing our production schedule, to sell twenty million inflatable boats to the United Nations. They must be delivered within six months, accommodate four to five adults, carry a week's emergency rations, and permit of automatic inflation with carbon dioxide cartridges in two to three minutes. Foolproof handling is an absolute must—to put it crudely, we should have to design them with illiterates in mind. The price mustn't exceed twenty-five dollars apiece. Planes chartered by the United Nations would drop them over the Nile Valley. Think what you like of the idea, but get this straight: if we don't join forces, the Americans will win the race . . ."

The formation of Euro-Tire was marked by a reception in Milan. Grosset, who delivered the inaugural address, said:

"It is an open secret that Operation Ark should not be regarded as anything more than a leavening agent in the new combine which was formed today. Now that the Ark production schedule has prodded us into amalgamation, we must use our combined potential to break into the American market. This is a European challenge, ladies and gentlemen. I raise my glass to Operation Ark, coupled with the name of Euro-Tire. Thank you."

Waiters opened the French windows and the curtains bellied in the night breeze. Grosset walked onto the balcony and leaned over the parapet. He felt surfeited with applause and back-slapping. Today is Monday, he thought. Simone comes back in ten days' time. We'll go to the sea and relax.

Someone appeared at his elbow and said, "Tell me, Grosset, what first gave you the idea?" He rested his glass on the marble coping.

"It was something I read in a newspaper. Some Jew in Cairo kept a rubber dinghy on the roof of his house because he had a thing about floods. I even fancy his name was Noah."

In the considered opinion of a team of scientists from Cambridge, Massachusetts, who had flown to Aswan at the invitation of the Egyptian government, the downstream side of the dam was so proportioned that it would theoretically withstand the water pressure even if the maximum permissible level of 597 feet was exceeded. The vital factor was how the filling material would behave under stress. As soon as earth pressure in the body of the dam exceeded the tolerance threshold, there was a danger that the sand and silt would lose their stability. This, in turn, would bring about the condition described by Jaecklin and Wahler of Stanford University—namely "liquefaction"—in which filling became transformed into a slush composed of sand and water.

F R I D A Y

LAKE NASSER: LEVEL RISING

Lake level: 591.07 ft. above sea level. Change: plus 1.04 ft. (Top water level: 597 ft.; crest of dam: 643 ft.)

The delegation from the Japanese Chamber of Industry and Commerce was received by Minister of Construction Ahmed Fuad that afternoon. Fuad said, "We have no time for the usual courtesies. I'm sorry, but in my opinion your scheme is utopian."

Eisaku Mitsui, President of the Chamber: "We expected this reaction. You have no need to apologize. We did not come here to do business, after all—our experiments have been financed by the Japanese Red Cross. On the other hand, if the survival of an entire nation is worth fifteen minutes of your time, you should hear what we have to say."

Fuad: "We tested your concrete models at the naval research center in Marsa Alam. The buoyancy shells do function under normal circumstances, I admit. That's to say, they float. If disaster struck, however, the water would wash over the sides. We need genuine aids to survival, not coffins."

Mitsui: "If I may draw your attention to our standard vessel—the *Nomus*. This is intended for use in villages and would accommodate thirty or forty people—five families, let's say. People would eat and sleep in their concrete shells. They could leave them to tend their fields up to a radius of several hundred yards and take refuge in them when the flood approached."

Fuad: "What matters is the buoyancy effect. Our experiments at Marsa Alam showed this to be virtually nil. The water simply flowed down the test channels and swamped the models."

Mitsui: "We have submitted the *Nomus* scheme to hydrodynamic analysis by a number of impartial authorities—the University of Cincinnati, for example. Their computations support the validity of the idea, which is quite simply based on the technique employed by any surfer. The flood wave will not surge down the entire length of the Nile Valley like a wall of water. It will flatten out after the first hundred or two hundred miles. The advance wave will shoot under the bows, lifting the shell like a surfboard. The occupants will be well afloat before the mud comes."

Fuad: "And before the water comes a blast of air. You know what that means?"

Mitsui: "No, we have been concentrating on the flood itself."

Fuad: "Quite so. Stay at the Hilton for another six months and you'll be able to witness the phenomenon at first hand."

Mitsui: "Your attitude surprises me, Minister. When may we expect a final decision?"

Fuad: "The Cabinet plans to re-examine all such schemes at the weekend. Your delegation will then be notified by the Secretary of State."

Mitsui: "What are our chances?"

Fuad: "We don't plan to buy any coffins, not even floating ones."

ASWAN!

S U N D A Y

LAKE NASSER: LEVEL RISING

    Lake level: 592.61 ft. above sea level
Change: plus 0.52 ft. (Top water level: 597
ft.; crest of dam: 643 ft.)

EARTH PRESSURE IN BODY OF DAM: INCREASING
(tolerance: 21 kg/cm^2)

Pressure gauges	A	B	C	D	E
kg/cm^2	19.36	18.17	18.99	9.31	13.29
Change	+0.04	+0.03	+0.03	+0.02	+0.04

SEEPAGE VELOCITY: CONSTANT

Near the village of El Ghayata in the Nile Delta, a forty-two-year-old peasant named Ahmed Fawzi collapsed beside the road on his way home from the fields. He was found writhing convulsively by the driver of an oxcart and taken back to his hut on a load of maize straw. Fawzi temporarily regained consciousness but was unable to speak. That afternoon, having bedded him down on some blankets in the aisle of the bus which plied twice daily between El Ghayata and Kafr el Dawar, his sons took him to the district hospital.

Fawzi had to be strapped to a stretcher while being examined. The doctors found signs of severe thirst, although his sons declared that he had drunk tea that morning as usual. When he was brought back from the fields and cried out for water, they had given him some mango juice.

The sick man arched his body under the leather straps and snapped at the medical assistant who was trying to take a specimen of his saliva. Although he temporarily reacted to the doctors' questions, he was unable to urinate into a bottle.

A nurse bent over the stretcher from behind as Fawzi rolled aside and inserted a cannula under his shoulder blade to draw off some tissue fluid.

"Clean again, clean again . . ." muttered the dying man.

The medical assistant asked his sons if they had ever seen him trying to lick crystallized salt off clods of earth.

The two youths replied that they had never seen him eat salt while working in the fields.

"Water," Fawzi muttered, "clean . . ."

Half an hour after the autopsy was complete, the medical superintendant of Kafr el Dawar hospital telephoned the Governor of Alexandria and informed him that the peasant Ahmed Fawzi of El Ghayata had died in a frenzy after licking crystallized salt off his fields.

"He died this afternoon. I'm sure his trouble was correctly diagnosed."

"What makes you so positive?" asked the Governor.

"I heard of a similar case at Shirbin two weeks ago. That's why I called you."

"If it's true and people get to hear about it, they'll go berserk. It isn't just mass hysteria any more—they're killing themselves. Tomorrow we'll have the students of Alexandria and Mansura breathing down our necks."

"It was a difficult case to diagnose at first. There's no medical precedent that I can recall—I mean, of someone eating salt in a frenzy until he dies. The human organism would normally protect itself."

"You say these people die of thirst?"

"In a sense. They become dehydrated."

That evening, the Governor had a hectographed memorandum sent to all district military headquarters and hospitals instructing them to be on the lookout for an increase in halophagy among the farming population in the next few days. "These cases are accompanied by delusions, because patients believe that they must continue to ingest sodium chloride from their fields until they have purified the allegedly contaminated soil. The illness follows the same course as cases of severe thirst and should be treated accordingly. The extracellular spaces in the human organism—in other words, those containing tissue fluids—hold twenty percent of the salt content of the human body. If the cells become saturated with salt, tissue fluid diffuses through the cell walls in accordance with the laws of osmosis and reduces the proportion of extracellular tissue fluid in the body. The salt content of the cells will combine with so much water that the affected person becomes, to all intents and purposes, dehydrated. Should any such cases occur, use must be made of conventional methods which have hitherto been employed in treating cases of polydipsia: increased water intake, coupled with the administering of preparations which increase renal activity. All cases of this nature are subject to the military pledge of secrecy."

According to particulars on the death certificate issued to the local authorities at El Ghayata, Ahmed Fawzi died of complications following an epileptic seizure.

The U.S. satellite Samos 19, which had been placed in an elliptical orbit over latitude 26°N. on New Year's Day, received a radio signal from ground station Rota, Spain, at 19.21.06 hours W.E.T. The impulse was stored in the satellite's computer and at 19.22.09 hours opened the shutter of its Zeiss-Ikon camera, thus recording on infrared film the thermal values of an area bounded by latitudes 27° and 36°N. and longitudes 32° and 35°E. The film was developed on board the satellite. The negative, examined when the satellite was recovered eight months later, disclosed a pale fan-shaped trace which branched off the Nile Valley south of Aswan, followed the Wadi Natash, skirted the eastern slopes of Mount Musirab, passed through the Wadi Gimal, and ended in the Red Sea.

Five orbits later, while the satellite was passing over Dallas, Texas, its computer ejected the capsule containing the infrared print. Two Phantom jets took off from U.S.A.F. base Andrea Five, New Mexico, and at twenty-five thousand feet extended their hydraulic nose hooks in readiness to retrieve the film capsule as it descended by parachute.

The cylinder had somersaulted on ejection and spun so severely that the traces became entangled and prevented its parachute from opening properly. It corkscrewed off course and struck a coral reef near the Caribbean island of Saint Alban.

The silk caught on a jagged rock. The radio beacon continued to chirp for another six hours and was picked up by a radio ham at Port Alvarez. By evening the batteries were exhausted.

Three days later, the wind plucked the parachute silk free and carried the capsule out into the bay. Sea water seeped through the fractured plastic cylinder and destroyed the film inside.

The loss of the film was reported to the Egyptian Ambassador in Washington by NASA director Brooks the same evening.

"We're truly sorry, Your Excellency. We know how much those pictures meant to you."

"My government took the precaution of asking for the experiment to be repeated if necessary."

"We can't try again until October. Samos 19 has run out of infrared film. Samos 20 is scheduled for launching in a few weeks' time."

ASWAN!

Next morning, General Fachallal telephoned Secretary of State Tewfik at the Ministry of the Interior.

"I knew it from the start. Nixon's crafty Jewboys have been celebrating all night, gloating over our films and slapping their fat thighs with glee."

The Minister pulled a yellow memorandum pad toward him while Fachallal was speaking. After he had hung up, he made the following note: "10:10. F. called. Sounded drunk."

A representative of Nazareth Iron United, Boston, called at the Egyptian Ministry of the Interior to submit specifications for a survival tower. The polyester model of the prototype, scaled to one-twentieth, was molded in four sections and stuck together with synthetic resin.

The survival aid which Nazareth Iron had developed for the population of Lower Egypt took the form of a platform mounted on three stilts and accessible by ladder. The steel floor could accommodate forty-five to fifty refugees.

As the board of Nazareth Iron stressed in its covering letter:

> The design of our survival tower takes account of recent discoveries in the field of aerodynamics and hydrodynamics. Its structure is based on the drilling-rig principle. Since the main stress may be expected to come from one direction only, we can guarantee sufficient stability to withstand the flooding that would follow the collapse of the High Dam.
>
> The survival tower is designed to resist a flood wave from thirty to, at most, forty feet high, and is thus intended predominantly for the populated area between Cairo and the coast—in other words, for an area where the flood wave has emerged from the narrows and begun to fan out across the Delta. Other survival systems—e.g., hydraulic platforms which can be jacked up the banks on tracks—must be developed with all speed.
>
> Assuming that the flood wave attains a height of thirty-five feet at Cairo, twenty-two feet at Tanta, sixteen feet at Mansura,

212

and eight feet when it reaches the coast, the height and thus the cost of the towers can be graduated accordingly.

For and on behalf of the Board,

WILLIAM D. MIRIATH

Boston, July 12   President

Gidaff stood staring at the plastic tower which had been mounted on a sheet of blockboard beside the south window of his office in the Ministry of the Interior. His fingers, which had been interlaced behind his back, snapped apart. His right hand came up and swept the glasses off his nose.

"That's the platform," said his deputy, "up there on top of the stilts. People are supposed to take refuge on it as soon as the sirens sound."

"How many ladders?"

"One to each stilt, so they can converge on the tower from all directions. I checked with the blueprints."

"A ghastly thought."

"I think we ought to discuss it in Cabinet. The Americans are waiting at the Semiramis."

Bending over the model, Gidaff inadvertently stubbed his cigarette on it. He saw the plastic discolor, melt, and break out in small white pustules as the glowing end bit into the platform.

"I find it gruesome, the whole idea. A steady decline in costs the further north we site the towers. According to their calculations, we can save two hundred lives at Mansura for every hundred people we leave to drown in Cairo."

Acrid smoke rose from the smoldering ember.

"Even so, we ought to submit it for Cabinet consideration," Gidaff's deputy said, and shrugged. "I couldn't take the responsibility for turning it down myself."

"What did they say about total cost?"

"Calculations are still incomplete. Mr. Liechtenstein said this morning that it largely depends on special equipment. Water filters and so on."

The glasses rotated round Gidaff's right forefinger. "A nation of undertakers," he murmured. The little bubbles on the sheet of plastic had congealed.

T U E S D A Y

LAKE NASSER: LEVEL RISING

Lake level: 593.63 ft. above sea level. Change: plus 0.62 ft. (Top water level: 597 ft.; crest of dam: 643 ft.)

An emergency meeting of the Egyptian Cabinet instructed Gidaff to obtain provisional estimates from Nazareth Iron United. He invited Nazareth Iron's senior representative, John Liechtenstein, to visit the Ministry at 2 p.m. and then put through a special priority call to the U.A.R. trade mission in Washington.

Pakistan's ambassador in Cairo wrote a personal letter to Foreign Minister Aya requesting his immediate recall. He explained that, according to information current in U.S. diplomatic circles, the collapse of the High Dam could be expected within the next fortnight. The commander of the 3rd Eskadra had already made preparations to evacuate the Soviet colony from Egypt. The operation would be camouflaged as a naval visit to mark the fifteenth anniversary of the Soviet-Egyptian treaty of friendship. Embassy staff would be summoned to Alexandria in a week's time, ostensibly to prepare for the festivities, and would later be taken aboard the destroyer *Krupskaya*. Seventy Russian advisers had already left Aswan and gone to visit geological field-research camps on the desert plateau. It was even rumored that a young attaché at the Danish Embassy had engineered his repatriation by infecting himself with tubercle bacilli purchased from a technician at the Quasr Eleni Hospital. The ambassador's letter concluded with the following words: "In the prevailing situation, subterfuges can benefit neither our own government nor that of the United Arab Republic. This being so, I formally request my recall. I do not propose to put myself or my family at risk for the sake of an utterly futile gesture of solidarity."

Professor Nuredin Saber, lecturer in marine biology at Mansura University, was flown to Heliopolis in a Ministry helicopter to give the President a progress report on research into developments at Aswan. The conference took place in the projection room of the President's villa, because Saber had brought diagrams and colored slides with him from Lake Nasser. It was attended by Minister of the Interior Gidaff, Defense Minister Nachram, General Boghdadi, and Secretary-General Sidki.

Saber began by stating that the steady rise in the level of Lake Nasser was attributable neither to an increase in the Nile's flow nor to the sealing of subterranean fissures. The President was perceptibly nervous, and interrupted Saber's opening remarks to snap at Gidaff, who was pacing to and fro between the rows of seats with his arms folded.

"Sit down, for God's sake. And tell them to put the lights out."

"I'd like to make one more point before we come to the slides," Saber said. "Assuming that the lake level is rising independently of any developments in the drainage basins of the Blue and White Niles, a total area of over 1,100,000 square miles—"

215

Sadat broke in again. "We know it isn't raining in the Ethiopian highlands. We also know that Lake Victoria hasn't overflowed yet. The question is, why has the water stopped evaporating?"

"If I may be permitted just one more interpolation: basing my estimates on changes in the gauge readings at Aswan—"

"In other words," said Sadat, "on the fact that the lake is rising."

"I calculate," continued Saber, "that the lake would still be rising even if we hadn't sealed the aquifers between Aswan and the Red Sea. That gives you some idea of the rate."

"I'm still waiting to hear why the water has stopped evaporating," said Sadat.

"There are three possibilities. As I explained in my last report, a sort of film—rather like an oil slick, for argument's sake—is resting on the surface of the lake and has suddenly inhibited the process of evaporation."

"And is that as far as you've got?" asked Nachram.

"Of course not. We're working on the assumption that an alien substance is coating the surface. Its specific gravity must necessarily be less than that of water, it is invisible because no optical reflexes are apparent, and it clearly retains its sealing properties when diluted to an almost unimaginable degree, or we should already have isolated it by chemical analysis."

Sadat frowned. "That goes without saying, I hope."

"Theoretically, this substance may inhibit evaporation in any one of three ways. First, though, I must say something about the principle of evaporation. Evaporation is the process whereby a substance passes from the liquid to the gaseous state without necessarily coming to the boil."

"We've yet to reach that stage at Aswan," observed Gidaff.

"The molecules on the surface of the liquid escape into the atmosphere. This results from an input of energy—sunlight, in our case. Energy must be exerted because the molecules lying on the surface are not surrounded on all sides by neighboring molecules. All the molecular forces which act on these surface molecules emanate from the interior of the liquid. It follows that there must be a force which in some degree binds the molecules to the surface. This is surface tension, which insures, among other things, that free-falling water assumes a geometrical shape of minimal surface area—namely, the sphere or droplet. It also follows that in order to overcome these internally directed molecular forces and detach molecules from the surface of a liquid, energy must be expended. Stefan's rule states that surface tension increases in proportion to the strength of intermolecular forces. It decreases, in accordance with Eötvös's rule, as the temperature rises. It is only marginally dependent on local gaseous pressure but is strongly affected by impurities in the liquid. This may well be a contributory factor at Aswan.

"I spoke of three possibilities. The first and least likely is that this film which coats the surface of the lake, evidently in monomolecular strength, may have the effect of filtering thermal energy from the air. I called it unlikely because the substance would itself have to evaporate at some stage if it continued to store energy without interruption.

"The second possibility is equally unlikely. This may be that the lake water and the substance coating it are held together by special forces of adhesion, like a liquid between two superimposed sheets of glass.

"The third and last hypothesis, on which we have been concentrating at Mansura in the past few days, is based on cohesion—on the attraction between the atoms and molecules that go to make up liquid and solid bodies. It is not beyond the bounds of possibility that the alien substance on the surface of Lake Nasser is affecting the molecular forces of the water, and consequently its surface tension, in such a way that virtually no molecule can detach itself . . ."

Saber went to the table to fetch a diagram of a water molecule, but Sadat rose with a murmured apology. He left the projection room and sat down in front of the teleprinter in his aide's office, waiting for the next readings from Aswan.

Basing their calculations on a minimum delivery of five hundred thousand survival towers, Nazareth Iron United estimated that a single twenty-two-foot tower would cost ten thousand dollars. Included in this price were erection costs, an automatic warning system which would summon people to take refuge before the flood wave arrived, filtering equipment for the preparation of drinking water, an emergency power supply, a first-aid post, seven inflatable boats per tower, chlorine chambers for the storing of dead bodies, a public-address system, and a ten-day survival store containing vitamin extracts, dehydrated protein and carbohydrate products, blankets, and plastic eating utensils.

The cost of each tower would increase by two thousand dollars for every three feet in excess of the base figure.

S U N D A Y

LAKE NASSER: LEVEL RISING

Lake level: 594.68 ft. above sea level. Change: plus 0.39 ft. (Top water level: 597 ft.; crest of dam: 643 ft.)

The Egyptian commercial attaché in Washington was instructed by the Ministry of the Interior in Cairo to inform Nazareth Iron United that Project Survival Tower had been

218

turned down. The government of the United Arab Republic was unable, for technical and financial reasons, to adopt the scheme.

The Sudanese newspaper *Omdurman Herald,* quoting sources close to the U.N. special representative Count Hengström, predicted that the High Dam would break even before the advent of the rainy season. The editorial of the morning edition read as follows:

"It now seems that there is no way of preventing what has long been dismissed as unthinkable. This leads one to ask which African country should inherit the bitter legacy of such a disaster. Whether this question should be raised before or after the flood is a matter of tact and delicacy, but raised it must be—and, in the interests of the Sudanese nation, not too late.

"If our Egyptian brethren cease to exist, over 386,000 square miles of territory will lie vacant, awaiting worthy heirs. They will inherit a desert, but a desert which the flood has once more coated with life-bringing mud. They will inherit an abode of blood and tears—tears not least because the people of Nubia have suffered there throughout the ages: under the overseer's whip in the quarries of the Pharaohs, under the arrogance of British imperialists, and, more recently, under the arbitrary dominion of an Arab ruling class.

"Africa is a black continent, black as our own skins. Africa belongs to Africans, not to pale-skinned Arabs, who have always, in their heart of hearts, remained alien to this part of the globe. They are foreigners who pass themselves off as rulers, just as they did in our own country before the Great Revolution. If our Nubian sons and brothers return to Egypt, it will not be as bellhops and doormen. They it will be who once more cultivate the neglected soil to the natural, fructifying rhythm of a mighty river which has burst its man-made bonds."

The same day, Libya's ambassador in Khartoum requested an interview with President Agal. He was informed that the President would be opening a new pumping station at El Manquil that afternoon, and was referred to Foreign Minister Shuchawi. After cabling his government, the Libyan envoy left Khartoum on a scheduled flight of Ethiopian Airlines.

Addressing a rally in Benghazi that evening, the president of the Libyan Revolutionary Council, Colonel Qadhafi, said: "We shall never join forces with the pack of ghouls who gloat over every drop of water that brings the High Dam closer to collapse. Nevertheless, when the hour of decision comes, our nation will know how to assert its sacred claim to Arab soil."

Qadhafi spoke from the hood of a jeep. He put his hands on his hips and surveyed the delirious mob that surged round him. "Libya is a big country," he said quietly. "We lay no claim to a square inch of foreign territory. If we fight for Egypt, it will be in the name of Pan-Arabism alone. As long as I still lead our Government of National Progress, no Nubian will ever set foot on the soil of an Arab brotherland. If we stand together, all who mask their primitive origins beneath a veneer of Islam will be driven back to the place from which they once crept forth—the African bush!"

In Cairo, Ambassador Raymond Boothe called on Minister Gidaff and told him that the U.S. government was prepared to meet 35 percent of the cost of implementing Project Survival Tower. The board of the World Bank was currently studying the terms of an international loan.

Appearing on an evening television program in Boston, Senator Kennedy declared that the survival system developed by Nazareth Iron United offered every country an opportunity of saving the Egyptian nation from the greatest catastrophe in human history by manufacturing the towers under license. The Senate of the Free and Hanseatic City of Bremen resolved at an emergency session to finance the construction of two survival towers in the neighborhood of Mansura. In London, a spokesman for the oil concessionaire Kaneki Moutafian announced that Mr. Moutafian planned to present the government of the United Arab Republic with three survival towers for erection within the city limits of Alexandria. Senator Goldwater and the president of the American labor federation A.F.L.-C.I.O. jointly sponsored a dinner at Sacramento, California, whose proceeds were to be devoted to the construction of survival towers in Port Said.

The Sheik of Hadhramaut cabled instructions to the Pollop Agency of Bristol to prepare a series of postage stamps entitled "Survival Tower."

The press agency MENA announced that the government of the United Arab Republic had decided to go ahead with the Nazareth Iron project. The announcement was withdrawn just before midnight. An hour later, Radio Cairo reported that the Cabinet had never even considered the implementation of such a scheme. Earlier reports were presumably due to deliberate misinformation on the part of American business interests.

The Venice office of the Banco del Santo Spirito informed the relevant department of the Sudanese State Bank by cable that there was no reason why traveler's checks issued in the name of Dr. Mario Angelo, born April 14, 1918, resident at Calle del Cristo 6065A, Venice, should not be honored.

ASWAN!

The government of the United Arab Republic instructed Nazareth Iron to erect four survival towers at a test site on Egyptian territory and subject them to stress by an artificial flood wave. The site proposed for the experiment was a valley near Beni Khalid, east of the Joseph Canal.

In a telex message to the Egyptian Embassy in Washington, Nazareth Iron replied that the test installations, including temporary dam and wind machines, would take at least eight weeks to complete.

That evening, Minister Gidaff invited the senior representative of the Boston firm, John Liechtenstein, to dinner at the club of the Egyptian Chamber of Commerce.

"Personally," he told Liechtenstein, "I'm dubious of a firm which plans to sell enough survival towers to accommodate twenty million people but finds it hard to build four of them in a matter of weeks. After its experiences with the High Dam, my government declines to adopt any scheme that hasn't been thoroughly tested. We refuse to be rushed into anything. We're well aware that we shall have to meet the cost of every dud investment we make, down to the last piaster, once the present boom in pro-Egyptian sentiment has waned."

A Boeing chartered by Nazareth Iron United took off from Boston at 11:10 p.m. local time, bound for Cairo via Rome. On board were President William D. Miriath, chief engineers Milton Ferryman and Jack Harper, and thirty-seven technicians. In San Francisco, talks on cooperation opened between Nazareth Iron, the Rockwell Steel Company, and a consortium of Japanese steel producers.

T H U R S D A Y

LAKE NASSER: LEVEL RISING

Lake level: 595.92 ft. above sea level.
Change: plus 0.68 ft. (Top water level: 597
ft.; crest of dam: 643 ft.)

Four survival towers took shape on Nazareth Iron's test site west of Beni Khalid, linked by footbridges at platform height and capable of accommodating two hundred refugees. The upper reaches of the valley were sealed off by a concrete dam, forming a reservoir into which American technicians had so far pumped over 7,060,000 cubic feet of water from the Joseph Canal.

After a second tour of inspection, Gidaff announced that he was willing to forgo the installation of wind machines on the slopes overlooking the valley. Instead, Egyptian army engineers sank four tons of dynamite into the ridges on either side of the reservoir. The charges were to be detonated at an interval of 0.5 second so as to simulate air blast. Test buildings of mud brick encircled the four survival towers over a radius of two hundred yards. The distance between the mock fields bordering the village and the nearest survival tower could be covered at a trot in less than two minutes. The fields and the tracks leading into the experimental village were outlined in brick dust and sawdust, respectively.

A week before the test, Gidaff made another tour of inspection at Beni Khalid.

"I'd like to emphasize once more," he told Liechtenstein, "that your company bears full responsibility for this thing. Your scheme is fundamentally sound—I see that now—but the introduction of Peace Corpsmen is an unjustifiable risk."

ASWAN!

"The suggestion came from us. We want to run through the whole sequence under realistic conditions. Besides, they're all volunteers."

"Even if you chased convicted criminals up the towers, it wouldn't—"

"My company wants to demonstrate the procedure *in toto* before it sells you a single tower."

"The Cabinet sees no point in using human guinea pigs. Our only concern is to make sure the towers stand up."

"The members of my board—"

"All right, but I'll say it again—the responsibility is yours. When are the youngsters due to arrive?"

"Middle East Airlines will land them in Cairo tomorrow midday. If the coaches are there on time, they should be in Beni Khalid by nightfall. By then, we shall have installed the television cameras, three daylight and two infrared, in case you want to carry out the test at night. You'll be able to monitor the whole proceedings from your Ministry by the day after tomorrow at latest."

They were standing on the track at the foot of the dam. Above them, pneumatic drills started up as army engineers sank shot holes into the concrete. As they walked back across the rails to the experimental village, Gidaff stumbled. Either he's drunk or he can't judge the distance between the sleepers, thought Liechtenstein. He said, "You can have three infrared cameras if you like."

"Could we run through the whole thing once more?" Gidaff said. "I left your list in the car. The test begins with—"

"As I told you, the Peace Corps volunteers are expected here tomorrow night. That's when it really starts. They've all been trained in advance."

"How much water will there be in the reservoir by Thursday night?"

224

"If the pumps hold out, over 27,550,000 cubic feet. We had trouble with the local governor the day before yesterday. Water shortage."

"So I heard," murmured Gidaff.

"Over 27,550,000 cubic feet. Given the dimensions of the valley, it means we can flood the test site to a depth of twenty-two feet. We've allowed for an initial wave thirty-six feet high, but that's an outside estimate. The test ought to take place within the next ten days."

"Isn't the preliminary phase rather pointless?"

"My board members don't think so. The Corpsmen will live here in the test huts and move about like Egyptian villagers. No sleeping bags, no radios, just the normal rhythm of existence. Mornings and late afternoons, they'll spend in the fields. In the evening, they'll sit outside their huts. We plan to simulate Egyptian village life in every detail, as you'll see when you're sitting in front of your monitors in Cairo. That's important because of the timing. You can start the flood any time, either at night or when they're working in the fields by day."

"Always assuming I press the button sometime and your four tons of dynamite go up. Always assuming the circuit doesn't—"

"We're taking no chances. The moment you detonate, you'll have simulated the atmospheric blast which would precede the flood in the event of a real disaster at Aswan. Atmospheric waves will activate the acoustic sensors on the four survival towers, the diaphragms will produce a short circuit, and the low-tension circuits will be interrupted. In other words, the switches will drop and set off the sirens."

"It makes me shudder to think of it," said Gidaff.

"Don't forget there are four independent alarm systems. One siren would be enough to wake the entire village, quite apart from the sound of the charges going off. There are twenty-four diaphragms and twelve sirens, and only one diaphragm has to respond."

"What about the lights?"

"Let's assume the ignition switches don't work and the diesel generators fail to start. In that case, the stand-by circuit will automatically switch to the dry-cell batteries beneath the platforms. The lights'll burn for six to eight hours."

Beads of sweat gathered on Gidaff's forehead.

I do believe he'll back out at the last minute, thought the American.

A blue cloud spurted into the air above the south bank of the reservoir. A moment later, the valley rang to the sound of an explosion.

"When do I blow up the dam itself?" asked Gidaff. He dropped his glasses in the dust.

"We're dependent on estimates, of course—my company has stressed that from the outset. Our assumption is that atmospheric blast and flood wave will hit the town of Aswan almost simultaneously. After sixty-five miles, the interval between blast and flood may have lengthened to two or two and a half minutes. It all depends on the sensors, because the water will propel the wave of air ahead of it, and the blast will, in turn, propel a build-up of air in their direction."

"But not with the same intensity," said Gidaff.

"Of course not. People in the path of the flood will feel an intermittent breeze to begin with, as though they were sitting on a swing. The breeze will become a wind, light at first but growing stronger every second. Birds will take to the air, cattle tug at their halters, roofs begin to shake. And then the roar of the blast itself—a sound like thunder, I guess."

"There'll be hundreds of false alarms, especially when the khamsin blows. In the end, the peasants won't bother to run to their towers at all."

"My company is still working on that. The U.S. Air Force

has assigned twelve experts to our aerodynamic research center at Brewhill. However, what matters is the towers themselves."

"Of course," Gidaff said wearily, "especially to Nazareth Iron. Very well, so I set off the blast wave. How long before I blow up the dam?"

"We've worked out some tables for you—only based on estimates, of course. You'll be quite safe if you give the people seven or eight minutes. We've even tried it out at walking pace. It takes five minutes to reach the nearest survival tower from the outlying fields. If the balloon goes up at night, they'll be out of their huts in half that time. The men and women will simply grab their plastic dolls and run for it. We reckoned on three or four infants per hut, and they'd all have to be carried up the ladders."

Perhaps I won't blow up the dam at all, thought Gidaff. His glasses were powdered with fine dust. Liechtenstein's voice sounded very remote.

"You'll see, Minister. The youngsters will be perched in their towers with minutes to spare, waiting for the water to shoot underneath. Then it'll all be over and they can climb down again."

Gidaff groped for a handkerchief. "You mentioned something about dolls. Was that why you tried to phone me the other day?"

"Yes, customs released them twenty-four hours later—your deputy got us an import license. We've already distributed them around the huts."

"Has it ever occurred to you that the refugees may panic and fight to get at the ladders, that they may even . . ."

"You want me to be frank, Minister?"

"Naturally."

"If you want the truth," Liechtenstein said, "I dreamed about that last night."

ASWAN!

. . .

Reconnaissance planes of NATO's Mediterranean Command sighted five old Liberty ships south of Cyprus. They were flying the Ceylonese flag and appeared to be sailing in convoy. Admiral Paoli notified NATO headquarters in Brussels the same evening.

The letter posted in Khartoum by Dr. Mario Angelo reached the New York office of the U.N. Secretary-General and was duly filed. Dr. Angelo had written:

Dear Secretary-General,

Having already sent you two letters which remain unanswered, permit me to make one final observation. You are not, of course, responsible for everything that goes on inside the Food and Agriculture Organization. Far be it from me to reproach you in any way, but if you knew what has happened in Khartoum you would find the knowledge hard to endure. I will not elaborate. Could you, however, see to it that the next Congress on World Hunger does not open with a working dinner? By so doing, you would deliver the world, if not from hardship, at least from a blatant piece of cynicism.

Sincerely yours,

Mario Angelo

The Egyptian Cabinet finally decided to drop plans to evacuate the population to the desert plateaus on either side of the Nile Valley. Cabinet members took the view that provisioning of refugees in desert areas would inevitably break down after two days at most. All efforts should therefore be centered on the establishment of survival systems in densely populated areas.

It was nightfall. Gidaff had closed the door of his office and was waiting in front of the monitor screens for the techni-

cians at Beni Khalid to switch to infrared. Beneath the monitors glowed the two detonator keys inscribed "ATMOSPHERIC
BLAST" and "DAM." An electrical timing device was built into
the base of the instrument panel.

Gidaff went back to his desk and fetched the tabulated
figures. Then he sat down in the swivel chair and stared at
the screens. In the left-hand monitor, he recognized Liechtenstein in the twilight, walking back from the dam toward
a group of pseudo-villagers. Gidaff said to himself, He must
think I'm afraid; otherwise he wouldn't be spending every
day at the test site. The Minister braced his left foot against
the parquet and swung the swivel chair to the right. He
pulled himself erect by the armrests and bent over the central screen, patting his pockets in search of cigarettes.

Liechtenstein had walked over to a mud hut and was
squatting on the threshold sharing a can of tea with a fair-
haired girl. He threw a stick over the roof and urged the dog
beside him to run after it.

Gidaff remembered the dog. It had come limping down
the slope toward them on his second or third visit to the
test site and refused to be chased away.

Gidaff's fingers crushed the empty cigarette packet. His
secretary had already gone home.

If the dog isn't back inside two minutes, I'll do it tonight,
he thought. The hand of the clock moved forward with a
jerk. Gidaff went to the door and bumped his forehead on
the paneling as he unlatched the chain. He eventually found
some cigarettes in the second drawer of his secretary's desk.

Or if the dog comes back without the stick, he thought.
They're all waiting, I suppose. It must be hard for them to
sleep. Suppose the sensors don't work . . . Gidaff subsided
into the swivel chair.

Liechtenstein had wedged the can between his knees and
was smoking. The girl disappeared into the mud hut and

came back with a blanket. Gidaff swung the chair around and scanned the left-hand monitor for the dog. They've even hung their flag from the tower, he noted. The chair swung back. On the center screen, Liechtenstein flipped his cigarette end onto the mud track that led past the hut.

Infrared, Gidaff reflected. That's how the Israelis spot our snipers. He wondered why they hadn't equipped the site with any charcoal grills.

The dog trotted diagonally into view from the bottom left corner of the screen. I just can't do it, he told himself. Not tonight. Maybe tomorrow morning, when the others are here. I ought to phone the Semiramis and warn the Nazareth people. His left forefinger shot out and pressed the button of the stopwatch. Abruptly, the sweep hand returned to zero.

He threw his cigarette into the night, spat after the glowing end, and slammed the window shut.

At 10:21 a.m. local time, John Liechtenstein, general representative of Nazareth Iron United, was standing beside the north leg of Survival Tower No. 3 with his hand on the ladder that ran up it. In a mud hut on the western outskirts of the village, philosophy student Edward Maddox, twenty-one, of Atlanta, Georgia, was rolling a sheet of paper into his typewriter. Nurse Ann Mayor, nineteen, of Granite City, Illinois, had just turned the valve of a propane cooker and sent gas hissing into the burner. The girl who had shared a can of tea with Liechtenstein the night before was reaching for her Alice band.

The dog stirred in its sleep.

In the hut below Survival Tower No. 2, water was boiling in an aluminum saucepan.

Mechanic Arthur Donovan, forty-three, of Springfield, Massachusetts, was tightening a two-inch bolt. His wrench slipped and fell into the dust.

Sociologist Ralph Abigail, thirty-three, of Florence, South Carolina, was neatly folding a handkerchief.

Twenty-nine members of the Peace Corps were out in the mock fields beneath sun umbrellas. They were sitting in canvas chairs, reading. Four Nazareth Iron technicians and two Peace Corpsmen were sprawled on air mattresses in the shade at the foot of the dam.

Three men were sitting on a stack of timber playing dice. The party in the fields had a number of plastic dolls lying in the sand beside their canvas chairs.

Student Mary Aitken, nineteen, of Bardstown, Kentucky, was balancing on a rail. The dog's legs twitched.

At 10:21 a.m. local time, in his Cairo office, Minister of the Interior Gidaff pressed the key marked "ATMOSPHERIC BLAST."

Dr. Angelo's coffin was put on board a freight plane of Middle East Airlines and flown from Khartoum to Cairo-Heliopolis. It was then transferred to a storage depot, because, thanks to an oversight on the part of the Sudanese Transport Ministry, the death certificate and other documentation had been sent back to the Italian Embassy in Khartoum.

Half an hour before the charges were detonated, Gidaff invited his deputy, counterespionage chief Ewal Hamid, two female secretaries, and seven executives of Nazareth Iron to join him in his office.

When interrogated at midday, they all testified on oath that the Minister had correctly operated the key marked "ATMOS-PHERIC BLAST." They further stated that they were grouped around him in front of the monitor screens.

.   .   .

231

Gidaff jerked his hand back when the secretary screamed. Almost subconsciously, he noted that the stopwatch had sprung to life.

The girl put her hands over her ears and screamed again. Gidaff straightened his left leg in an attempt to swivel the chair. As he was turning to look at the girl, his eye caught one of the screens and saw the concrete apron fold up.

For a moment, the wall of water seemed to hang poised in midair. Then it bellied in the middle and spray exploded over the rocks.

The men on the air mattresses raised their heads.

The girl on the rail stumbled.

The dice rolled out of the cup. The dog leaped to its feet. Water surged down the valley. Liechtenstein hauled himself two rungs up the ladder before the flood wave tore his legs away. A roof skated across the boiling surface, the youngsters tumbled from their canvas chairs, the dog raced down the village street and somersaulted as the wave hit him, the secretary screamed again, and the television images danced as a wall of water thundered against the survival towers. One of the Americans pushed Gidaff aside and inverted a wastepaper basket over the "DAM" key, showering the Minister with scraps of paper. Sun umbrellas whirled through the air. Gidaff cried out as two arms emerged from a vortex of water. The dog was tossed into the air. Someone struck the secretary across the mouth with the back of his hand. Gidaff slumped forward, striking his head on the stopwatch. The dogs was again thrown into the air by the flood and fell back with its legs retracted. Gidaff felt a moment's astonishment that he was capable of registering so much detail. The vibration of the television images dwindled. Scraps of clothing and rucksacks floated past; a man crawled to the crest of the south bank, flopped on his stomach, and lay staring into the valley. The secretary sobbed. Gidaff reflected that the towers must still be standing or the cameras would have gone. Roof timbers and palm fronds shot to the surface. Four or five bodies sank from view and reappeared, tumbling over and over. "I'm going out of my mind," Gidaff said aloud. An arm broke the surface and the girl started to scream again. The shattered base of the dam came into view on the left-hand monitor, also an overturned crane with its stays entangled in the rocks. The hand of the stopwatch scurried around the dial. Gidaff groaned. Two corpses were hanging from one of the towers. The girl whimpered. The man on the bank slid down the slope on his knees. Like that lame dog, Gidaff thought.

WEDNESDAY

LAKE NASSER: LEVEL RISING

Lake level: 596.84 ft. above sea level. Change: plus 0.36 ft. (Top water level: 597 ft.; crest of dam: 643 ft.)

PORE-WATER PRESSURE IN BODY OF DAM: INCREASING (tolerance: 11 kg/cm^2)

Main piezometers	A	B	C	D	E
kg/cm^2	9.03	9.24	8.92	6.89	7.02
Change	+0.05	+0.03	+0.02	+0.04	+0.04

EARTH PRESSURE IN BODY OF DAM: INCREASING (tolerance: 21 kg/cm^2)

Pressure gauges	A	B	C	D	E
kg/cm^2	19.67	18.64	19.02	10.50	14.12
Change	+0.07	+0.07	+0.06	+0.07	+0.07

ASWAN!

SEEPAGE VELOCITY: SLIGHTLY INCREASING

In alluvium   (tolerance: 9 thousandths
(subterranean)   of a mm/sec)

West bank	Valley center	East bank
5.9 thou- sandths of a mm/sec	5.8 thou- sandths of a mm/sec	6.0 thou- sandths of a mm/sec

Change
+0.004   +0.005   +0.006

In apron   (tolerance: 5 thousandths
of dam   of a mm/sec)

West section	Dam center	East section
3.6 thou- sandths of a mm/sec	3.9 thou- sandths of a mm/sec	3.9 thou- sandths of a mm/sec

Change
+0.002   +0.004   +0.003

SEEPAGE OUTFLOW: SLIGHTLY INCREASING

Drain well A	3.3	Drain well B	4.2
	1/sec		1/sec
Change	+0.3		+0.4

The board of inquiry appointed by President Anwar el Sadat discovered, while checking the cables linking the Ministry of the Interior in Cairo with the test site near Beni Khalid, that the team of American technicians at the Atfih substation had switched two terminals. The board stated: "The electrical impulse which should have detonated the dynamite charges on the banks, thus simulating atmospheric blast, was inadvertently transmitted to the shot holes in the dam itself. Conversely, manipulation of the key marked 'DAM' would have detonated the charges of dynamite in the banks."

. . .

Minister of the Interior Gidaff was transferred by Red Crescent ambulance from Cairo's Northern District Military Hospital to the Behman Clinic for Nervous Diseases at Helwan. "I saw it," he muttered to the orderlies who strapped him to his stretcher. "I saw it, you must tell him I saw it, you must tell him . . ." He stretched, sighed stertorously, turned his head to one side, and lapsed into unconsciousness.

That evening, in a television address recorded at San Clemente, his Western White House, President Richard Milhous Nixon commented on the disaster as follows:

"If the death of our young brothers and sisters has any meaning at all, it may be that our great and proud nation does not win or lose its battles in the jungles and paddy fields of Southeast Asia alone.

"We could have given any one of many names to our volunteer organization for aid to the developing countries, but we decided to call it the Peace Corps—an appropriate name, because mankind will never overcome the deadly dissensions of our age as long as our fellow-men elsewhere in the world know for a certainty that, tomorrow as today, they and their children can hope for no more than a bare subsistence level; a subsistence level which—in terms of calories or other, similar criteria which pour scorn on the rights and expectations of the individual—amounts to a handful of rice.

"Fifty of our brothers and sisters have died for a great ideal.

"May God bless them and take them to His eternal home.

"May God bless you all."

Liechtenstein's trousers were found entangled in the rudder of a small freighter which had been anchored at Samalut since Monday because of a broken camshaft. The trousers, which had caught between gudgeon and pintle, tore when two sailors retrieved them from the water with a boat hook.

The captain had himself rowed across to Samalut and went to the local police station, where he handed over Liechtenstein's passport and an ivory rosary.

Nurse Ann Mayor had been lifted by the flood wave and smashed against a rock north of Beni Khalid. She was found lying in the mud with her back broken.

The man who had watched the disaster from the bank was Melvin Kennedy, a twenty-two-year-old student who had left camp in search of botanical specimens. The sound of the explosion brought him running back to the ridge. He started down the slope in a state of shock, then wandered screaming through the sand until some Bedouin tied him to a donkey and brought him to Beni Khalid.

Edward Maddox was floating face down beneath the date palms bordering an irrigation ditch.

Richard Huston, a radio technician, had been washed up against a stack of sugar cane belonging to an agricultural cooperative near Beni Khalid. His body was conveyed to town on a water buffalo.

On returning to the Cairo East depot, bus driver Yussuf Ahmir found a plastic bag containing hectographed leaflets on a window seat and handed them in at the manager's office. Half an hour later, Ahmir was recalled to the office and asked how long the bag had been in his possession.

"I saw it lying on a seat when I walked down the aisle to the rear exit."

"You didn't bring it with you when you came on duty?"

"No, I found it."

"Have you read the leaflets?"

"I only saw there was something written on them and stuffed them back inside the bag."

"Do you have any witnesses—I mean, that the bag was lying there already?"

"Not really. There was only a mechanic on board when I drove into the garage."

"Someone you know?"

"No. I think he left the garage and headed for the canteen."

"Would you recognize him?"

"I don't know. I could try."

"Do that."

Ahmir failed to find the man. As he was walking back to the office, it occurred to him that he had stopped a little way past the terminal and gone to the rear door because he could hear a hiss of escaping air from a pneumatic tube. At that moment, the mechanic had tapped on the rear window and asked if he might hitch a ride to the depot. Ahmir paused on the office stairs, closed his eyes, and tried to visualize the rows of seats. There were two policemen waiting for him in the manager's office.

"So you don't know what's in the leaflets?" asked one of them, who was perched on the edge of the manager's desk.

"No idea. I only glanced at them."

"Then we'll read you some extracts," said the other policeman. "For yet seven days, and I will cause it to rain upon the earth forty days and forty nights; and every living substance that I have made will I destroy from off the face of the earth . . ."

"Does that ring a bell?" asked the policeman sitting on the desk. Ahmir shrugged and shook his head.

"And the waters prevailed exceedingly upon the earth; and all the high hills, that were under the whole heaven, were covered. Fifteen cubits upward did the waters prevail; and the mountains were covered."

"That's taken from a Jewish book," said the man on the desk, "translated into Arabic, run off on a duplicating machine, and addressed to the citizens of Cairo. Leaflets. Interesting, don't you agree?"

"If you say so." Ahmir made another effort to picture the interior of the bus.

"And all flesh died that moved upon the earth, both of fowl, and of cattle, and of beast, and of every creeping thing that creepeth upon the earth, and every man," read the policeman. "Almost every sentence is numbered." He turned the leaflet over.

"I'm pretty sure the seats were empty when I drove back from the terminal. Perhaps the mechanic forgot to take the bag with him."

"It wasn't forgotten, it was left there on purpose. Ready for tomorrow morning's passengers," said the second policeman.

"If it belonged to me," said Ahmir, "why would I have handed it in?"

"We're only asking. And reading you extracts."

"Listen to this," said the first policeman. "All in whose nostrils was the breath of life, of all that was in the dry land, died. And every living substance was destroyed..."

"We've been looking at your work permit. How long were you employed as a truck driver in Aswan?"

"Two years or so. I moved back to Cairo in spring, 1970."

"Scared of all that water, eh?"

"I don't know what you mean."

"I mean, weren't you afraid the High Dam might break? That there might be a flood?"

"I never gave it a thought. It was a lot of water, sure, but—"

"Then why carry these leaflets arounds? Some might call it incitement to public disorder."

"All I did was find the bag and hand it in."

"All right, you can go."

238

On the third day after the disaster, the bodies of seventeen members of the U.S. Peace Corps and four employees of Nazareth Iron United were retrieved from the Nile. Army vehicles brought them to Heliopolis, where they were soldered into zinc coffins.

The U.S. Ambassador in Cairo, Raymond Boothe, announced at a press conference in the Semiramis Hotel that the dead had been posthumously awarded Medals for Merit by President Nixon.

At 8:10 p.m., a U.S.A.F. DC-8 received landing clearance from the control tower at Heliopolis and was directed to the hangar where the twenty-one flag-draped coffins lay.

The news agency MENA reported that the government of the United Arab Republic had decided to drop Project Survival Tower.

F R I D A Y

```
LAKE NASSER: LEVEL RISING
        Lake level: 597.43 ft. above sea level.
Change: plus 0.72 ft. (Top water level: 597
ft.; crest of dam: 643 ft.)
```

PORE-WATER PRESSURE IN BODY OF DAM: INCREASING
(tolerance: 11 kg/cm^2)

Main piezometers	A	B	C	D	E
kg/cm^2	9.12	9.29	9.01	7.11	7.15
Change	+0.05	+0.05	+0.04	+0.04	+0.03

EARTH PRESSURE IN BODY OF DAM: INCREASING
(tolerance: 21 kg/cm^2)

239

ASWAN!

Pressure gauges kg/cm²	A	B	C	D	E
	19.98	18.92	19.32	10.96	14.86
Change	+0.07	+0.06	+0.07	+0.05	+0.07

President Sadat drove to Helwan that morning. His air-conditioned Mercedes drew up on the slope below the Behman Clinic for Nervous Diseases, and the escorting vehicles followed suit. Putting on his dark glasses, Sadat climbed out.

"I've come to see a patient," he said. "Yussuf Gidaff." The doorman nodded and stuffed a handful of nuts into his mouth.

Strange how they keep the loudspeakers blaring all day long, Sadat thought. A Nubian orderly shuffled from behind the reception desk.

"Yussuf Gidaff," Sadat repeated.

He waited in the stone-flagged corridor. There was a metal plaque screwed onto the wall at eye level. The inscription read: "The bars which are indispensable to the safe-keeping of certain patients have been artistically designed so as to resemble a form of decoration only ... U.N. World Health Organization for the Eastern Mediterranean." A Palestinian with an Al Fatah badge sewn to his shirt limped past Sadat. He carried a riding crop with a carved handle and swung it exaggeratedly in an attempt to correct his lopsided gait.

"I'm looking for a patient named Yussuf Gidaff," Sadat told the Nubian as he tried to brush past him. "My secretary phoned yesterday to say that I was coming." At a window on the other side of the paved courtyard, a patient started wrenching at the artistically designed bars.

Gidaff was strolling among the rhododendron bushes in

240

his pajamas. Sadat walked slowly down the steps. If only they'd turn off the music, he thought.

A male nurse padded across the flagstones. Sadat paused to let him pass. Gidaff chuckled. The patient at the first-floor window threw a paper cup into the courtyard.

Gidaff showed no sign of recognition. Sadat said, "Good morning, Yussuf. I came to see you."

The sick man turned away and sat down among the bushes. The male nurse padded back again.

"He doesn't like you," he said to Sadat. "You can see he doesn't like you."

"We're friends," the President replied. "Go away, we're friends, I tell you. Look at me, Yussuf."

Gidaff raised his head, drew up his legs, and heaved himself forward into a kneeling position. He said, "I saw it all. I saw the flood. You must tell him. The button . . ." Sadat bent over him.

"It's me—Anwar. You've had a shock. Look at me."

"The button . . ." Gidaff started to weep.

The male nurse gripped Sadat's shoulder. "I told you he didn't like you. Leave him alone or I'll call the superintendent."

The Canadian newspaper Toronto *Star* announced that the President of the World Bank, Robert McNamara, had commissioned a report from the World Health Organization. On the basis of this study, all promises of credit for a scheme which envisaged the installation of concrete buoyancy chambers in Egyptian villages had been withdrawn. The U.N. special representative Count Hengström was summoned to the Egyptian Foreign Ministry. One of McNamara's senior advisers told a correspondent that the United Arab Republic's latest credit applications were still under review.

A spokesman for the World Health Organization emphasized at a press conference in Geneva that there was no substance to reports to the effect that the WHO had been commissioned by other international bodies to study the reaction of the human organism to changes in atmospheric pressure resulting from flood waves. "To be more explicit, at no time have any studies been made of the extent to which, from the medical aspect, technical aids to the survival of the Egyptian people in the event of a breach in the High Dam might, or might not, repay the cost of their manufacture."

The five Liberty ships hove to at regular intervals along the coast from Tobruk to the Gaza Strip. The commander of the U.S. Sixth Fleet sent a destroyer to reconnoiter the area. Its captain radioed back: "Purpose of Liberty operation obscure. Remarkably few men on board. Awnings amidships may conceal helicopters. No evidence that ships are armed."

In response to a query from the U.S. military attaché in Colombo, the Foreign Ministry of the People's Republic of Ceylon stated that no information was available about the cargoes or destination of the freighters in question. The Italian newspaper *La Stampa* reported that the Soviet admiralty was preparing to intervene should the government of the United Arab Republic make an attempt to demolish the High Dam at Aswan. The five Liberty ships had, it went on, been leased to the Soviet Union during World War II.

On Wednesday night, the American satellite Samos 20 recorded an explosion on board the Liberty freighter *Grey Princess,* one hundred and twenty miles south of Cyprus.

The Soviet Ambassador in Washington was summoned to the State Department. The representatives of Italy, Greece, and Turkey protested at a meeting of the NATO Standing Group against Admiral Brugg's proposal that the Liberty ships be searched by boarding parties from the U.S. Sixth Fleet. They justified their attitude by arguing that in the prevailing mood of crisis the situation in the Eastern Mediterranean should not be aggravated by political factors.

Giovanni Andreali, the Italian Foreign Minister, and Defense Minister Berlinguer attended a meeting at the President's official residence. Berlinguer recalled Admiral Paoli to Rome. Evaluation of infrared films taken to Erzurum by jet fighters of the U.S. Sixth Fleet confirmed that the crew of the *Grey Princess* had recently extinguished a fire in the forecastle.

Twenty minutes before the departure of United Arab's Cairo-Athens Flight No. 745, an electric trolley brought Dr. Angelo's coffin from a stores shed at Heliopolis to the rear of the Ilyushin 18. It was then loaded into the baggage compartment by a forklift truck.

Egyptian army engineers, assisted by a group of Russian explosives experts, sank chambers into the banks of the Nile at five points between Idfu and Asyut and filled them with massive quantities of dynamite. These charges were to be detonated if the High Dam collapsed, setting off man-made landslides which would, it was hoped, block the riverbed and reduce the initial momentum of the flood wave.

Professor Saber, head of the Marine Research Institute at Mansura University, flew to Aswan and El Diwan to supervise the collection of water samples.

Anwar Heikal was appointed to succeed Yussuf Gidaff at the Ministry of the Interior.

ASWAN!

WEDNESDAY

LAKE NASSER: LEVEL RISING

Lake level: 598.55 ft. above sea level.
Change: plus 0.52 ft. (Top water level: 597
ft.; crest of dam: 643 ft.)

PORE-WATER PRESSURE IN BODY OF DAM: INCREASING
(tolerance: 11 kg/cm^2)

Main piezometers	A	B	C	D	E
kg/cm^2	9.22	9.39	9.18	7.76	7.37
Change	+0.03	+0.03	+0.02	+0.01	+0.03

EARTH PRESSURE IN BODY OF DAM: INCREASING
(tolerance: 21 kg/cm^2)

Pressure gauges	A	B	C	D	E
kg/cm^2	20.01	19.15	19.88	11.12	15.02
Change	+0.04	+0.02	+0.02	+0.02	+0.02

Leaflets bearing excerpts from the seventh chapter of Genesis translated into Arabic were found in a changing room at the Tewfikieh Tennis Club on Gezira Island, on a counter in the Aeroflot office in Shari'al Nil, on the steps of the Arab League Headquarters, and scattered around the Ibn Tulun Mosque. Unidentified persons threw more such leaflets out of a train—the 1:18 from Helwan—as it was traveling between the stations of El Saida Zeinab and Bab el Luk.

The leaflets had been hectographed on two different machines. One batch was inscribed, "To the Inhabitants of the Capital of the United Arab Republic." The second version read, "To the Doomed People of Egypt." Noah's name did not figure in either group of quotations.

.   .   .

The board of Inter-Mediterranes, meeting in special session at Corfu, debated whether a collapse of the High Dam might lead to an epidemic incidence of bilharzia in the Mediterranean area. In an unpublished resolution, the board urged the government of the United Arab Republic, even at the expense of curtailing outflow from Lake Nasser, to restart the turbines of the Aswan station. "There is a chance that, if only in the upper reaches of the river, the snails that act as hosts to the larvae of the blood fluke may be destroyed by the turbine blades."

The bodies of three seamen were washed ashore at Limassol in Cyprus. On the basis of an identity card found in the pocket of one of the dead men, the Cyprus authorities identified him as a Libyan citizen named Gawir Nohmad. The two other bodies exhibited acid burns so severe that the musculature of their arms and backs had been eaten away to the bone. Their clothing fell to pieces when they were recovered from the water.

A lecturer in forensic medicine at Nicosia University declared that the burns could only have been caused by hydrochlorous acid.

Some Lebanese fishermen reported that, two days earlier, the crew of the Liberty ship *Grey Princess* had torn down the forecastle rails and pushed the wreck of a burned-out helicopter into the sea.

Answering questions put to him by the U.S. Secretary of State, the Soviet Ambassador said, "Even assuming for one moment that your theory is correct, my government has less reason than ever to intervene in the internal affairs of the United Arab Republic now that the evacuation of Soviet citizens is almost complete. Any reports to the contrary can only be intended to damage the friendly ties between our two countries at a crucial stage in their relationship."

An Italian research team had for the past three years been employed by the Food and Agriculture Organization to plot the movements of migratory locusts in the Red Sea area. After flying back to Port Sudan from Kuwait via Jidda, its members drove northward along the coast road. At Marsa Sha'b, just short of the Sudanese-Egyptian border, the party split up. Four jeeps drove through the Wadi Hodein to Aswan and Idfu, and three went on to Foul Bay, where the research ship *Miramar* was waiting to pick them up. Having camped for a night on Philadelphus Point, at the extremity of the crescent-shaped peninsula which juts into the bay, the second group boarded the *Miramar* near the ancient sulphur mines.

Interviewed after a reception at the Waldorf-Astoria in New York, a spokesman for Robert McNamara announced that the second devaluation of the U.S. dollar had compelled the World Bank to defer the U.A.R.'s latest credit applications. He further intimated that West Germany's abandonment of a floating exchange rate might, under present circumstances, create a new situation.

The London *Sunday Times,* quoting informants in the British chemical industry, reported that the Secretariat-General of Inter-Mediterranes had for some weeks been buying up bleaching powder in Europe and the United States. Vast stocks of this substance had been accumulated at Amsterdam, Bilbao, Boston, Cádiz, and Toulon, there to be loaded into Liberty ships which the Secretariat-General had chartered via a licensed firm in Ceylon. Working on the assumption that between twenty-five and twenty-seven million people would die if the High Dam collapsed, the association of Mediterranean countries was taking steps to prevent massive contamination of the sea.

"If the worst happens," wrote the *Sunday Times* correspondent, "it is envisaged that the Liberty ships will be scuttled off the Egyptian coast and their crews flown by helicopter to Ierapetra in Crete. The member countries of Inter-Mediterranes are assuming that the tens of thousands of tons of bleaching powder in the holds of the scuttled freighters will steadily dissolve in sea water and rise to the surface. This would, for a considerable period, isolate the Nile Valley dead from the rest of the Mediterranean by a sort of disinfectant film—a *cordon sanitaire* in the literal sense. Clearly, the Secretariat-General of Inter-Mediterranes would rather lay waste the Eastern Mediterranean by impregnating it with chemical compounds than risk creeping death from putrescent matter. The French government, which is now said to be contemplating a withdrawal from Inter-Mediterranes, has allegedly underwritten one-fifth of the total cost of the scheme."

The *Sunday Times* correspondent went on to observe that while this could certainly not be numbered among the most tasteful ventures in the history of mankind, it was unfortunately one of the most inescapable.

At a press conference in Rome, the Secretary-General of Inter-Mediterranes flatly denied having sent freighters laden with bleaching powder to the area of the Nile Delta.

Referring to recent developments in a special evening broadcast, a Radio Cairo commentator said: "It is clear that the seamen hired by Inter-Mediterranes have not been skulking off our shores for the good of their health.

"Seldom in these times of trial was there a more brutal

demonstration that the world has long ago written off the Egyptian nation. We found it quite inconceivable that our neighbors could be buying up bleaching powder at inflated prices and hoarding it out of concern for their bathing beaches. We found it equally inconceivable that the Egyptian people should represent no more to their neighbors than a health hazard, or that the marine protection charter of the United Nations could ever be implemented in this gruesome fashion. From today, we know the truth. We also know that we must and shall overcome the present crisis by our own unaided efforts."

Shortly before midnight, a page entered the bar of the City Center Hotel in Munich and summoned the President of Inter-Mediterranes to the telephone. The President listened in silence for about forty seconds, then rushed gesticulating from the phone booth, leaving the receiver dangling at the end of its cord. He missed a step on the way to the foyer, was taken to the hospital with a fractured thigh, and died an hour later of fat embolism.

T U E S D A Y

LAKE NASSER: LEVEL RISING

      Lake level: 600.91 ft. above sea level. Change: plus 0.88 ft. (Top water level: 597 ft.; crest of dam: 643 ft.)

PORE-WATER PRESSURE IN BODY OF DAM: INCREASING

EARTH PRESSURE IN BODY OF DAM: INCREASING (tolerance: 21 kg/cm^2)

Pressure gauges kg/cm^2	A	B	C	D	E
	20.19	19.37	20.02	11.33	15.17
Change	+0.04	+0.05	+0.05	+0.05	+0.03

Dr. Bustelli spotted the first swarm of locusts at 9:47 a.m., on the radar screen of the Italian research vessel *Miramar*. At this juncture, the wind was easterly and traveling at a speed of 18.7 feet per second. The swarm originated in the central desert of Saudi Arabia and had left the mainland between Mecca and Rabigh.

The insects headed first for the Jebel Asoteriba in Northern Sudan, swung north-northwest over the Red Sea, and were finally picked up by radar off the island of Zebirget. Other swarms followed throughout the afternoon at intervals of seventy minutes. Members of the FAO research team at Aswan and Asyut were informed by short-wave radio that desert locusts would descend on the Nile Valley in thirty-six hours' time, if not sooner.

Government spokesman Quaruni confirmed that the Egyptian Cabinet had, after an emergency meeting, instructed an international consortium to begin dismantling the Great Pyramid of Khufu and the Step Pyramid as Saqqara. The blocks of stone would be used to construct a breakwater for the protection of Cairo in the triangle Helwan–El Ma'sara–Ausim. This would, it was hoped, split the flood wave and deflect it across the west bank of the Nile. The intention was to transport the blocks by means of a roller system which would take advantage of the difference in altitude between Giza and the riverbank.

Addressing journalists at Shepheard's Hotel, Quaruni said: "The Great Pyramid alone has a volume of almost 3,270,000 cubic yards. This is our builder's yard, gentlemen, and the world must excuse us if we clear it in our hour of need. If we are to save the capital, we need every stone. The project will be tackled at once. Preparations have already been in hand for two weeks."

. . .

ASWAN!

The MENA wire service put out its news flash at 11:20 a.m. local time. At 3 p.m., the Presidential secretariat received McNamara's cabled announcement that the World Bank would finance the construction of the breakwater by means of an interest-free loan.

During the late afternoon, tens of thousands of demonstrators assembled in Alexandria and surged toward the Governor's official residence, chanting "Why drown the Delta so that Cairo may live?" Police fired tear-gas grenades into the crowds. Stones rattled against the front of the building when the Governor appeared on the balcony, and several ground-floor windows were shattered. Two students carrying a banner inscribed "The Flood Belongs to Everyone!" were beaten to the ground by guards at the south gate.

Units of the 7th Division left Cairo and erected barbed-wire roadblocks on the approach roads to Giza. The Ministry of Tourism canceled all further *son-et-lumière* performances and confiscated the tape recordings. A soldier tossed a hand grenade onto the console of the lighting system. At 6 p.m., the Pyramids and Sphinx at Giza were declared a restricted area. Troops guarding the road stopped a coach-load of tourists returning to Cairo and emptied their cameras of film. A party of American engineers were landed by helicopter at the foot of the Khafre Pyramid. West of the Menkure Pyramid, army scrapers began to level the ground for an emergency airstrip.

On the London Stock Exchange, shares in Plant Chemicals, Ltd., the largest cement-producing company in Great Britain, rose fourteen points in a matter of hours. The staff of Rome University's Institute of Oriental Studies passed a resolution protesting the destruction of the Pyramids. "Even in the face of a crisis whose extreme gravity is apparent to all, it cannot be regarded as other than a product of hysteria that twentieth-century technology should find its *ultima ratio* in the destruction of some of the most grandiose relics of human civilization."

Aristotle Onassis offered the Egyptian government 380,000 tons of shipping space for the transportation of cement at special rates. Navy Minister Fawzi, who was handed the teleprinted message at a reception given by the Spanish Ambassador, decided that the government's acceptance of a prior offer from Niarchos should stand.

Egyptian and Soviet surveyors staked out the lines of a breakwater in the suburbs of Helwan. Loudspeaker cars summoned the inhabitants to leave their homes.

Albrecht Tschugg-Brey, the celebrated Bernese Egyptologist, walked the streets of the Swiss capital handing out duplicated leaflets to passers-by. "How," the leaflets demanded, "does President Anwar el Sadat imagine that he can evade the inevitable? Death will come quickly to him who disturbs the Pharaohs' repose. Tutankhamen took revenge on those who despoiled his sarcophagus. They all died, even Nasser. Does Sadat believe that he is above this law?"

A Beechcraft courier plane belonging to shipping magnate Aristotle Onassis crashed on landing at Heliopolis. The pilot and Evdoros Demetriou, one of his directors, were burned to death.

The port authorities at Alexandria requested the captains of all ships currently berthed there to clear the quays within forty-eight hours so that cement freighters could take their places. The Polish cargo ship *Wroclaw*, lying at anchor with engine trouble, was towed out to sea. Engineers of the 7th Division blew up eighteen houses on the outskirts of Helwan.

The Orientalist Otto Bahrenwald shot himself in a Bremen car park. Emerging from his left temple, the bullet passed through the driver's window and dented a van belonging to Nordfisch AG. Herds of lowing cattle waded northward along the irrigation ditches as members of the Egyptian youth movement helped to evacuate villages between Helwan and Ausim. A peasant from El Badrashein decapitated forty doves with his sickle and was that evening committed to the Behman Clinic for Nervous Diseases at Helwan.

The International Archaeological Association, based in Paris, passed a resolution approving the steps taken by the Egyptian government but requested that the demolition work be monitored by a scientific committee. "Only thus, at the eleventh hour, can at least some undiscovered relics of Pharaonic civilization be preserved for posterity."

A contributor to Radio Copenhagen's evening news roundup commented: "So now mechanical excavators will forge a path for us into the burial chambers which scholars have been seeking for generations past. The world will at last be permitted to gaze upon the countenance of the sun-gods. The secret of the Great Pyramid will at last be laid bare, though not in circumstances of which mankind could ever have dreamed. In this hour of expectation, one is overwhelmed by a bitter sense of the irrevocable."

Troops of the 7th Division fired maize fields outside Helwan and used their tanks to mow down date palms. Frantic peasants clawed onions out of the ground and stripped their tomato plants of unripe fruit.

Shortly before midnight, the automatic fire alarms went off at the British Museum. Members of the London Fire Brigade discovered night watchman Maurice Lempton, aged sixty-seven, burned to death in the Egyptian Collection. Lempton's hands and feet were charred and his skull had burst in the heat. Employed in the Egyptian Collection since World War II, Lempton had sat down beside the mummified body catalogued as "Male Adult Lying in a Flexed Position," poured gasoline over himself, and struck a match.

By dawn, clouds of smoke from burning maize fields were drifting over Cairo.

Twenty-six radar posts had been installed in the Aswan-Asyut section of the Nile Valley to record the movements of migratory locust swarms. Watching through binoculars at Idfu and Luxor, members of the FAO research team observed the arrival of the first swarms from Saudi Arabia.

Team director Guglielmo Malfatti recorded his impressions on tape. "It was the usual picture to begin with. First the vanguard, like black smears on the horizon, then the high-pitched hum of the approaching swarms, then the eerie silence that descends immediately after they land, and finally the munching of countless mandibles. In the Aswan-Asyut area, the behavior of *Schistocerca peregrina* displayed certain anomalies which attained significance only when taken in conjunction with the events that followed. These ranged from diminished appetite to sexual passivity and a reluctance on the part of swarms to take wing.

"In the observation area north of Aswan, density was three to four insects per square yard. As many as eight per square yard were counted at Idfu. These were solitary locusts, for the most part, though some transition to group formation was already taking place.

ASWAN!

"In the course of the day, solitary locusts of pronounced maturity began to desert the swarms near Aswan and move westward. This phenomenon, which is usually confined to individuals and can be traced to vibration stimuli—e.g., the hoofbeats of cattle—spread to most swarms within a very few hours.

"Although the fields had not been picked clean, the locusts formed new swarms and abandoned the Nile Valley less than seven hours after their arrival. Skirting the principal ridges bordering the river, they flew westward in a huge fan-shaped formation. As far as we can reconstruct their route from recordings made by our radar posts, the swarms then turned south halfway between the Nile Valley and the Kharga oasis. The reasons for this premature departure of locust swarms from the Nile Valley have yet to be established."

A confidential World Health Organization report was published in facsimile by the Canadian newspaper Toronto *Star*. The document had been signed at Montreux on June 12 by Professors Fontain of Marseilles, Livingstone of Boston, and Kuhn of Vienna. Section 3 of the study read as follows:

"The committee has assumed that the surge of atmospheric pressure preceding such a flood will attain a maximum of ten atmospheres. These figures will decrease as the Nile Valley widens to the north (lateral displacement of air). The undersigned are nonetheless of the opinion that the inhabitants of populated areas on the lower reaches of the Nile will suffer from acute nitrogen poisoning ('the bends'). No account has here been taken of mechanical injuries occasioned by impact with walls, trees, vehicles, et cetera.

"After studying autopsy reports on flood victims at Longarone (Italy) and Fréjus (France), the undersigned consider it improbable that there will be any general incidence of alveolar rupture or bronchial damage, because disparities of pressure between thorax and external atmosphere are automatically adjusted by the respiratory ducts. A more real danger appears to be that the abrupt rise in atmospheric pressure just prior to the arrival of the flood wave will so saturate the blood of those affected with nitrogen that symptoms of depth intoxication will manifest themselves; that is to say, loss of ability to concentrate, delusions, and diminished proprioceptive capacity of the peripheral nervous system. There will, at best, be a delay in the transmission of cerebral impulses to the end organs by way of the motor and sensory nerve fibers. To construct an example: just as a diver suffering from depth intoxication loses his sense of danger as a result of nitrogen saturation and performs uncontrolled movement (diving to greater depths, severing of safety lines, etc.), so the group of affected persons will no longer be capable of carrying out relatively simple maneuvers. In other words, being in a state of nitrogen narcosis, people exposed to a surge of atmospheric pressure of the sort which must ensue on the collapse of the High Dam would be incapable of, say, leaving their places of work and seeking refuge in concrete buoyancy shells. Instead, to put it crudely, they would await death in an exalted mental state.

"Even assuming that they survived the atmospheric pressure and the flood wave itself, one is led to wonder how the danger of air embolism could be averted after so rapid a normalization of the relationship between intrathoracic and external air pressures. The committee would point out that divers whose blood has become saturated with nitrogen cannot be hauled to the surface at once, even in cases of dire emergency, because the rapid expansion of nitrogen bubbles in their blood would inevitably prove fatal. With regard to the survival system under review, the committee would sum up by saying that the above-mentioned group of persons would be afflicted during the primary phase of such an abrupt fluctuation of pressure by nitrogen narcosis, and, during the secondary phase, by general air embolism."

In identical notes addressed to Cairo, Rome, and the U.N. Secretary-General, the Sudanese government complained that the FAO's Italian-manned research team had used a network of infrasonic transmitters to divert swarms of migratory locusts from the Nile Valley to Lower Sudan. In the Wadi Halfa-Atbara area alone, damage to crops exceeded last year's losses by 900 percent.

The Egyptian government replied the same day that installations along the Aswan-Asyut section of the river were merely radar tracking stations whose purpose was to plot the flight of locusts, not influence it. The equipment in question had already been in use for two years. The swarms' change of direction was a phenomenon which the FAO team was currently investigating. Cairo invited the Sudan to send observers to the Nile Valley to check the radar stations for themselves.

At about 7 a.m., while cycling to a bridge construction site from the Provençal village of Saint-Martin-de-Londres, the laborer Georges Michelet caught sight of a Citroën sedan parked some distance up a cart track with its headlights on. The other feature that struck him, as he later told the police, was that it seemed to be canted forward.

The front tires were riddled with bullets. On the back seat lay a woman's handbag and two rugs. The car was registered in the name of Michel Tontain, a second secretary at the French Embassy in Cairo. Tontain had returned from Egypt on leave the previous week and driven with his wife and daughter to Saint-Pierre-sur-Mer, where he had purchased a bungalow in August, 1970. On Thursday, he had told acquaintances at Saint-Pierre that he intended to take his family to Montpellier for a few days.

At midday, the Citroën was released by the police and towed away. *Le Soir* reported that tire tracks discovered near the abandoned sedan indicated that another car had turned in the field and driven off. It further hinted that the diplomat's disappearance might have undertones of espionage. Tontain, alleged *Le Soir,* had been involved in recent negotiations for the sale of Mirage fighters to the United Arab Republic. By this time, the French Foreign Ministry had already received an anonymous letter demanding three hundred thousand francs for the release of Tontain and his family.

The toads began to take flight when the mating season came. Fisherman at Daraw reported that they were drifting down the Nile in huge clusters.

The first toads emerged from their burrows before sunrise and crawled to the bank. They scraped hollows in the mud with their hind legs and lay in the water that seeped into them. Toward midday, more toads converged from fields and inlets, clambered across the toads in the hollows, and spilled down the bank in long brown skeins.

The military commander at Idfu radioed the Defense Ministry in Cairo that unrest among the peasants was growing. Phenomena of this kind had not been observed within living memory.

The Sûreté was called in to assist with the search for Tontain, his wife, and his daughter. Officials in the Quai d'Orsay mailing department found a second anonymous letter reiterating the offer to release the diplomat and his family against a ransom of three hundred thousand francs. The text was pasted together out of characters clipped from newspapers and the envelope had been posted in the city of Arles, in southern France. The letter stipulated no time limit and contained no instructions about the method of exchange to be adopted.

That night, the croaking of a myriad toads could be heard along the banks of the Nile. The first wave had reached the town of Tahta at dusk and was drifting down to Asyut. By this time, hundreds of thousands of the creatures had been thrust underwater by sheer weight of numbers and lay, pale bellies uppermost, on the backs of their fellow-fugitives. A second wave followed in the course of the morning.

Second Secretary Tontain was sighted by a gendarmerie patrol in the Cévennes Mountains of southern France as he was carrying an aluminum can to the spring below the derelict village of Miremont. He tossed the can into a clump of ferns and raised his hands.

"I'm glad you've come," he said. "I was going to give myself up anyway."

Tontain led the gendarmes through gorse bushes and undergrowth to a dilapidated peasant shack. "Take care," he warned them, "I've scratched myself to ribbons every day." He walked ahead of them, holding branches aside and shielding his face with his hands. His wife was waiting at the door. The little girl was asleep on an air mattress in the stable.

Even before he was driven to Arles for questioning, Tontain confessed that he had staged the kidnap attempt to avoid having to return to Cairo. The High Dam was on the point of collapse and the whole of Egypt might be flooded at any moment. In a signed statement made at the prefecture in Arles, Tontain said: "I was haunted by this dilemma for weeks. On the one hand, I wanted to leave Cairo at once for my family's sake. On the other, it would have meant the end of my diplomatic career if I had officially cited developments at Aswan as my grounds for requesting a transfer. There is a growing mood of panic among members of the diplomatic corps, and my Ministry is anxious at all costs not to start a chain reaction in the Egyptian capital. I even had difficulty in taking my annual leave at this juncture. I am aware that, by abandoning my car under suspicious circumstances and sending two anonymous letters to Paris, I have committed what amounts to a criminal act.

"I should like, nevertheless, to emphasize that in view of my Ministry's attitude, which is designed to cement Franco-Egyptian relations at the expense of its own personnel, this seemed to be the only available means of taking myself out of circulation, as it were, and salvaging my career at the same time. I should also like to take this opportunity of stressing, formally and for the record, that my plans were aimed solely at deferring my return to Egypt until the situation at Aswan had resolved itself, and that they were not associated with any intention to blackmail. Had I genuinely meant to convert ransom money to my own use, I should have stipulated some method of exchange in my second letter, which I succeeded in posting incognito from Arles. Signed: Michel Tontain, Second Secretary."

Tontain, who was released after questioning, went on to tell the police inspector that his kidnapping maneuver had begun like a summer holiday of indefinite duration. He spent the time reading and carving little animals out of juniper roots. After five or six days, however, the solitude started to tell on his wife. "It was all the old stones and clumps of fern. In the end, she couldn't even stand the cries of the gulls that occasionally strayed there from the Rhône. I sat on the window sill for hours, chasing the birds away with a catapult.

259

Next, it was the scent of lavender that got on her nerves. She grew quite hysterical. If your men hadn't come when they did, we'd have given ourselves up."

"Yes," said the inspector, "so you said."

The Egyptian Ministry of the Interior sent biologists from Alexandria University to Aswan and Luxor. The mayor of Isna reported that toads were coating the entire width of the river like a living carpet. "They're converging from all directions and heading for the Nile. Six miles south of here, the banks are ankle-deep in toads which can't get into the water for lack of space. Every five or six hours, they try to climb ashore and block the sluices of the side canals. At Asfun, El Mata'na, peasants have been busy with shovels and baskets for the past sixteen hours, throwing the toads back into the Nile. In some villages, the people are lining the banks and killing them with sticks."

The first team of scientists flew back from Luxor to Cairo at midday. Its spokesman, Professor Hassuni, called on the Minister of the Interior and told him that the toads' death march was a phenomenon for which he could find no immediate explanation.

"So it's a phenomenon," said Heikal. "If that's all you can tell me, I needn't have bothered to send you to Luxor."

"One can't help being reminded of the lemmings and their suicidal migrations into the sea."

"So you account for one inexplicable phenomenon by quoting another."

"We could send to Stockholm for Professor—"

"How much time do you think we have left? I asked for your expert opinion."

"This death march—"

"You keep on talking about a death march. Are you so sure?"

"I don't quite follow, I'm afraid."

"The creatures are running away. They're trying to escape, not kill themselves—they even copulate on the move."

"To be absolutely frank, Minister—"

"I took your frankness for granted from the outset."

"Very well. The facts seem to confirm what you say. Just before I flew back here, I received a report by telephone from my colleagues in Aswan. The behavior of the toads south of the dam is entirely different. They're completely apathetic and take no nourishment. Some of them die because they interrupt their spawning."

"Northern toads and southern toads . . . Tell that to the next learned congress you attend and they'll recommend you for psychiatric treatment."

"If I ever do attend another. As of now, Minister, I'm convinced that the dam will succumb to water pressure within the next few days. Structural changes are already taking place in the body of the dam."

"You obviously know more than the High Dam Authority."

"Yes, I suspect I do."

"What makes you think so?"

"The contrasting behavior patterns I mentioned."

"In other words, the toads in the lake sense that they can't escape. The dam at their backs, desert on both sides, and another three hundred and ten miles of it between them and the Sudan. A depressing thought. Is that what you mean?"

"Not exactly. Let me restate the problem. We've compared the various phases in the behavior of the toads traveling downstream. The first accumulations occurred in the neighborhood of Daraw, close to the dam. The creatures formed small groups and waited. They didn't begin to swim downstream until the day was well advanced. These groups must have functioned as a sort of primer, because the number of fugitives increased hour by hour. As soon as the first wave had crossed a section of bank, others struggled to reach the water, too."

"And what do you infer from that?"

"It may have something to do with the ossicles in the middle ear of the order Salientia. They not only confer an extremely acute sense of balance but appear to be sensitive to seismic disturbances. That's why I spoke of structural changes occurring in the body of the dam."

"You mean the toads near the base detected tremors of some kind?"

"Yes, sections caving in, earth and rubble being displaced by water pressure. At all events, the creatures were alarmed by something and fled. These were individual decisions on the part of small groups, if you like. The huge masses of toads downstream were subsequently alerted by their calls as they drifted past."

"We could still send for a psychiatrist," said Heikal.

"You asked my opinion. What recommendations will you make to the Cabinet?"

"None at all. We shall string nets across the Nile. My department can at least do that much."

The first fires were started that morning. A cotton warehouse went up in flames on the western outskirts of Cairo. Between the main station and Heliopolis, five Nubians cut through the wire mesh enclosing the railway embankment, punctured the fuel tank of a diesel locomotive with pickaxes, and threw wads of burning rag into the escaping gasoline. Near the Opera House in Shari'al Gumhuriya, an army patrol shot four men who had overturned a taxi. Two more men dashed across the street into Ezbekiya Gardens and hid among the rhododendron bushes. Fifteen minutes later, they slipped back across Shari'al Geish and set fire to the pool of gasoline by the taxi while the soldiers were still searching the gardens.

A sergeant emptied his tommy gun into the flames and the burst caught one of the men, who threw up his arms and fell backward into the blaze.

In Bab esh Sha'ira, the mob stormed a supply depot belonging to the Egyptian army. Screaming women hurled sacks of flour from the windows. The guards fled down Sharia Klut Bek, were driven back to their posts by military policemen, and used their rifle butts on the white-powdered children who were dancing under the warehouse windows.

In the inner courtyard, some youths set fire to a stack of tires. The flames licked through the flour dust that was pouring from the windows, rolled across the ground, and expanded into a yellow fireball. The explosion knocked the children flat and left one little girl spread-eagled across the hood of a truck. Stunned faces stared down into the courtyard from the gaping windows. An officer ran at two soldiers, belaboring them with his rubber truncheon, and tripped over a child who was crawling back into the yard.

That afternoon, the bus driver Yussuf Ahmir sat down in the middle of Liberation Square, drew up his legs, and propped his head on his knees. He was carried back to the pavement by passers-by, lashing out in all directions, and remained prostrate beside the curb for a quarter of an hour. Just before 4 p.m., he stood up, reeled down Shari'al Zahara, and after two hundred yards threw himself in front of a truck which was delivering vegetables from Warraq el 'Arab to Shepheard's Hotel. The driver wrenched his wheel to the right, Ahmir rolled aside, and the truck rammed a stationary taxi. Crates of tomatoes cascaded into the road and burst, showering Ahmir's prone form with ripe fruit. The offside rear wheel of the truck had caught him above the hip. He got to his feet and staggered, with the breath rasping in his throat, toward a group of pedestrians who were watching from the pavement, collapsed, shuffled another five yards across the asphalt on his knees, stood up for the last time, and vomited blood over the man who went to catch him as he fell.

Found in the pockets of his bus driver's tunic were a phylactery, seven pound notes, a clay pipe, and four hectographed leaflets bearing quotations from the Old Testament.

That evening, an air force officer walked into Shepheard's Hotel and tried to book a room on the third or fourth floor. His wife and two sons waited on the steps outside the glass doors while he was speaking to the head porter. The head porter said that all the rooms on the upper floors were booked until December. The officer pulled a wad of pound notes from his breast pocket and shouted that he must have a room. The Nubian commissionaire who had been pacing up and down on the top step paused to watch. The officer's wife turned, took her children by the hand, and walked across the street to a hairdresser's shop. The woman assistant in the hotel jewelry boutique propped herself on her elbows and leaned over until her breasts touched the glass-topped counter. The page boy deposited a suitcase on the carpet and smoothed his galabieh.

"I need a room on the fourth floor," the officer said, quietly now.

"I'm sorry, we're booked solid."

"See those boys? They're twins—they'll be five next week."

The head porter drew the hotel register away from him, the page boy came to life with a jerk and picked up his suitcase, the woman in the boutique craned across the glass slab with her mouth open. There was no sound in the foyer except the footsteps of the Nubian commissionaire pacing to and fro on the top step. A taxi drove up. The lift doors opened silently and closed again. The officer tossed the pound notes into a key compartment, muttering, "Five years old, can you imagine that?" He gripped the head porter's sleeve.

"I said, can you imagine that?"

"I don't know what you're talking about."

The officer turned and walked across the red carpet to the glass doors.

"Your money, sir," called the head porter. The page boy vanished into a niche beside the newspaper kiosk and the woman in the boutique straightened up with a sigh. The officer crossed the street, led his wife and children from the shopwindow to the car, which was parked at the curb, and opened the door for them. He hurried back into the hotel foyer, took the money which the head porter pushed across to him, then ran back to the car and threw the wad of notes into the trunk. He bent over and tapped on the passenger window, but while his wife was winding it down he turned and made for the hotel once more. Running up the steps, he thrust the Nubian aside and burst into the foyer. "Give this to my wife," he told the the head porter, tossing his key ring on the carpet.

Then he walked over to a wall mirror, drew his service revolver, and shot himself through the right ear.

Addressing a conference at the Ministry of the Interior, the British consultant psychologist Anthony Wainwright declared that the present wave of incendiarism could not be attributed to political motives. If his theory was correct, these seeming acts of aggression were only an outward symptom of underlying panic. He quoted a study made in 1938 by Brancson, who had observed that natives in the vicinity of Mongalla in the southern Sudan set fire to their fields for fear that the White Nile was about to flood. "Yesterday fields, today locomotives," said counterespionage chief Ewal Hamid. "Thank you, I've a lot of time for theories." Wainwright said, "I thought you wanted an explanation. At all events, I feel bound to draw your attention to a possible link with Ptolemy's theory of the elements, which probably spread inland from Alexandria in the wake of trading expeditions and may now have returned to its place of origin. I refer to the theory that fire and water are mutually counteractive."

Outside the Ibn Tulun Mosque, an army jeep ran down a man who was making for Shari'Assliba with a can of gasoline. Shots fired from the offices of the Automobile Club killed the driver of a fire engine which had been summoned to the Egyptian Museum by an anonymous phone call. In Shari'al Giza, a cyclist hurled a blazing bundle of straw under a horse-drawn cab and rode off across the El Gama'a Bridge. Thirty yards short of the east bank, he was caught in the beam of a spotlight and cut down by a burst of submachine gunfire from the lieutenant in command of the bridge picket.

At 9 p.m., the crew of a police helicopter radioed that a truck depot on the eastern outskirts of the city was on fire.

A Nubian butcher's boy, who was supposed to be delivering a side of mutton to a bazaar cookshop on the carrier of his bicycle, rode back along the Shari'el Muski to the Bridge of July 26th. Squatting beside the balustrade, he started to dismember the meat and throw the pieces into the river. He continued to do so until kicked and beaten by an angry mob, then collapsed in the roadway and pulled his galabieh over his head. The crowd fell back in silence, but he died some minutes before an ambulance arrived.

A few hundred yards short of the Jewish quarter, four military policemen on patrol in El Saida Zeinab noticed a stench of burning hair. Tracing the smell to its source, they came upon a blood-smeared doorway in a lane leading off Sharia Quadri. All the lights in the house went out when patrol commander Abdel Sarwat kicked the door with his boot. Sarwat ordered his men to break the door down, and, after uttering three challenges, sprayed the passage with bullets. Then he sprang back and waited for the others to fetch flashlights from the jeep. Soon afterward, a young Jew came shuffling out of the house. He put his hands over his eyes because the lights dazzled him. The soldiers pinned his arms behind his back and pushed him ahead of them down the passage. Sarwat caught him by the beard and twisted it so that he faced into the beam. The young man kept his eyes shut while being interrogated.

"Where did the blood come from?" asked the patrol commander.

"We slaughtered a young goat."

"Are you sure it isn't human blood?"

"No, we slaughtered a kid."

Upstairs, a child started to wail. A sergeant appeared in the doorway and reported that the doorposts of five other houses in the same alley were similarly smeared with blood.

"They've been burning their dead," said Sarwat. "We first smelled it a quarter of an hour ago."

"We only threw the hide and head into the fire. It is the Lord's will. And that which remaineth of it until morning, ye shall burn with fire."

"Are you crazy?" Sarwat demanded, relaxing his hold. The young man bowed his head.

The child on the landing whimpered. The men in the downstairs passage heard a patter of bare feet on the boards. Then a door slammed.

"Should we inform headquarters?" asked the sergeant.

"I haven't finished yet," Sarwat said. He laid his hand on the young Jew's shoulder. "It was a kid, you say?"

"A male of the first year: ye shall take it out from the sheep, or from the goats."

Sarwat hit him in the face.

"Open your eyes!"

"And ye shall take a bunch of hyssop, and dip it in the blood that is in the basin, and strike the lintel and the two side posts . . ."

"He's crazy," said the sergeant.

"For the Lord will pass through to smite the Egyptians."

"Let him go," ordered Sarwat. The prisoner clasped his hands behind his back.

"And when he seeth the blood upon the lintel, and on the two side posts, the Lord will pass over the door and will not suffer the destroyer to come in . . ."

"That's enough," Sarwat said. "Take him to the jeep."

Searching the house, the MPs found the forelegs of a young goat. Beside the hearth lay a can half full of congealed blood, a bowl of water, and a bloodstained brush. Some shabby suitcases bound together with rope were stacked beneath the stairs. There were clay pitchers slung from the handles on leather thongs. Just as the soldiers were smashing them with their rifle butts, they heard the child start crying again.

During a reception given at the Nile Hilton by the Egyptian Chamber of Commerce, the Pakistan Ambassador walked up to Muna Fuwasi, wife of the Egyptian Minister of Power, and bowed.

"A thousand apologies for intruding on your conversation. I have something to tell you."

Handing his glass to a waiter, the Pakistani lifted her necklace with one forefinger and said, "You have breasts like a sow." He withdrew his hand, leapt onto the buffet, and shouted to the room at large, "I always knew it—Madame Fuwasi has breasts like a sow."

A network of short-wave transmitters and receivers was installed for the use of military personnel assigned to detonate the charges in the riverbanks between Idfu and Asyut. Each post was provided with an emergency generator to power its radio installations and detonating circuits.

At the Marine Research Institute in Mansura, eighty foreign scientists collaborated with Professor Saber's team in evaluating water samples from Lake Nasser. Spectroscopic experiments reinforced an existing suspicion that the surface was coated with a monomolecular film. Reports from international institutes which had also requested water samples contained no additional information of value.

At nineteen points on the desert plateaus above the Nile Valley, army engineers bulldozed troughs in the sand and lined them with plastic sheeting. Drinking water was to be pumped into these man-made reservoirs shortly before a general evacuation took place.

The Foreign Minister of Pakistan summoned the Egyptian chargé d'affaires at midday and apologized for the incident at the Nile Hilton. The Pakistan Ambassador had, he said, already been recalled to Karachi to render an account of his behavior. The diplomat, his wife, and three sons left for Beirut by Air France at 11:30 a.m.

A steel net spanned the Nile south of Abu Tig. Engineers had anchored four pontoons in the river and passed the main cable over improvised T-rail supports. The net extended below the surface to a depth of six feet and the diamond-shaped interstices were an inch across.

Fire trenches ran up to the plateaus from the abutments on each bank. By afternoon, army half-tracks had hauled six thousand gallons of kerosene to the heights overlooking the river. Abu Tig buzzed with rumors that a ferryboat had cap-

269

sized in a welter of toads seventy miles upstream. Most of the passengers had drowned, and two crew members who struggled ashore had allegedly died of massive ulceration some hours later. The boat was said to be drifting down to Abu Tig, its exposed keel thick with tens of thousands of toads.

On arrival in Beirut, the Pakistan Ambassador to Egypt cabled his Foreign Ministry and asked to be permanently recalled from Cairo. His request was turned down. Secretary of State Buttol cabled back that information gleaned in Moscow did not suggest any immediate threat to the High Dam. No one disputed the gravity of the situation. "However, the very possibility of such a threat renders the presence of a representative of the Republic of Pakistan an essential symbol of the solidarity prevailing among the nonaligned nations of the world." The ambassador and his family caught the next plane back to Cairo.

The first toads drifted into the net at Abu Tig shortly after 10 a.m. Within fifteen minutes, the creatures were piled high against the pontoons and dark-brown water was gushing through the wire mesh. On either bank, troops pumped kerosene into the fire trenches and ignited it. Tongues of flame darted down the slopes toward the Nile.

Just before 11 a.m., the crew of a helicopter reported that the creatures were starting to turn aside and head for shore. They swarmed out of the water on each bank, recoiled when they met the fire trenches, and crawled up the slopes. "From up here," said the helicopter pilot, "they look like streams flowing uphill."

Male toads were dragged through fields by their mates; females left skeins of spawn adhering to stones and grass stems. They poured through canals, swarmed across roads and embankments, mowed down corn and tomato plants. Under pressure from other toads still swarming from the turbid river, they eventually breasted the gravel slopes and debouched onto the plateaus. There the horde divided into columns which crept across the dunes like black fingers.

Early that afternoon, the living tide began to ebb. The flames in the fire trenches subsided, soldiers amused themselves by rolling empty kerosene drums down the slopes, and the croaking died away. Countless toads expired in the sun's heat, swelled up, and burst. Two transport planes swept low over the plateaus dropping bleaching powder.

By eight o'clock on Thursday morning, the surface of Lake Nasser had risen to within five feet of the crest of the dam.

At 9 a.m. on Thursday, the government lifted the curfew that had been imposed in all governorates after the spate of arson and looting in Cairo, Alexandria, Asyut, and Luxor.

Broadcast proclamations invited people to leave their towns and villages if they so wished. The situation at Aswan was exceptionally grave, though rumors that water had already overtopped the dam were unfounded. The proclamations concluded with a warning that martial law would be enforced throughout the Nile Valley in areas where drinking water was distributed by the army. In Cairo, units of the 7th Division stood guard over the Nile bridges after refugees fleeing from the western quarters of the city to the desert plateaus in the east had increased tenfold in two hours.

Two coaches took the foreign scientists who had been working at Mansura to Port Said, where an Air France Caravelle had been awaiting to evacuate them since early that morning.

•   •   •

ASWAN!

The High Dam Authority reported westerly winds, Force 3–4.

Troops on duty at Athens airport during the twelfth day of the flight controllers' strike loaded the zinc coffin containing Dr. Angelo's body into the freight compartment of an Alitalia aircraft. After declining to make an intermediate stop at Heliopolis on the flight from Karachi to Rome, the pilot had changed course for Athens over Beirut.

The reading of verses from the Koran over Radio Cairo was discontinued after fifteen minutes by order of the Minister of the Interior. The BBC's correspondent in Cairo reported in his midday bulletin that the anomalous feature of the whole situation was general vacillation rather than universal fear of a flood. "It has not been said that the High Dam will break—and this assessment conforms with the fatalism of the population. If people were to flee in millions to the desert plateaus, they would die of thirst in a day or two—that is, if they had not already been trampled to death at the dozen or so reservoirs improvised and supervised by the army. In other words, they would be fleeing from an uncertain fate only to die in the desert. If they remain and the dam breaks, their chances of survival are equally slim. The bald choice between these two alternatives has generated a nationwide psychosis such as the world may never again witness. The government information services are being quite fair. Everyone has been put in the picture and allowed to decide for himself, but there is no official guidance. Only this can account for the present mixture of panic and apathy. This morning, I watched refugees streaming eastward to the bridges past shopwindows behind which people were working with every appearance of normality. The street vendors are crying their wares as usual. The waiters in my hotel show no signs of panic. It has just been reported that refugees are pouring back into the city from the east. On the other hand, others are said to be heading west in the direction of the Pyramids."

Dr. Angelo's coffin was transferred at Rome-Fiumicina airport to an Alitalia freighter which took off for Venice at 6:17 p.m.

The High Dam Authority reported westerly winds Force 5–6. The first flocks of birds appeared over Cairo. At Mansura University, Dr. Elbrem concluded a series of experiments with essential oils extracted from cacti. Addressing the people of Egypt on radio and television, President Sadat told them that their hour of supreme trial was at hand.

A hearse conveyed Dr. Angelo's coffin from the airport to the Stazione Marittima on the northern outskirts of Venice.

Latest reports from the High Dam Authority spoke of wind speeds varying between Force 8 and Force 9.

That night, the wind veered northward, piling water against the dam. A dark cloud of birds circled the sky above Cairo.

The wind-lashed lake spilled over the crest of the High Dam. Soldiers abandoned their machine-gun posts and started to wade, knee-deep in swirling water, to the bank. The first parapet stones worked loose and were swept away.

At Daraw, where the southernmost charges had been laid, a lieutenant rushed into his radio hut and tore the microphone from its stand. "The storks are coming," he yelled, "thousands of them! The storks are coming . . ." A wall of air wrenched the door off its hinges. Over Asyut, a helicopter carrying the final batch of water samples to Mansura was caught by the surge of atmospheric pressure that raced ahead of the flood wave.

Birds perched by the thousands among the steel stays and girders of Radio Cairo's transmitting tower. Output dwindled, and Minister Heikal sent for flamethrower units to drive the birds away.

Between Idfu and Asyut, three dynamite charges were detonated and sections of hillside slid into the valley.

Clinging to wires and insulators, birds hung like clusters of grapes from the high-tension cables which led through the Nile Valley to Cairo. Clouds of them swept down on the pylons, causing them to arc across, and knots of burning flesh and feathers tumbled to the ground. By 11 p.m., three-fifths of all high-tension transmission lines had been put out of action by short circuits. Cairo was plunged into darkness.

Dr. Elbrem repeated his evaporation experiment with cactus extracts in the presence of Professor Saber, head of the Marine Research Institute at Mansura University. Twenty minutes before midnight, satisfied that perymethylene ether had been isolated at last, Professor Saber decided to inform the President. He asked the switchboard for a call to Cairo.

Two minutes later, the girl called him back. "Cairo isn't answering."

Professor Saber walked out into the grounds of the Institute. The air was filled with the sound of beating wings. A million birds were flying out to sea.

Next morning, a pall of mist hung over the Nile Delta and

the stretch of coast where the flood wave had spent itself in the sea.

The Lufthansa Boeing *Richard Wagner,* bound for New Delhi from Rome, was scheduled to make an intermediate stop at Heliopolis. As it descended through the haze, the navigator saw the water.

"What do you mean?" he said. "Of course I'm sure."

The captain said, "If we can't raise the tower, we should at least be getting a radio fix by now."

"Look at all that water, for God's sake."

The Boeing flew above the muddy yellow deluge at a thousand feet.

The navigator said, "Tell me I'm not crazy . . ."

The passengers peered out of the windows.

Someone said, "I thought we were over Cairo."

A woman screamed, "They're going to make a forced landing! In the sea!"

The co-pilot said to the captain, "I've got my binoculars on it now. It's the roof of a car. There's a car floating down there. And look at those cows. . . ."

The Boeing continued to drone low over the surface of the water.

The co-pilot said, "There's a tree trunk with a cat clinging to it. No, it's a child—no, a cat."

The navigator whispered, "So I'm not crazy . . ."

The captain spoke into the microphone. "Ladies and gentlemen, I'm afraid we have a minor fault in our navigational system. We're changing course for Beirut. Meanwhile, light refreshments will be served."

Dr. Mario Angelo was buried at San Michele that morning. The gravediggers had prepared Plot No. 16, Row 13, Section Q, to receive his coffin. Twelve hours later, the water level in Venice rose six inches.

A Note on the Type

The text of this book was set in a face called Times Roman, designed by Stanley Morison for The Times (London) and first introduced by the newspaper in 1932.

Among typographers and designers of the twentieth century, Stanley Morison has been a strong forming influence, as typographical adviser to the English Monotype Corporation, as a director of two distinguished English publishing houses, and as a writer of sensibility, erudition, and keen practical sense.

Composed by Cherry Hill Composition,
Pennsauken, N.J.
Printed and bound by
The Haddon Craftsmen, Scranton, Pa.

Typography and binding design by
Virginia Tan

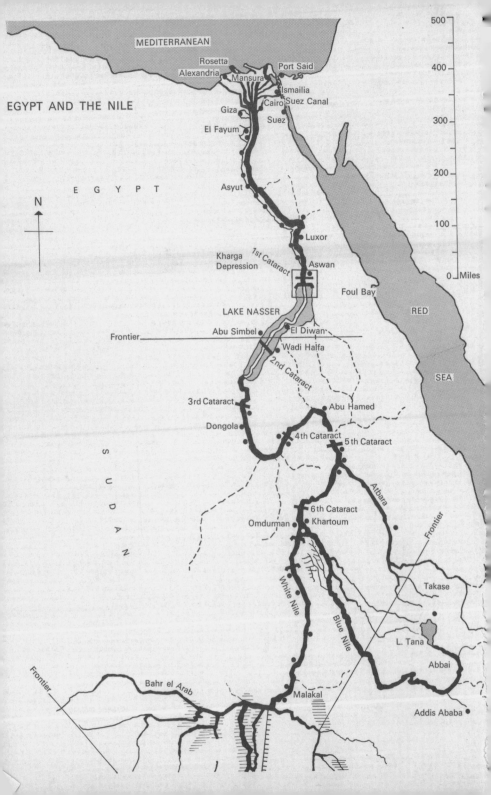